Copyright © 2021 by Janet Elizabeth Henderson

All rights reserved.

No part of this book may be reproduced in any form or by any electronic or mechanical means, including information storage and retrieval systems, without written permission from the author, except for the use of brief quotations in a book review.

RUN

BENSON SECURITY 6

JANET ELIZABETH HENDERSON

ALSO BY JANET ELIZABETH HENDERSON

Invertary Romantic Comedy Books

Lingerie Wars

Goody Two Shoes

Magenta Mine

Calamity Jena

Bad Boy

Here Comes The Rainne Again

Caught

Invertary Too

Come Fly With Me

Here Comes Trouble

Sinclair Sisters Romantic Comedy Books

Can't Tie Me Down

Can't Stop The Feeling

Can't Buy Me Love

Romantic Suspense Books

Reckless

Relentless

Rage

Ransom

Rich

Run

And more on my website

Janet Elizabeth Henderson

1
———

Elle Roberts was bored. And that was never a good thing. Usually, she loved team meetings, as it was like one big dysfunctional family forced to socialize together every week. They'd bicker about someone eating more than their fair share of the snacks. Or tease each other about something stupid they'd done. Or poke their noses into each other's business, offering unwanted advice. But today, the meeting was all about the run-of-the-mill operations they had going on. And none of it interested her.

If she had to do one more background check on a prospective employee for a generic financial company, she would jump into the Thames. For weeks, all they'd dealt with was Instagram influencers who felt they needed personal protection from their hordes of fans because they were *like, so popular and totally misunderstood* (a direct quote from the last lipstick guru who wanted a bodyguard), businesses that thought they were so important someone might steal their ideas (spoiler: they weren't, and no one wanted anything they had), and people who needed security systems installed by *the best*.

Dull. Dull. Dull. Dull. Dull...

Where were the flying bullets? The international travel? The life-or-death situations? And, best of all, the call for her to hack her way into places very few people could enter? There was no getting past it—the glory days of Benson Security seemed to be over. Maybe it was time to move on...

"We boring you, Elle?" her boss, Callum McKay, barked, making her jump in her seat. Although, his tone wasn't a sign he was annoyed with her, it was just a sign that he was a grumpy-arsed Scotsman.

"Not you," she said honestly. "The jobs. They're mind-numbing. I'm fed up with background-checking boring people and combing through crappy private networks for bugs. Can't we infiltrate an oppressive regime somewhere and bring down a dictator? Or even negotiate for a hostage or two? Surely someone, somewhere, has been kidnapped and needs our help."

Callum stared at her like she'd grown two heads. Meanwhile, Ryan Granger, the ex-soldier and native Londoner she considered a younger brother—despite him being marginally older—pointed at her. "What she said," he told their boss before reaching for the last Danish pastry on the meeting room table.

"I'm with Elle." Megan Raast nodded. "I haven't shot at anyone in months."

The Scottish bombshell had been Benson Security's first trainee—which had only happened because she was too dangerous on her own not to train her. Megan seemed to think that a bad temper, an inability to feel fear, and questionable ethics were a good substitute for the military training the rest of the team had. Well, not *all* of the team. Elle's expertise lay in computer hacking, coding, and her encyclopedic knowledge of the *Star Wars* universe. Oh, and Julia, their office manager, was hell on wheels with a whiteboard.

Dimitri, Megan's American husband, cocked an eyebrow at his wife. "You shot at me last week."

Megan waved a hand. "That doesn't count. I wasn't really aiming for you."

"You barely missed my leg," the former army ranger pointed out.

"Exactly." Megan tossed her long blonde hair over her shoulder. "I *didn't* hit you."

Dimitri's grin summed up their marriage—crazy did it for him.

Callum, who stood at the end of the table because sitting meant he couldn't pace when something annoyed him, pinched the bridge of his nose. It was his go-to move when their lack of professionalism frustrated him. Even after countless operations together, he still wished his team would behave like the SAS soldiers he used to command.

It was a foolish wish. While his old commandos had worked like a well-oiled machine, his Benson Security team worked like a cobbled-together MacGyver project. Although, to be fair, much like MacGyver's improvisations, the team got the job done. And hardly ever blew things up while doing it.

"I like the jobs we've been doing," Julia Barone, their office manager, said.

It was still strange to hear shy Julia talk during a meeting without being forced. It was even stranger to see her sitting at the table with everyone else instead of hiding behind one of the huge plants she'd positioned throughout the building. But then, she did have her husband at her side, and Joe wouldn't let anything, or anyone, intimidate his wife. Ever. There were days when watching Joe and Julia together was just too cute for Elle to bear.

"That's because you're up to your eyeballs in schedules and paperwork, baby." The former Marine's eyes lit up when he looked at his wife. "It's your happy place." His eyes cooled as he turned to the rest of them. "I, on the other hand, wouldn't mind seeing some action for a change."

"For a change?" Callum exploded.

Honestly, it was a miracle he'd lasted that long. And it was a welcome sound. It had been weeks since his temper had gotten the better of him during a meeting, which was another sure sign that things were far too quiet.

"Come on." Ryan looked around for more food. "Nothing interesting has happened since we helped Rachel out with her problem."

"Nicely understated. I like." Elle grinned at him. "Although, I don't like that sorting Rachel's problem meant she left us. Meetings aren't the same without her."

Rachel Ford-Talbot had once been a partner in Benson Security but was now CEO of her family's pharmaceutical company. It didn't stop her poking her nose into her former business, but it wasn't the same as watching her ongoing power struggle with Callum.

"It's like Mum and Dad got divorced, and she doesn't live with us anymore," Ryan said.

"I miss their fights," Elle said wistfully.

"I miss having to come up with creative threats for when she crossed the line with her bitchiness," Megan said morosely.

"It's her complete lack of tact I miss the most," Dimitri

added. "Never met anyone who cared less about what they said."

"I miss having access to her family jet," Joe said with a grin.

Callum slammed his hands down on the table. "Will you listen to yourselves? You sound like a bunch of spoiled teenagers who only want to whine about their lot in life. 'Boo-hoo, poor me. I wish somebody would shoot at me. Why can't my life be in danger? I miss my old boss's toys.'" He slapped the table again. "Cry me a bloody river. You're professionals. Do your job and shut up about it."

There was a beat of silence before Elle said, "I forgot Isobel was still visiting her sister. Want me to call and get her and the kids to come back early?" She wasn't joking. Elle saw herself as the carer of the team, and Callum's mental health was directly tied up with his love for his wife. Only she could calm his wild inner beast.

"This is not about my absent wife!" He pointed at them. "It's about you lot."

Ryan pretended to cough. "Yeah, right."

"Get a grip," Megan told Callum. "They're only in Scotland for two weeks. If you're suffering from withdrawal, go up and see them. We can cope without you."

Everyone nodded.

"What could go wrong?" Elle said. "The Instagram Queen takes a bad photo? A background check shows that some guy's bought too many bottles of wine? Somebody hits their thumb with a hammer while installing a security system?"

"I swear," Callum growled at her, "if you jinx us with your attitude, I *will* fire you."

"No, you won't," Elle said cheerily. "You love me too much. Anyway, you need me around for a female opinion. Megan doesn't count, her viewpoint leans more toward anarchist than female, and Julia is still too scared of you to tell you what she really thinks. Without me, you'd be lost." She beamed at him. "You also wouldn't be able to access your email. Or work your computer. Face it, if I didn't change your password for you every week, it'd still be *password*."

Ryan gaped at him. "Your password was password? Dude, you run a security company."

Callum's face turned red, and it wasn't clear whether he was embarrassed or about to explode. But they didn't get to find out which way it would go because Elle's ever-present laptop emitted a loud wailing sound.

"Crap!" She grabbed the machine, flipped it open, and typed fast, her stomach a tornado within her. "Oh no, that isn't good." Code streamed across the screen before her, and none of it was good. "Damn, damn, damn."

"Elle," Callum snapped. "What's going on?"

She couldn't answer; her whole focus was on shutting down the threat in front of her. Someone had backtraced a hack she'd instigated in her attempt to uncover which organization employed her favorite sexy spy.

"Elle!" Callum shouted.

"Someone's trying to hack us." Elle spat out the words as her fingers flew over her keyboard. "They can't get past our firewalls, so they're searching for a soft target. Shit! They're attacking the Wi-Fi. Julia, shut it down while I deal with this."

"How?" Julia rushed to the meeting room door.

"Cut the power to the building!" It was the fastest way to turn everything off.

Julia ran for her office and the control panel.

But it was too late.

Elle slammed her laptop shut and shot to her feet, her eyes flying to all the personal phones sitting on the table.

Each one of them hooked into the office Wi-Fi. "The hacker was searching for our physical location. Check your phones. Make sure the GPS is disabled. If it isn't..." She wrapped her hands around the bunches on either side of her head and yanked them hard, feeling the bite in her scalp. Oh boy, she'd totally screwed up this time.

"I thought you gave everyone a program to protect their GPS," Joe said as he reached for his phone. "To stop people from turning it on remotely."

"I did. But it doesn't stop them from gaining access if you've turned it on yourself."

"We know enough to keep it disabled." Megan checked her phone. "I'm clear."

"Me too," Dimitri added.

"Shit." Ryan paled as he stared at his phone screen. "I'm sorry, Elle."

Callum let out a stream of curses. "Why the hell would you have it enabled anyway?"

Ryan turned a deep shade of red. "Tinder."

There was a moment of stunned silence.

"You compromised all of us to get laid?" Joe demanded.

"I thought I'd switched it off after the last time I looked at it," Ryan said.

"It doesn't matter." Elle's brain raced. "Accidents happen. It's not your fault." She swallowed hard. "It's mine."

Callum let out an almighty growl. "What did you hack this time, and which government agency should we expect to come after us?"

"It wasn't the government." She shuffled nervously, her pink Dr. Martens thudding on the thick carpet. "It was a dark web chatroom. I was following up on a lead I got in my search for info on—"

"David? Right?" Callum started pacing like a mad man.

"Damn it, Elle," Dimitri said. "David warned you about

this. He told you not to search for him. You told us you'd given up on trying to find out who he works with."

"And I had. Until I got bored and started looking again." She threw her hands in the air. "He shouldn't have asked me to stop anyway. It was like waving catnip in front of my face. I mean, a problem I need to hack to uncover? Involving a sexy, dangerous spy who kisses like a god? Of course I'm going to keep on searching for the man." She hung her head. "I have issues. There should probably be an intervention and some intensive therapy in my future."

"Kisses like a god?" Megan asked, making her husband frown at her.

"I did *not* need to hear that." Ryan had turned a little green. "First, no guy wants to hear about another guy's performance in anything. Second, you're like a sister to me, which means you are never to tell me that your lips or any other part of your body have touched anyone." He shuddered.

"Focus!" Callum roared as he came to a halt at the end of the table. "Do you have any idea who was tracking you and why they'd want your location?"

Elle shook her head, but a heaviness in the pit of her stomach made her want to curl into a ball. "I've seen that hacking technique before, though. A hacker or a group of hackers for hire that goes by the name of SurfNinja. I don't know much about them other than they're scary good and don't care who pays them. I think they might be Russian."

"How much time do we have until somebody turns up here?" Callum's eyes were laser hot.

"I don't know. They could be hacking us from anywhere. Hell, they could be next door or on the other side of the world. Worse, they could be working for anyone, and the person they're feeding information to could be on their way already. If we're lucky, we've got days before someone turns up. If we aren't"—she wrapped her arms around herself—"ten, fifteen minutes, maybe? I have no idea."

Her boss ran a hand down his face. "Wipe this place down, dump all devices with Elle for disposal, and get to the safe house out by the airport. Until we know what we're dealing with, our priority is to protect our clients' information. Got it?"

They were running before he'd finished barking orders.

2

———

Monday 10 a.m.
Amsterdam-Zuidoost, Netherlands

David Knight had been trained to withstand torture. When being interrogated, he knew how to turn the tables in order to obtain information from his interrogators. And he knew how to compartmentalize physical pain in order to endure. It wasn't the first time he'd been tortured in the hope he'd betray a colleague, or worse, his country. It was, however, the first time in a very long time that he'd been asked to betray someone he cared about. Because, until a cute little hacker with a penchant for pop culture, fifties dresses, and blue hair walked into his life, David hadn't let himself feel anything for anyone in years.

Not that he was *letting* himself feel for Elle now. It was just that, no matter how hard he fought it, the feelings wouldn't die. And they had to. Because the last time he'd felt for someone, he'd managed to get them killed.

A body blow from a guy with mallets for fists knocked the air from his lungs and brought his attention right back to his most pressing problem—torture, interrogation, and protecting Elle Roberts' true identity.

Damn it, *everything* led back to his hacker.

No.

Not *his*.

Not since his boss at MI6 had been killed and his off-the-books job watching Elle had suddenly ended. And yet... he hadn't been able to walk away from her. He'd told himself he was just ensuring he did his job well, even though he wasn't getting paid for it. When that hadn't worked, he started telling himself that an honorable man would make sure she was safe before walking away. In the end, he'd had to be honest and admit to himself that he watched over her because he cared about her.

That's when he'd started keeping his distance.

Which was exactly why he now hung from the ceiling in an abandoned Dutch bar—because Elle didn't like the distance he'd put between them and had stepped up her search for him.

"You are only hurting yourself with your refusal to tell me what I want to know, my friend." Henk Bakker, drug dealer, information broker, and all-around asshole sat at the bar, sipping cheap Scotch. His silver-colored suit was pristine, and his shoes shone—because the Dutchman never did his own dirty work. He waved a hand toward the dumb grunt beating David. "Azzo could do this all day. He's being careful, making sure he doesn't damage anything vital. That can change if you don't answer my question. Where is the hacker who is searching for you?"

"Don't know who you're talking about," David said again.

A fist struck his jaw, knocking his head to the side and

making the room blur for a second. He spat blood on the floor as he raised himself onto his toes, attempting to ease the pressure on his shoulders from having his arms stretched tight above him while he hung from a hook in the ceiling. A bruised face wouldn't slow him down, but a ripped tendon would. And he knew from experience that his shoulders would tear if he hung there long enough.

As he breathed through the latest bout of pain, he calmly cataloged his injuries. It was a relief to find nothing that would hamper his walking away.

Because he would walk away.

There was always an out. He just hadn't found it yet.

"David, David, David, you must stop doing this to yourself." Henk sauntered toward him, glass in one hand, the other in the pocket of his pants. His open jacket exposed a gun sitting snug in its shoulder holster—strapped in nice and tight. *Idiot.* In the time it took Henk to free his gun, David would have broken his neck.

"Last I checked, it wasn't me doing this," David said, purely to keep Henk talking. To draw him nearer still.

Azzo smirked his amusement while, no doubt, planning where he'd place his next strike. Even though the enforcer was more flab than muscle, his prison tattoos bore testament to years of experience in his chosen profession. One he clearly enjoyed.

"David," Henk said, "we have been friends for many years and I don't want to hurt you. But you must understand, there are several interested parties who'd like to know what I can learn from you. Make this easy on both of us and give me what I ask. Tell me where the girl is."

"Friends," David mumbled, speaking softly to entice his prey closer. "You keep using that word. I do not think it means what you think it means." If Elle had been there, she would have laughed her ass off at him for quoting *The*

Princess Bride. Thankfully, the reference went over his interrogators' heads and didn't prompt them to hit him harder.

Henk sauntered forward. One more step was all David needed. He wrapped his hands around the chains suspending him from the ceiling, gripping tight. His ankles were in the same shackles as his hands, a long chain between them linked around a hook in the floor. A hook screwed into wood. A hook David had been loosening with each jerk of his legs. He was dealing with amateurs.

"Give the girl up," Henk persuaded. "We know you know who she is and where she's hiding. Otherwise, why would she be searching for you and leaving such personal messages everywhere?"

"I don't know what you're talking about." David stalled as his mind raced for a plan to get him out of there.

Henk pulled his phone from his pocket and tapped the screen. "This was left on one of the message boards you use for contracting work: *Blue girl still seeking partner in crime. Fluffy pink handcuffs included.*" He gave David a look that said he pitied him. "She used your contact code."

"It must have been a mistake. That message was meant for someone else because it means nothing to me." Other than David planned to use those handcuffs on Elle when he next saw her, and it wouldn't be for pleasure. No, that woman deserved a spanking. Big time.

"Perhaps, but my contacts tell me that the style of hack used to get into this board is the same one several interested parties have been tracking for a very long time. It's the same one that keeps popping up in relation to you. There are no coincidences in our line of work; you know that."

"Then this is a first," David said.

A fist came from the side and struck his kidney with practiced precision. David breathed through the pain. He'd be pissing blood for a week from that blow alone.

Henk's look of concern was as phony as a three-dollar bill. "What is she to you that you want to protect her? She isn't protecting you. She's leaving a trail all over the web pointing right at you."

"I'm telling you." David spoke quietly. "I don't know her."

Azzo shifted, no doubt intending to beat David for yet another denial, but Henk held up his glass, signaling for his henchman to wait. "I'm afraid that isn't good enough. You see, there's a lot of money on the line for information regarding this hacker. A *lot* of money. I would very much like to be the person who collects it."

David hung his head as though losing strength. Damn stubborn woman. He'd told her time and again to stop searching for information on him. But no, she treated the whole thing as a game, a puzzle she needed to crack. As though her life would fall apart if she didn't know which government agency pulled his strings. Sure, he'd played along for a bit, mainly because there was a novelty in someone wanting to play with him. Although, it hadn't taken him long to warn her to back off—which she'd ignored. It was enough to drive a man insane.

"Don't tell me you'd sell out a *friend* to cash in, Henk," he said, making sure to slur his words and appear weaker than he felt.

Henk waved a dismissive hand. "This is the business, is it not?"

Yeah, which is why David should have been more careful when he turned up for his meeting with a snitch. There was a possibility he was slipping, becoming soft in his job, which could get him killed.

Or worse, get Elle killed.

Letting his head loll to one side, David acted as though

keeping his eyes open and staying focused was difficult. "If she's that important, I'd have heard of her, and I haven't."

"I once told you that your stubborn streak would get you into trouble one day," Henk said with a shake of his head. "Today might very well be that day." He motioned to Azzo, who struck David in the ribs again.

Yeah, he felt that.

"This won't do you any good," he gasped, hoping like hell his ribs weren't cracked. "I can't tell you what I don't know."

"Stop lying and help me to help you. It's clear you want a way back into your organization. I have the contacts to make it happen. You could come in from the cold. No more freelancing. Your slate would be wiped clean, and your government would welcome you with open arms. Isn't that what you want?"

David kept his head down, groaned something nonsensical, and went over his plan of escape until he could carry it out without thinking. He'd only have one chance to make this work. He did *not* want to waste it.

"What did you say?" Henk pressed. "Azzo, you hit him too hard. I told you I needed him to talk."

Azzo didn't reply.

"My friend, tell us where the girl is, and this will all stop." Henk sounded as though it pained him to see David beaten.

Yeah, right. Not as much as it pained David.

He mumbled something, making sure he included a woman's name, one he'd plucked from thin air.

"That's it," Henk said eagerly. "Speak up, and I promise you I will help you to get back into the job you love. Vindication will be yours at last. All you have to do is reach out and take what I'm offering." With clear impatience, Henk took that final crucial step toward his prey.

And his prey struck back.

With an almighty kick upward, the hook flew out of the floor as David's feet connected with Henk's Scotch glass. It shot straight up in the air. Clutching the chains above him, he used his upper body strength to swing his legs in a showy soccer kick. His aim was perfect, hitting the glass and sending the shattered shards straight into Azzo's face and throat.

The big man wailed as his meaty fingers clasped his throat, blood running through them. Henk didn't react. Instead, he gaped at Azzo. *Untrained idiot.* David lifted his knees to his chest and looped the chain between his ankles around Henk's neck.

Henk clawed at the chain, clearly forgetting he had a gun that could neutralize the threat to him within seconds. Using the struggling man's shoulders, David launched himself upward and unhooked his wrists before somersaulting over Henk in one smooth motion. The sound of his *old friend's* neck breaking was loud in the empty room as, together, they toppled to the floor.

It took only a second to relieve Henk of his gun. One more to shoot Azzo between the eyes. Then, it was a matter of aiming at the door, ready to deal with anyone who heard the shots and ran inside.

No one appeared.

Obviously, Henk had assumed two men were enough to deal with him. Calmly, David dragged Henk's body toward him and searched his pockets. He found the key to his restraints—along with a phone, a money clip, and the fob for Henk's car.

After freeing himself, he limped behind the bar and smashed what bottles of liquor remained before taking one to douse the dead men.

"We were never friends," he told Henk's body. "I don't

have friends. But if I did, I wouldn't choose a drug-dealing snitch as one of them."

Pressing his hand against his side to give his bruised ribs some stability, he made his way to the back door. As he pushed through it, he struck a match from a book he'd found on the bar, lit the remaining matches, and tossed the whole thing back at the bodies. The sound of the hungry flames followed him out into the fresh air.

Smashed bottles, used condoms, and spent syringes littered the cracked concrete surface of the parking lot. Shadows from the surrounding tower blocks blocked out the sun as David crossed to the silver Porsche sitting in the middle of all that garbage.

With disgust, he climbed into the vehicle, every bruise on his body protesting as he curled into the narrow space behind the wheel. "You couldn't have had a nice spacious SUV," he grumbled, "or at least something that didn't scream you were compensating, could you?"

It was a testament to Henk's reputation that his Porsche was still in one piece and right where he'd left it. The Bijlmer, as the locals called it, hadn't got its reputation as one of Amsterdam's most dangerous areas by chance.

A quick glance around told him that doors had been shut and curtains pulled, probably at the sight of Henk's car. There would be no witnesses to his taking the Porsche— none that would speak to the cops, anyway.

Clenching his jaw as pain began to register, he pulled out Henk's phone and dialed the London office of Benson Security. There was no reply. Cursing himself for not memorizing Callum's cell number, David called the only cell he had committed to memory—Elle's. It went straight to voice mail.

The hairs on the back of his neck stood on end as the bar's fire alarm started to wail.

Quickly, he typed out a text message to Elle—knowing she'd check that during a meeting, whereas she wouldn't answer a call. *Urgent. Several interested parties after you. Call me. David.*

No reply.

In the distance, he heard sirens. It was time to get out of Dodge. But first, he gave the office line and Elle's number one last try. Nothing. With no other choice but to hit the road, he put the car in gear and headed for the nearest train station. From there, he'd catch a train to Schiphol and then the next flight to London. He'd never been more grateful that the flight between the two cities was often less than an hour long.

As he drove, he called the final number he knew from memory and almost sagged with relief on hearing the voice on the other end of the line.

"Lake Benson." The English accent was crisp.

"It's David; we've got a problem."

As he spoke, he put his foot down and made the most of stealing a high-performance car.

3

———

Monday 10:20 a.m.
Benson Security
London

Every handheld device in the building, including Elle's beloved laptop, was locked inside the industrial-sized drawer of the degausser machine that stood in the corner of Elle's office.

"Goodbye, old friend," she said as she pressed the On button.

The machine would expose the devices to a powerful targeted magnetic field, wiping out their hard drives and rendering them unusable. It was inhumane.

"Your laptop deserves to die," Megan said from beside her. "Whereas my new phone never did anything wrong. Now all those photos I took of Dimitri last weekend are gone."

Elle knew better than to ask what photos. Instead, she

pointed at the message scrawled across her T-shirt, the one she wore to every team meeting as a reminder they should save their stuff to the cloud. It said, *Back up or you'll be sorry*.

"I'm already sorry," Megan said in disgust. "Sorry someone didn't take away your internet privileges before the rest of us suffered."

"I was weak." Elle returned to her desktop setup and checked that the program her old boss, Harry, had written had done its job. Which it had. Their local network was now wiped clean in such a way that even the best data-specializing forensic scientists on the planet wouldn't get anything from it.

"For almost three years? That's a long time to have no impulse control." Megan was clearly unconvinced.

"I've learned my lesson. From now on, I'll only be a good little hacker."

With everything safely backed up to a secure server in a country that didn't recognize UK court orders, all Elle needed was a new laptop to get them up and running again. She gazed longingly at the machine where her old laptop lay dying. It'd been state of the art, custom-built, and set up to perfection. It was quite possible she'd never get over its loss.

"Serves you right." Megan accurately read the puppy-dog eyes Elle was giving the machine of death. "You wouldn't listen to reason. Or threats. Or even logic."

"Do you realize how long it took me to get that laptop exactly how I wanted it?"

"A better question is, do you realize how little I care?"

"Now you sound like Rachel." With a scowl at Megan, Elle tugged her messenger bag on over her head. It felt far too light without the weight of her laptop pulling it down.

"Rachel? My sarcasm has nothing on how she's going to

react when she finds out about your latest screwup." Megan mimed explosions and choking—for some reason.

"Whatever," Elle grumbled as they headed downstairs.

Julia stood by the main door, holding a tray laden with paper bags. She handed one to each of them.

"Your burner phone, cash, and the keys to the car you'll be using are inside the bag," she told Elle. "It's in garage A, down the street. Just drive in and swap out your car for the junker." It had been Julia's idea to keep an assortment of untraceable cars in different parking garages close to the office. They used them for surveillance but also as a fail-safe in case they were compromised and had to escape unnoticed. "I've preprogrammed the phone with the numbers of the other burners and disabled GPS."

"You couldn't have disabled everybody's phones before Ryan sat down at the meeting?" Megan grumbled as she took her bag.

"It's possible office policy will change to include that happening from now on," Julia said.

"Paperwork's in the furnace," Ryan called to them as he rushed into the foyer. "With time to spare. Gimme my phone, so I can get out of here." He held out his hand, and Julia gave him the paper bag with his name on it. "I don't suppose there are two safe houses? One for Callum and one for the people he'll want to shout at?" He pointed at himself and Elle—just in case there was any confusion.

A door slammed behind them, and a scowling Callum strode out of his office.

"Too late," Ryan muttered.

"Why are you hanging around in the foyer?" Callum asked.

"Waiting for Dimitri and Joe," Megan said. "They're doing one last sweep of the building, making sure the weapons are locked up tight."

"What about your house?" Julia asked, referring to the converted carriage house at the bottom of the garden, where Callum lived with his family.

He glared at Elle. "Everything that might be sensitive is locked up or binned. Which I'm none too happy about."

"I'm sorry, Callum." Elle hit him with her best contrite expression, which included anime-sized eyes. "I'll make it up to everyone. I won't ever search for David ever again, I promise."

Whatever Callum planned to say was lost when a gunshot rang out and a bullet struck the wall behind the reception desk with a loud smack.

"Take cover." Callum ducked out of sight of the door.

Ryan shoved Elle away from the door, while Megan yanked Julia back against the wall.

Elle couldn't tear her eyes from the bullet hole above reception. What kind of idiot shot at a business in the center of London? In the middle of the day?

"Is this real?" Elle asked no one in particular, so she wasn't surprised when she didn't get an answer.

"Sitrep?" Joe demanded as he hurried down the stairs with Dimitri.

"Somebody's shooting at us." Megan sounded quite pleased about it too.

Joe made his way along the walls to his wife. "Hit the alarm, Jules."

Julia reached up to the panel behind her and triggered the silent alarm that went straight to the local police station. Meanwhile, Joe darted out to slam the doors shut.

They'd barely closed when another bullet shattered one of their glass panels.

"Why the hell aren't those doors bulletproof?" Callum demanded.

"Because you wouldn't sign off on the quote, you cheapassed Scot," Joe said. "Julia told you the glass was a wise investment, but you said, 'Who's gonna shoot at us in a London street?' Good call."

"Aye," Callum said. "I may have made a mistake with that decision."

"Anybody see anything?" Dimitri fired a warning shot through the door. "I can tell there's more than one of them, but that's about it."

Another bullet blasted through the glass and embedded itself in the wall beside reception.

"Who the hell are these people? And why are they still here? Don't they realize the cops will be here any minute?" Ryan fired another warning shot to keep their attackers from coming inside.

Elle wanted to shoot too. She really needed a gun. Why didn't she have a gun? It wasn't like this was the first time she'd been shot at. She was damn well going to start carrying her own gun. A pink one. Or maybe blue. So what if it was pure luck when she hit whatever she aimed at? If worst came to the worst, she could always throw the gun at her attacker. Or pistol-whip them. She was rambling. Again. At least this time, it was in her head and not out loud.

"Get to the basement and hole up in the panic room," Callum ordered. "I'll cover you."

"What about you?" Elle didn't want anyone left behind. Especially Callum. Isobel would not be pleased if her husband ended up with holes in him.

"Don't worry; I'm right behind you." Never before had he looked more like a Highlander ready to wage battle. She found it kinda comforting.

"We don't want to hurt anyone," a voice shouted from outside the building, making them pause. "We only want the girl."

By the Hoary Hosts of Hoggoth!

She knew that voice.

Almost as well as she knew her own.

As though in slow motion, a bullet floated through the air and sank into the front of the reception desk with a muted thud.

"If you don't want to hurt anybody, why are you still shooting?" Ryan's voice sounded like he was underwater. Distorted. Dull. Drawn out.

"I said we don't want to hurt anyone," the voice called out again, the words strangely slow and stretched. "Not that we won't."

"Just tell us what you want." Callum's bellow echoed around in her head.

The reply took ten years. "We...want...Elle."

Just like that, a switch flipped. Time rushed at her. Speeding up in a way that made her wobble on her feet.

"Elle?" Callum frowned at her. "They want you?"

No, no, no, no, no...

This wasn't happening. She'd run away from this. She'd been careful to stay hidden—mostly. Crap, Elle just bet it was that mostly part that'd bitten her on the butt.

"Elle," the voice shouted, "get out here, or we're coming in to get you."

The word roared through Elle's head a second before it exploded out of her mouth: "No!"

She was up before she'd even registered she was moving. Running toward the main doors instead of away from it—as any normal person would do.

"Get down now," Callum ordered as the rest of her team called her name in alarm.

She heard their fear. Anger. Confusion. It only inflamed the reckless outrage driving her actions. Chest heaving, Elle screeched to a halt in front of the shattered doors. Furious, she glared out into the street beyond. Straight at their attackers.

Straight into the eyes of her brother.

4

"Marcus, don't you dare hurt anyone. I'm serious. Put those guns down right now," Elle demanded of the brother she'd once adored. The brother who'd embraced everything she hated. The brother she thought she'd never see again. "I swear, if you harm one hair on the heads of the people in here, I will rain down hell on you and the family."

"Elle," Joe hissed. "Get out of the way before you get shot."

She barked out a laugh. It was brittle and tinged with hysteria. "He won't shoot me. They need me alive too badly for that."

Her brother heard her. "No, we won't shoot *you*. But we will shoot anyone who gets between us and you. Come out here before someone gets hurt."

"Elle? What are you doing?" Ryan demanded. "This is insane. Who's Marcus? How do you know these guys?"

Elle tuned him out, her focus on her older brother. He'd aged in the years she'd been gone, looking older than he should. It appeared being heir to one of the worst crime families in Europe took its toll.

Marcus spread his arms wide, a gun in his hand. "I don't want to hurt your people. I just need to you come with me before the cops get here."

"Yeah, I bet you do," she scoffed. "Do you know you even look like him now? Dressed in your tailored suit, with your slick haircut. Next it will be a platinum pinky ring and pretensions of playing the godfather. I *am deeply* disappointed in you, big brother."

"Big brother?" Julia squeaked.

"Holy shit," Ryan said. "I know who that is now. It's Marcus James. As in, the James Family Syndicate, one of the biggest crime organizations in Europe. He can't be her brother. Right?"

"Elle," Marcus called to her. "I'm losing my patience. Get out here now."

"Not on your life," Elle bellowed. "Go on home to Darth. Tell him I'm keeping the plans to the Death Star, and there's nothing he can do about it."

"Bloody hell," Callum said. "Does anyone know what she's talking about?"

"It sounds like she's got information her brother wants," Megan said.

Ryan cursed. "If that's really her brother, then Tommy James is her father. Tommy makes Darth Vader look like Father of the Year." He raised his voice and used the singsong tone someone would use to talk a crazy person off a ledge: "Elle, don't wind up the psycho mobster, honey. Callum, you might want to do something here before things get seriously out of control."

"Good idea," Callum rumbled.

There was movement behind her, which Elle ignored as her focus was on her brother. "Go home, Marcus," she called. "Tell Tommy I'd rather die than come back to the family."

"Fucking shoot her." A head appeared from behind a car. Leo Trainer—one of her father's pet psychos. "Take out her knee, then scoop her up. We'll carry her out. The cops are coming."

"Nobody shoots my sister," Marcus bellowed as his second-in-command and lifelong best friend, Abasi Otieno, aimed his gun at Leo instead of Elle.

"I am not your sister," Elle shouted at him. "Not anymore. I resigned from that position years ago. Take your wannabe army and get out of here before the cops arrive; otherwise, I swear you'll regret it. I've left you alone these past years, but I can change that with a keystroke. Do you really want to mess with me? You know I can bring you a world of trouble. Do you hear me, Marcus? You have seriously irritated me this time!"

Someone grabbed her around the waist, making her squeal, and the next thing she knew, Ryan was carrying her like a rugby ball as he ran for the stairs to the basement.

"Let me down!" She kicked and fought, furious at Ryan for taking control out of her hands. Furious at Marcus for turning her life upside down. And furious that her team was in danger because of her—because she'd been born as Elle James.

"Not going to happen." Ryan sounded bizarrely unfazed as he took the stairs two at a time. "You need to be saved from yourself. Trust me on this."

"Let me go and give me a gun," she half-pleaded, half-ordered. "A big gun. I'm going to shoot him in his stupid head. I don't care that he's my brother. Okay, I do. Which means I'll probably shoot him in the shoulder instead. Either way, he totally deserves to be at least a little bit shot. I can't believe he attacked us like that. I mean, I knew he was hunting for me, but I never thought he'd do something like this. He put my friends in danger. My *people*. I've changed my mind. I'm going to shoot him in both thighs, so he can't run while I tell him what I think of him. Let me down, Ryan, or I'm shooting you too."

"You know"—Ryan pushed through the door to the basement stair—"I'd worry about your threat if I didn't know you couldn't hit the side of a bus from two feet away. You're the worst shot I've ever seen—and I once saw a monkey pick up a pistol the team dropped in the rainforest and fire until it was empty. The monkey had better aim than you."

"That's it," she roared. "I'm freezing your bank accounts. I'm putting you on the No Fly List. Your credit rating is toast. Not only you; I'm doing this to the whole damn team. You're all complicit in keeping me from shooting my no-good criminal of a brother!"

"I feel like one of those parents you see in the supermarket with a screaming toddler under their arm," Ryan said.

"That's it." Elle glared up at him. "I'm shutting down all of your gaming accounts and having you blacklisted."

"With what? You had to fry your laptop because you have impulse-control issues."

"I'll get another one, and when I do, I'm going to rewrite all of your online dating profiles as well as screw with your gaming sites. Every woman in England will know that you're a hound dog who'll eat them out of house and home."

Ryan slammed his palm onto the side of the bookcase that covered the door to the panic room. "Does David know about this mean streak of yours? I'm guessing not, or he wouldn't be flirting with you quite as much."

As the door swung open and he carried her inside, a huge blast rocked the building.

"It's okay," Joe said as he rushed in behind them. "Callum blew the doors to buy us some time."

"There were explosives in the doors?" Julia's voice was high-pitched as Joe dragged her into the room with him.

Joe nodded absently, his gun trained on the door as Megan and Dimitri joined them. "It's procedure for something like this."

"Something like this?" Julia's voice lifted an octave. "We planned for this?"

"We plan for everything, baby." Joe tore his eyes from the screens showing video feeds from the cameras upstairs. He smiled at his wife. "You know that."

"I didn't know there were explosives in the doorframe. What if we'd accidentally set them off?"

"We didn't want to worry you," Joe soothed. "Trust me, they were safe. I rigged it myself."

"You and I are going to have a long talk about this later, Joe." Julia tucked her hair behind her ears and frowned. "As office manager, I should be kept informed about which parts of the building are stuffed with C-4."

"You're right, baby. It won't happen again."

Of course, Julia's anger fizzled, and she smiled at her husband, which was beyond pathetic. "There goes the discussion I planned on having."

"Seriously?" Elle shouted. "You're letting him off the hook? Just like that?"

"Can we gag her?" Ryan said. "Do we have any gags? Or a bandage? A tea towel? Anything to stuff in her mouth. Anything at all."

"I want out of here," Elle shouted. "I have a brother to shoot!"

But it was too late. Callum ran into the room and slammed the door shut, sealing them in. Now, even if Ryan set her down, she'd have to make it past four well-trained men and Megan to make it back upstairs. She let out a long scream of outrage and tried to kick Ryan. He tossed her away from him and hid behind Megan.

The coward. The two-faced, interfering, annoying coward.

She pointed at her team, swinging her arm wide. "I am very annoyed with every single one of you right now."

There was nothing to do but pace the small space, making Elle feel like a caged tiger. Only, instead of a fake savannah, she had two sets of built-in bunk beds behind her, a table and chairs in front of her, and a wall of screens above a long desk. Oh, and the kitchen area, where Julia was quietly rearranging all the spices in alphabetical order while waiting for the kettle to boil.

"Have you calmed down enough to talk yet?" Callum asked, making her want to hit him over the head with a chair.

"Did you know that the computer in your bionic prosthetic legs can be hacked?" She narrowed her eyes at him. "Tell me to calm down one more time, and you'll dance a jig every time you put them on."

"Stop scaring the boys." Megan pulled out a chair at the table and sat. "Lucy, you got some 'splaining to do. You've been keeping secrets from your team, and that's all kinds of wrong. If my family happened to be the English Mob, I'd have told you. I'm really quite hurt that you didn't confide. Just sayin'."

Elle snorted with outrage. "Yeah, right. I can hear that conversation now: 'Hey, guys, did I mention that I'm on the run from my psychopathic gangster father and his adoring son? No? Well, let's discuss it over cookies and tea.'"

"That would have worked," Megan said with a nod.

"Who's that with Marcus?" Ryan pointed at the main screen, which showed the decimated foyer. Her brother and his right-hand man stood in the middle of the debris—looking pissed.

Good.

"That's Abasi Otieno," Elle snapped. "He's Marcus' second-in-command. Or understudy. Whatever. I never could get my head around the organizational structure."

Abasi was a lithe and compact black man whose family hailed from Kenya. If Marcus was heir to the James throne, Abasi was prime minister-in-waiting. She'd liked Abasi when they were kids. Back when she'd also liked her brother.

While Elle continued to pace, Joe tapped the keyboard on the desk, and the audio from the camera came on.

"Cops will be here in a couple of minutes," Abasi said. "We're cutting it close."

Marcus planted his hands on his hips, his face a mask of tightly controlled rage—an expression that reminded her far too much of their father. The sight pulled the rug out from under her own anger. She did *not* want to be like them —another James family member with anger-management issues. No, she never wanted to be like any of them. Her shoulders slumped as the last reserves of rage fled her. Now she just felt sad.

On the screen, Marcus said, "Need to get to her first."

"I know, brother." Abasi checked his phone. "Police are a couple of minutes away. You can't be here when they arrive."

"Do they know who Elle Roberts really is?" Marcus' cold eyes met his friend's.

"They do now. Somebody talked."

Marcus swore. "If they get to her before we do, this whole thing will go to hell."

"I'll contact our man on the inside. Make sure that doesn't happen." Abasi was already sending a text.

"Great," Megan muttered. "Guess we can totally trust the cops then."

Callum's grim face said he agreed with her sarcasm. "We're not without our own connections in the force, though."

"There must be another exit," Marcus was saying. "No way they got past the men stationed out back, and we sure as hell won't find anything searching this place."

"I'm confused—" Ryan said.

"It's because you have a teeny, tiny brain," Elle told him sweetly.

"I don't mean confused generally," Ryan corrected. "I mean, I'm confused about this. If he thinks searching the building is a waste of time, why did he send his men to do exactly that? I saw him point to the stairs." Ryan gestured to the other screens, showing men in several rooms. "They're definitely looking for you in the offices."

"Maybe it's a case of covering all their bases?" Joe mused. "Making sure he hasn't missed anyone?"

On the main screen, Abasi cocked his head. "You hear that? Sirens. Time to get out of here."

Marcus holstered his gun under his suit jacket and fastened it. "Let's go." He turned and strode toward the door.

Abasi followed, his gun still in his hand. "Do I tell the team to pull out?"

Marcus paused in the doorway. "Where's Leo?"

"Searching the apartments he found on the top floor." He lowered his voice. "Nowhere near an exit."

"Then we let the cops deal with that bastard. He's out of control."

"But he's one of Tommy's pets."

"Which makes him even more of a liability."

"You know he'll sell you out to the cops," Abasi said.

"I have witnesses who'll testify I was elsewhere when this went down."

Abasi pointed to the camera in the stairwell. "And that?"

Marcus strode over to stare up into the lens. "Elle, I know you're watching. Delete this footage." With that, the two men disappeared out of camera range.

Ryan gaped at the screen, a custard cream biscuit halfway to his mouth. "Does he seriously expect you to do what he says? Does he even know you?"

Elle let out a long, frustrated groan. "He's right. The cops can't get the footage. I'm on there too, telling the world I have something on the James Syndicate. But it's more than that; he's sacrificed one of Tommy's favorite psychopaths—the guy, Leo, they mentioned. If that gets out, there's no telling what Tommy might do in retaliation."

"Are you saying that you care if they take each other out?" Megan sounded incredulous.

"I care about all the innocent people who'd get harmed while they did it." Elle felt suddenly weary beyond her years. "The stuff you see in the media about the James Family? It doesn't even scrape the surface. Everything you've read or heard about them? That's the sanitized version. Tommy and Marcus are both power players. If they take each other on, there will be city-wide casualties. It wouldn't take much to set Tommy off. He thrives on violence.

"Tommy doesn't only eliminate those who cross him. He takes out their family and friends first. What he calls soft targets. He told us to always hit a man where he's weakest and would feel the most pain, and to make it last. The longer, the better. It sends out a message, he said. He's unpredictable, and there's no way of telling how he'd react to this footage. He could go nuclear or laugh and pat Marcus' shoulder for being a bastard."

She'd been thirteen when she'd first Googled

psychopath and realized the definition fitted her father to a tee. It hadn't surprised her. By then, she'd known Tommy delighted in other people's pain and enjoyed the notoriety that came with being vicious in his dealings with those around him.

Including his family.

Elle caught Callum's eye. "You're all on his radar now. Tommy will go after Isobel...the kids..." She took a deep breath and turned to Ryan. "Your grandparents aren't safe either. And, Julia, your family's high profile and easy to find. I'm so sorry for all of this. Sorry that I've put all of you and everyone you care about in danger. Megan's right: I should have come clean about my past long ago."

Julia paled, but she forced a smile. "Don't worry about my family. They might be in the spotlight, but they can also afford the best security on the planet, and we'll warn them to be careful. Right, Joe?"

He nodded as he put an arm around his wife.

Callum pulled out his phone and tapped the screen. "Isobel, love," he said when she answered. "Take the kids and your sisters, all of them, and head for Invertary. Lake will be expecting you. We've run into a wee bit of trouble here, and his team will keep you safe." He lifted his chin at Elle when he finished.

"Cops are here." Ryan pointed at the screen.

Together, they watched as the armed response squad rounded up what remained of the James Syndicate men.

Once the intruders were disarmed and secured, a familiar figure strode into the building—Tessa Sharp, commander of the Serious and Organized Crime Unit of London's Metropolitan Police. Tessa had worked with Benson Security on a number of cases and was a trusted contact of Lake Benson. She was smart, relentless, and respected within the ranks. She also didn't suffer fools gladly, which was probably why she was one of the few people Callum could tolerate.

"Who are we dealing with here?" Tessa asked as she picked her way through the rubble, her uniform making her rank clear to everyone around her.

"James Family Syndicate, ma'am," the nearest officer said.

Tessa cocked an eyebrow. "Benson Security staff?" She surveyed the damage with a keen eye.

"Aren't in the building."

"Were they in the building when this happened?"

"Hard to tell, ma'am. We noticed they have cameras, and we're working to access their feed."

"Good luck with that," Elle muttered.

The video feed was saved on a server outside of the building, and the only live screens—now that Elle had worked her magic—were in the panic room with them.

Tessa lifted her phone to her ear. "Callum, when you get this message, call me back immediately." She ended the call, unaware that Callum's phone had been fried along with everyone else's in Elle's handy magnetic machine, and no one outside of the team had the numbers of their burner phones.

Then, as they watched, Tessa seemed thoughtful before her eyes narrowed, and she headed for the stairs to the basement.

"You are so busted," Ryan said. "You never should have shown her the panic room."

Callum frowned as the screen showed Tessa marching down the stairs. "No matter what that woman says, we aren't leaving this room without our lawyers. Is that clear?"

Everyone nodded.

Callum focused on Elle. "There's goin' to be a lot of people desperate to get their hands on you. I imagine you'd be quite the resource for several government agencies. Whatever you do, make sure you have at least one Benson Security lawyer with you at all times. I don't want you disappearing into the bowels of MI5, never to come out again. Got me?"

"Yes. But I don't think the lawyers will hold them off for long." Elle was no idiot. As soon as word got out that the police had Tommy James' daughter in for questioning, every agency on the planet would swoop in to claim her. All they had to do was mention that she had information in relation to terrorist activities—Tommy had brokered for several terrorist groups—and the intelligence agencies could hold her indefinitely. She'd be answering questions for years, and there wouldn't be anything anyone could do about it.

"They'll hold them off long enough for us to come up with another way to deal with things," Callum said as Tessa began pounding her fist on the bookcase-covered door.

"Open up," she shouted. "I know you're in the panic room."

"She doesn't know anything," Megan mocked. "She's guessing."

"I swear I will charge everyone in there with obstruction if you don't answer me," Tessa threatened.

"Bloody woman would, an' all." Callum hit the intercom button. "What?" he barked.

"Get your backside out here right now," she ordered. "Along with whoever else is holed up in there with you. I've got questions for you all."

"Aye, I bet you do. Unfortunately for you, we're staying put until our lawyers get here."

"Why exactly would you need your lawyers?"

"Don't play games, Tessa. It's beneath you," Callum grumbled.

She heaved a sigh. "You can't protect Elle for long. There

are people with a whole lot more influence than I have who'd like to talk to her," she said, proving she'd known exactly who Elle was before even setting foot in the building.

Word was well and truly out about the location of Tommy James' daughter.

Callum was immovable—the big, stubborn Scot that he was. "Aye, well, they can talk to her with our lawyers present. Now, if you don't mind, my tea's getting cold." He cut the connection and dug out his phone again. "Need to give Lake a heads-up that the Sinclair sisters are on their way," he muttered.

"I should run," Elle whispered, but there was no conviction in her voice. Or her heart. She didn't want to run. She wanted to stay with the people she loved, doing the job she —mostly—loved. She didn't want to lose everything again.

"It's too late for that," Joe said softly. "All they'd do is work their way through the people you love until you came back."

He was right. Elle bent over and rested her forehead on the table with a groan. "I've made such a mess," she wailed.

"Yep," Megan agreed. "But we're good at cleaning up messes, and we were all bored anyway. If you think about it, ending up at Benson Security was the best thing you could have done. You're surrounded by bona fide commandos... and Ryan."

"Thanks," Ryan said. "Remind me, what are you again? Oh, yeah, the *barely qualified* team member."

"The *trigger-happy* barely qualified team member," Megan corrected. "Never forget that part."

"It doesn't matter how skilled our team is," Elle said into the table. "We'll never be able to take on someone who's willing to cross lines we would never cross. The James Syndicate is above the law. It's fearless and has more money than you can imagine. They have connections in every law enforcement agency in the country, which makes playing by the rules when dealing with them even harder. Trust me, I've spent years thinking this through, trying to figure out what I could do to bring them down, and all I came up with was hiding and holding information over their heads. Even then, I don't think the information would cause much damage. Tommy James is untouchable."

"No, lass, everyone has a weakness." Callum sat down at the table. "All we need to do is find his. You cannae choose your genetics, but you can damn well choose your family. Sit up and look around you."

Reluctantly, Elle did as she was told.

"See these people? They're your family. Not that crapfest you grew up in."

Joe grinned at their boss. "I knew Benson Security would get you to connect with that sensitive core of yours one day."

Callum glared at him while making that low growling noise of his that made kids cry.

"Joe's joking," Megan said. "You're big and bad. Ooo, scary. Can we stop growling now?"

Callum sighed but carried on talking. "Lake says he got a call from somebody with information to share. His contact's on his way here to tell us what he knows. Hopefully, the man's got a way out of this situation that doesn't involve us hiding forever. I don't see Isobel and her sisters going for that plan."

"Do we know this contact of Lake's?" Ryan asked. "Can we trust him?"

"Aye, we know him." Callum pinched the bridge of his nose. "Jury's still out on whether we can trust him."

"Are you going to tell us who this savior is or make us

extract the information from you a sentence at a time?" Megan snapped.

Callum let out a heavy sigh. "It's Elle's very own personal spy."

For the first time in her life, Elle was completely at a loss for words.

5

"You know," Elle said to the lawyer Benson Security had provided for her, "I think the police are going about this whole interrogation room thing the wrong way. I mean, wouldn't people be more likely to talk if they were comfortable? They should get rid of the boring table and chairs and puke-green walls and instead go with pastel shades. A comfy sofa, an Espresso machine, and snacks would be good too. They could even add a TV and some magazines." She grinned at the woman, who was staring at her like she was talking Chinese. "You know? Like a posh doctor's waiting room. Don't you think that would work better on the criminal psyche?"

"I think," Ms. Patel said in all seriousness, "that I have no idea how the James family gene pool produced someone like you. Or, more importantly, how you made it to adulthood."

She seemed genuinely mystified, so Elle answered honestly, "Online gaming, *Star Wars* movies, and *Buffy* comic books. Never underestimate the influence of decent geek culture on an impressionable young mind."

"Fascinating," the lawyer muttered as she stared at Elle.

Elle beamed at her. "It's a good job that I have zero self-esteem issues because you have a seriously elitist, authoritarian vibe going on." From her long, poker-straight, shiny black hair to her pristine black suit, everything about Ms. Patel suggested she was going over dissection techniques in her head while staring at you. "Now that I think about it, you remind me of someone I know. Have you ever met Rachel Ford-Talbot?"

"Can't say that I have."

"You should. If you added some vamp-red nail polish to your look and swapped out your warm skin tone for milky white, you'd get Rachel. It's uncanny. You two could be the same person in alternate realities." Elle folded her legs underneath her on the seat, tailor-style. "I need to see how far this goes. Do you come from money? Are you related to Prince Harry? Do you think tact is only for the lower classes?"

Ms. Patel blinked several times, reminding Elle of the reptile house at London Zoo. No matter who was caged, you knew who the true predator was. She cocked her head as she considered Elle. "Usually, I intimidate people."

Elle laughed and flapped a hand. "Don't worry; it's not you. It's me. You've still got it. It's just that when you've grown up around the London Mob and then had Rachel as a boss, you're pretty much immune to the whole intimidation thing. Although I pretend to be intimidated sometimes. Mainly for Callum. He'd be hurt if he knew I saw him as a big grumpy teddy bear." She glanced around. Still the same boring room. "Do you think they've given up asking me questions?"

Ms. Patel's eyes narrowed. "No, it's more likely they're scrambling for some cause to hold you. Don't worry. It won't work." She glanced at her Cartier wristwatch. "Another half an hour, and I'll inform them you've finished cooperating with their inquiries, and we're leaving. After that, they can contact you through me. They've already let everyone except Callum go. There's no need to keep you two any longer."

"I'm pretty sure they don't think I've been cooperating with anything. You've barely let me answer a question."

"That's what your employer pays me to do."

"Doesn't it make me look guilty when I don't answer their questions?"

"It makes you look smart and protected. The last thing you want is to appear vulnerable. Sharks can smell blood in the water for miles."

"You really are kinda scary," Elle assured her.

There was a knock at the door, and one of Ms. Patel's minions stuck their head into the room. "May I have a word?" he said. "I need your input on something."

"Of course." The lawyer stood and faced Elle. "Don't talk to anyone without me. Not one word."

Elle nodded solemnly. "You're the boss of the firm, aren't you?"

"Of course," Ms. Patel repeated as she sailed from the room.

Elle sighed. The police had confiscated her burner phone, and her laptop was dead. She felt naked without a device in her hand—and strangely nervous. She was sure a good psychiatrist would have a field day with that.

The door opened, and an older police constable walked in. He had the whole Santa vibe going on as he smiled warmly at her. "There will be no more questions today. You're free to go—however, please keep us informed of your whereabouts in case we have any further questions. I've been sent to escort you to the front door. Ready to go?"

"Yes!" Elle was out of her chair and running before he'd finished talking. "Wait, what about my lawyer?"

"She's helping a colleague and said to tell you she'll call you as soon as she's finished."

"Great. Where do I collect my bag and phone? Someone took them off me when we arrived."

"Front desk. We'll pick up your things on the way out." He held the door open for her. "Looks like you're eager to see the back of us," he teased.

"It's nothing personal," Elle informed him as they walked down the corridor and through the doors to the stairs. "I'm all for cops. Yay, the cops. Go, cops, go. But I've got places to be and things to do."

"Legal things, I hope?"

She grinned at him. "Of course, Officer."

When they reached the door at the bottom of the stair-well, he held it open and motioned her through. She'd already taken several steps before it registered that she wasn't in the reception area.

"I think we've gone down one flight too many," she said. "This is the garage."

She turned back toward the door but didn't make it. A hand yanked at one of her blue bunches, almost ripping out her hair, and the tip of a knife bit at her throat. Her eyes shot to the police officer, whose friendly smile had evaporated.

"Thanks for the delivery," the man holding her said. "Tommy's been hunting everywhere for this one. You can expect a bonus for this."

"It's a pleasure doing business with you boys." The cop turned away.

"Wait," Elle called to him. "You're just going to hand me over to them? Don't you care what they'll do to me?"

He shrugged. "Not really." And then he was gone, the door slamming behind him.

Elle frantically scanned the walls for cameras, hoping someone would notice she was being kidnapped. But the only one she spotted was clearly broken, hanging loose on its fittings.

She took a deep breath and did the only thing left to her: she screamed. "Help! I'm being kidnapped. Help!" She slammed a heavy Dr. Martens boot down on the toes of her captor.

He grunted in pain, but his hold on her tightened. "Do you want me to slice you, bitch? Tommy doesn't care what condition you arrive in. He only cares that you can still talk." The cold steel of his blade slid over her throat and down to the curve of her breast. "Lots of places I can cut that won't interfere with your voice."

He shoved her toward a blue minivan parked beside the stairwell door. A baby on board sticker in the back window made her wonder what'd happened to the mother who usually drove the van. A young guy she didn't recognize stood beside it, dressed in jeans and a hooded sweatshirt rather than the suits worn by the gang's more influential members.

His grin as he opened the van door for her made it clear he was happy with his life choices. Gang life suited him. It was in the gleeful appreciation written all over his face as he watched her struggle against the knife.

"Hurry up," another man called from inside the vehicle.

"Three men to pick up little old me." Elle hated the quaver in her voice. "I'm honored."

"Shut up, bitch, and get in the car." The guy holding her hair propelled her toward the open door.

Then he stumbled.

The knife fell from her throat, and Elle was shoved hard behind a nearby car, where she fell to her knees. By the time she'd scrambled around to see what was happening, a man stood behind her attacker, who'd been stabbed in the chest with the same knife he'd used on her.

The man had his arm wrapped around her attacker, holding him up as a shield. In his other hand, he held a silenced pistol. It took Elle a second to realize he'd already put a bullet between the eyes of Tommy's young recruit, who now lay motionless on the ground by the car. Stunned, Elle watched as the man hid behind his human shield while leaning into the van and shooting once.

Just like that. All three men were dead.

Her savior tossed his shield away before calmly striding over to Elle and crouching in front of her. "You hurt, Ellie?" he asked in that nondescript accent that could have been from anywhere.

David.

She blinked several times, swallowed with a dry throat, and said, "My knee's scraped."

His smile was so dazzling that it took a second to see past it to the bruises on his face.

"Oh!" Her hand shot out, fingertips tracing the cut at the corner of his mouth and the blackening bruise on his cheekbone. "You're the one who's hurt."

"Safe location first. Injuries second." He threaded his fingers through hers and stood, taking her with him. "Come on. I have a vehicle."

They hurried through the garage to a nondescript rental car, where he opened the passenger door and helped her inside.

"I jammed the signals from the cameras," he said. "We need to get out of here before they come to see what's happened to them."

Elle watched him jog around the front of the car and climb behind the wheel.

Like everything else he did, David's driving was efficient. No movement wasted. Awestruck, she swiveled in her seat and stared at him as he wove through London's traffic.

"We need to swap out this car," he said as he turned into one of the big parking garages. "'Fraid we won't be renting our next ride."

Elle was too scared to speak in case this was all a dream, and she woke up to find herself sitting alone in a cell with no David in sight. Or worse, lying on the floor in one of Tommy's many wet rooms.

They parked on one of the middle levels, walked up a level, and helped themselves to a small blue Honda. David broke in and hot-wired it in no time at all, then they were on the road again.

"You alright, Ellie?" he asked as they wove through traffic.

She twisted her fingers in the hem of her T-shirt. "I'm in a bit of a pickle."

His lips curved up again, making her melt. "So I hear."

Blinking to clear her mind, she took in her surroundings. They were heading west. "Where are we going?"

"Benson Security safe house."

Her eyebrows shot up. "You know where that is?" She'd thought its location was limited to their team.

"I know lots of stuff."

He negotiated the chaotic London traffic with ease, keeping one eye on the rearview mirror, watching for trouble.

"David," Elle asked because she couldn't wait any longer. The question was burning a hole in her stomach. "Why are you here?"

He glanced over at her, his dark eyes burning. "I'm here for you, Ellie Blue," he said before returning his attention to the road.

Elle reached out, flicked the air-conditioning to icy cold, and blasted it at her face.

6

———————

James Family Home
North London

"What do you mean, you don't have her?" Tommy James tossed his napkin onto the table beside what remained of the lunch his five-star chef had prepared for him.

"Cops turned up." Marcus stood at the other end of the dining table, his face an emotionless mask as usual.

Equally familiar was the sight of his son's best friend, Abasi, at his side. Those dark eyes of his stared through Tommy. One day, he'd remind Abasi who was boss, and he'd do it by plucking out those insolent eyes.

He glanced behind his son, but no one else walked through the dining room doors. "Where the fuck is Leo?" He'd sent Leo along on the pickup job because he knew that, unlike his son, Leo wouldn't hesitate to put a bullet in Elle if it made bringing her back easier.

"Cops got him," Marcus said, as though commenting on the weather.

Tommy stood, rolling down his shirt sleeves. Beside him, Arnold "Cutter" Matthews, his trusted advisor, pushed back his chair and casually swept his jacket aside to reveal his gun.

"You think I need protection from my own son?" Tommy mocked him.

Cutter shrugged, making Tommy laugh.

"Paranoid bastard," he told his oldest friend as he snapped his fingers, and his butler scurried away to retrieve his jacket from the closet off the dining room.

Although there wasn't one drop of Italian blood running through his veins, Tommy had styled himself, and his empire, on the portrayal of Sicilian Mafia ubiquitous in the movies of his youth. To that end, he always wore custom-made three-piece suits, favoring a silver-gray with a darker gray pinstripe and crisp white shirts. Of course, he needed a little bling too, so he wore a platinum ring on his pinky finger, and around his neck hung a medallion depicting St. Jude Thaddeus—the patron saint of lost causes and criminals. The most expensive barber in London's West End maintained his thick silver hair, and twice a week, a girl came in to give him a facial.

Tommy James hadn't made it to the top of his chosen career by looking like a common thug. Or by acting like one. He was smart, ruthless, and vain. And he saw nothing wrong with any of it.

As he shrugged into his jacket, he focused on his son. "Where is she now?"

"Can't be far," Marcus said. "They had another way out of the building, or we would have had her."

Cutter stirred beside him. "What I want to know is how she's managed to hide in London all this time. Right under our fucking noses." He narrowed his eyes at Marcus. "Thought you said she'd skipped the city."

Marcus appeared bored. "Must've come back."

"Bullshit," Cutter snapped. "She's been here all the time; you screwed up looking for her—if you even tried."

"I know you have problems with arithmetic, Cutter," Marcus said, "so I'll help you out. There are nine million people in London. Say a third of those nine million are kids, and another third men, that leaves three million women spread out over roughly six hundred square miles. You might have time to check every single one of those women to see if they're my sister, but I've got a business to run."

"You've got a business to run?" Cutter looked as if he was about to reach for one of his famous knives. "This search was top fucking priority, and last I checked, the business belonged to Tommy, you jumped-up little prick."

"Later," Tommy ordered Cutter. "We got photos of our girl?"

Abasi pulled out his phone and tapped the screen. A few seconds later, Tommy's phone chimed. He took it from his pocket and flicked through the images Abasi had sent him. It was the first time he'd set eyes on Elle in years, and she'd changed. Gone was the waist-length auburn hair with its fiery red streaks, and in its place was a jaw-length, dyed blue mess. She wore pale purple fitted jeans, a green T-shirt with a slogan across the chest, and pink boots. Every item of clothing was too short or too tight. She looked cheap and garish.

For a second, his vision clouded with red. This wasn't how he'd taught her to dress. Where were the designer clothes he'd bought her? The ones that covered her up and made her look classy? Like a good girl. A rich girl with privileges. Ones she'd thrown away when she turned her back on the family. In a fury, he tossed his phone at the wall and watched it smash and fall to the floor.

"Your sister's turned into a slut," he spat in disgust. "Just like her mother."

Silence was thick in the room as the men tensed, hands on weapons.

Tommy adjusted his suit jacket before eyeing his son. "Go through everyone she knows. Take them all out. Anyone who's ever helped her. Her friends. Her coworkers. All of them."

"The cops..." Marcus said.

"Fuck the cops." He had them in his pocket anyway. "Do what I tell you. Just don't get caught. I want that little bitch's life shredded around her. I want her drowning in blood by the time you get your hands on her. You understand me?"

Marcus gave a curt nod and strode from the room, followed by Abasi.

Tommy watched them leave before turning to his most trusted man. "Watch them," he ordered Cutter. "I got a feeling in my bones I don't like. Something isn't sitting right. Make sure the job gets done."

"You got it, boss," Cutter said as he got to his feet.

7

Benson Security's London safe house was located in the suburb of Bedfont, right beside Heathrow Airport. It was a high-traffic area, with seasonal and shift workers aplenty, which meant a bunch of new faces wouldn't attract too much attention. The location also made it easy for them to access several different escape routes if necessary.

The house itself was nothing to write home about. Built by the government in the seventies, it was exactly like the hundreds of other government-built houses in the area—white stucco walls, gray tile roof, and a small garden. It had three small bedrooms and a bathroom upstairs, and a kitchen, a second bathroom, and a living room downstairs. Benson Security had put in the second bathroom upstairs at the same time they converted the attic into a fourth bedroom. The house was boring and functional. It was also safe.

David parked their stolen car on the street, and they walked up the path to the house, where Elle let them in using the access code for the lock. Everyone except Callum was already there, and nobody seemed particularly surprised to see David enter the living room with Elle.

"What happened to your jeans?" Megan asked from where she sat curled up in the corner of one of the large gray sofas. The rest of the team was scattered in various seats around the room.

Elle glanced down at her favorite jeans. Lavender with Minnie Mouses (mice?) embroidered on the back pockets, they now had a hole ripped across the knee. And not in a cool, intentional way.

"David shoved me to the ground so he could take out three of Tommy's men, who'd grabbed me in the police station parking garage after a corrupt constable handed me over."

Five identically stunned faces stared at her, making her explain further: "He went all Ethan Hunt on them. Killed one guy with his own knife and shot the other two. Then we stole a car."

Mouths opened and closed, but no words came out, so Elle carried on. "The dirty cop's still alive, but I'm not sure my lawyer is. I don't know if they conned her out of the room so they could get to me, or if she left for a totally legit reason, and the cop just took advantage of her being gone. I should probably call someone to check she's okay."

Still nothing from the team. She pointed at her leg. "And I scraped my knee."

Joe cleared his throat. "I don't know where to start unpacking that."

With a grin, David took her hand. "Come on, Ellie Blue, you're freaking everyone out. Let's get you cleaned up before Callum arrives." He gently steered her toward the door, calling over his shoulder as he went, "If somebody wants to make coffee, I wouldn't say no."

Behind her, Julia said, "Who's Ethan Hunt?"

"Spy from the *Mission Impossible* movies," Megan replied. "Scarily skilled."

"Oh, okay," Julia said. "I'll make coffee then."

Elle heaved a sigh. There were days when she despaired of her teammates. "You know who Ethan Hunt is, right?"

"Yeah." David's bruises were getting worse, with a massive black eye blooming above the cut on his cheek. He pushed open the door to the ground floor bathroom. Finding it first try either by the use of X-ray vision or pure luck. "He takes down fake terrorists, using a combination of carefully designed stunts, imaginary tech, and special effects."

"Whoa, touchy much." She sat on the edge of the generic white bathtub while David searched under the sink for a first aid kit. Of course, there was one sitting there waiting for him.

He crouched in front of her and unzipped the kit. "Real spies don't wear masks."

"They do, you know." Elle wanted to run her fingers through his chocolate brown hair. It was short on the sides, a little longer on top, and a tad too neat for her liking. "I watched a TED Talk by a woman who helped develop masks for the FBI. Or was it the CIA? All I can remember is she wore one during a meeting with one of the President Bushes, and he couldn't tell her face wasn't real."

"That might have more to do with the President Bushes than the mask."

"Whatever. I saw the photos, and the mask totally rocked. What do you think of James Bond?"

He didn't hesitate. "Misogynist with a drinking problem."

Elle couldn't help but beam her approval. "You know, I think we might be made for each other."

His gorgeous lips quirked as he held up a pair of scissors. "We have two options here. I can cut the leg of your jeans to get to the graze, or you can take them off. Which will it be?"

Had the temperature in the bathroom suddenly spiked? Could you have hot flushes in your twenties?

"I like these jeans," she said.

"Then take them off."

For a second, it felt like a lens had focused in on him. All she could see was his features in high definition.

"Did you know," she said, "that the brown of your eyes is so dark it looks almost black?"

"I might have noticed that on occasion." Those black eyes of his sparkled with amusement.

"Are they contacts, or is the color real?"

"Elle, stop stalling and take off your jeans."

"I'm not stalling."

"Your jeans are still on. Take them off or lose them." David held up the scissors to make his point.

"Okey-dokey," she said as she stood.

His eyes stayed on her face as she unbuttoned her jeans.

"Why does this feel weirdly kinky?" she asked. "Like we're playing doctor."

The panty-melting smile was back again. Which did *not* help at all.

She let the jeans fall to her ankles and sat back down with a thump before her legs gave way. The cold enamel edge of the bath bit into the backs of her thighs.

"Here, let me." David reached for a fluffy white towel and folded it in half. "Lift," he ordered.

She rested her hands on his shoulders to steady herself as she lifted her backside from the bath. As David leaned in to slip the towel under her, his breath fanned out over her chest, and she swore she could feel it through her T-shirt.

"Better?" he asked when she sat back down.

All she could do was nod and swallow hard.

"This will sting." He ripped open an antiseptic wipe.

With one hand cradling her calf, he gently dabbed the graze on her knee. She barely felt it as she watched his hands on her skin. Strong, slender hands. Hands that were skilled and capable, yet oh so careful when they touched her.

His thumb stroked her leg as he tended to her wound and Elle found herself wriggling in place. How could one innocuous caress make her want more? It was as though every nerve ending in her body was primed for his slightest touch. The feel of his skin brushing against hers. The warmth of his breath on her bare flesh.

Tingles ran up her leg to the V of her thighs, making her hyper aware that she was sitting in a skimpy pair of lacy blue panties—in front of the man who'd starred in her fantasies for years. Her fingers curled into the cool plastic of the bath's rim. Holding on tight to stop herself from reaching for him and pulling him closer. She wanted those hands to slide up her thighs as he widened her knees and leaned into her...

"All clean," he whispered, before blowing on her paltry wound.

The chill of air over sensitive skin made her tug her bottom lip in between her teeth to stop from moaning aloud. All the while her eyes ate up the way his shoulders flexed as he ministered to her. And the solid strength in his thighs as he crouched before her. Her gaze meandered down from his glass cut jaw, over his firm chest, and along his arms until she was back where she started—those glorious hands.

That's when she noticed his wrists.

With a gasp, she grasped his right hand in hers and pushed up his sleeve. There were bruises around his wrist.

Dark, purple, angry bruises. All of the burning desire that'd been building within her was suddenly gone.

"Show me the other one," she ordered.

Without making a performance of it, he rested his other hand on her knee. She pushed up his sweater sleeve to reveal identical bruising.

"David," she whispered. "What happened?"

"Nothing that hasn't happened before and will probably happen again." He removed his hands from hers and continued to clean up her pathetic little graze.

She studied his face as he carefully smoothed ointment over her wound and applied a soft dressing. His focus was absolute.

"Okay, we're done here." He stood and turned away to wash his hands in the sink.

Elle pulled up her jeans and refastened them. "Your turn. Take off the sweater." No playfulness in her voice now; she was genuinely worried about what she might find.

"I can take care of my own injuries, Elle. Go get a drink, and I'll meet you in the living room."

"No." She picked up the scissors. "I'll cut the damn thing off you if I have to."

His eyes met hers in the mirror. They both knew she didn't have a hope in hell of carrying out her threat unless David wanted her to. Slowly, deliberately, he turned to face her. Then, just as slowly, he reached for the bottom of his black sweater and, taking the black T-shirt underneath with it, he pulled it over his head.

She sucked in a breath, tears filling her eyes. There were bruises everywhere. A rainbow of color spread across his ribs and kidneys. She glanced back up at his face, then again at his wrists. He'd been strung up and beaten. The sight made her want to weep and rage in equal measure.

David placed his clothes on the edge of the sink before

taking the scissors from her tight fist. She'd been holding them like a weapon. As though she could stab the person who'd done this to him.

"It's okay," *he* consoled *her*. "Nothing's broken."

"It's *not* okay. Nothing about this is okay. Who did this to you?" The words came out clipped as anger coiled around her throat.

"It doesn't matter. I dealt with them."

"It does matter." Tentatively, she reached out and traced the damage along his ribs with a barely there touch. "You matter."

David held her wrist to halt her exploration. "You can't say something like that to a man like me."

"I don't understand," she said as she searched his expression for answers.

All she saw was a man who seemed bewildered by his own reactions. A man who was used to being hurt and coping with it on his own. Her heart physically ached at the thought, making her want to press soft kisses to each and every injury—as though that would make it all better.

"Elle," he said evenly. "Men like me, we're nothing more than blunt instruments. There's nothing about us that can't be replaced. Nothing that would be mourned if we were gone. We're trained to suffer for the cause, and we're good at it, but we don't matter. Never think that we do. It'll just end up with you getting hurt."

"No." She shook her head, unable to believe what he was telling her. All the while seeing that he meant every word. It was clear, he thought he was educating her in the reality of life. Breaking an awful truth to her as gently as possible.

Well, he was wrong.

"Don't say that," she scolded. "You matter. Everybody matters. You believe that, don't you?"

He studied her for a second. "You're a helluva girl, Ellie Blue," he said as he shrugged back into his sweater.

"That's a non-answer if ever I've heard one," she muttered.

"Go sit with the others." He opened the door for her. "I'll be out in a minute."

"I can help with your injuries. Let me care for you the way you did for me."

"I've got this," he said.

"No, really I—"

He raised his voice to call out to the team. "Can somebody come get Elle? She's unsteady on her feet. A cup of sugary tea would help too."

The words were scarcely out of his mouth before Ryan appeared. "Do I need to carry you?" he asked Elle.

"No." Her reply was terse.

"Yep." Ryan put an arm around her shoulders and led her from the room. "That's her hangry face. Don't worry, we have Snickers."

But David wasn't worried. He'd already closed the door.

As soon as he'd locked the bathroom door, David let out a shaky breath and grasped the edges of the sink. Holding on tight, arms tense and straight, he stared at his reflection in the mirror.

"What the hell are you doing?" he asked himself.

Elle would never understand his place in the world, while he'd accepted it long ago. He shouldn't even have brought the subject up with her. But more than that, he shouldn't have touched her. And he sure as hell shouldn't have been flirting.

"You're being an asshole," he told himself.

Especially when he knew he couldn't go there with Elle. They didn't have a future together and all he was doing was teasing them both. Yet, he couldn't seem to stay away from her either. It was torture. Hanging his head, he let out a low groan. *Irresistible.* That's what she'd been since the moment he'd set eyes on her. And talking to her had only made it worse. He never should have agreed to that first meeting in South America. Up until then, he'd been able to keep it professional.

A vision of Elle appeared in his mind. She sat tailor-style on the hood of a beat-up SUV in Middle-of-Nowhere, Peru. It was nighttime, and he'd been brought in to help Lake Benson's team retrieve a kidnap victim. Elle's bright blue hair had bounced around as she explained how she'd hacked an unhackable closed system. Then she'd asked him which agency he worked with and, when he didn't give an answer, had requested some fingerprints and DNA so she could do some digging into his background. Like a fool, he'd left her a sample of his DNA after the mission ended. All because he couldn't resist playing with the fearless blue-haired girl.

He'd known then that he had to stay away from her. And he had. Until the need to see her, hear her...touch her had become too great. He'd told himself he was only chasing her down to warn her to stop searching for him—a feeble excuse at best. The truth was, he'd been weak. She was a light in the darkness of his life. The warm, flickering flame of a candle behind glass. Enticing him to come closer, to sit awhile, to relax. When relaxing in his profession could get him killed.

Or worse—get her killed.

And he couldn't be responsible for the death of another person he cared about.

David pushed away from the sink and pulled off his

sweater. It was black. Like his jeans. His shoes. His life. A life lived in darkness. A life spent hiding in shadows, hiding his identity, being invisible. There were days when he wondered if there was anything of substance left of him.

He barely registered the sting of the antiseptic; his mind was so deeply entrenched in his thoughts of Elle. She was everything David wasn't. Color to his black void. Light to his darkness. She was bright, full of life, bubbling over with joy. Even now, when her world was crashing down around her and the people she loved were in danger, she still couldn't help spreading sunshine. It was in her teasing jokes and witty sarcasm, her self-deprecating comments, and the way she cared for those around her. What could a man like him offer someone like her? A bitter laugh escaped him at the thought.

With no family, no friends, and no government willing to accept his service, he was as far from a catch as a man could get. His enemies were legion, his sins a stain that tainted anything he touched. He was a man whose past had been erased and whose future was uncertain.

A man who got his own wife killed.

Damn. He hadn't let himself think about Celeste in years. Nineteen years old and married to the first woman who'd loved him. The first *person*. Even now, he still wasn't certain he'd felt the same way about Celeste as she had about him. All he remembered was that he'd found something he'd never had before, and he'd wanted to keep hold of it.

Then, the government had recruited him.

Work had followed him home.

And Celeste had paid the price.

No, he'd never put someone he cared about in danger ever again. He'd never watch them die. All he could offer any woman was his ability to act as a weapon in her defense.

After all, he was a blunt instrument, one his government had pointed at the enemy—until his handlers had turned their backs on him. Washed their hands and left him alone to deal with the price on his head.

David stared at his scarred hands. They'd been drenched in blood for most of his life. A stream of it from the bodies he'd left in his wake. Hell, today alone, he'd killed five men. There was no getting around the fact he was a monster. In any other line of work, he'd be labeled a serial killer and locked away indefinitely.

And yet, he'd let his blood-stained hands touch Elle. Let his lying lips kiss hers. Twice. He'd given in to temptation twice and craved her ever since. His eyes closed with the heaviness of it all. He never should have kissed her. Never should have teased her. He blamed his lapse in judgment on the shock he'd felt when she treated him as a playmate rather than a killer. An enemy. A target.

Had he ever had a playmate? Not that he could remember. There'd been no carefree laughter in his childhood. No fun of any kind. Even Celeste had been careful around him, as though he were broken. Then Elle had appeared, all wild blue hair and teasing smile. With sparkling eyes filled with mischief, she'd challenged him to play with her.

And he'd been weak, given in to temptation.

It couldn't go on.

If losing Celeste had nearly killed him, losing Elle would destroy him completely.

Taking a deep breath, David tugged on his sweater again and faced himself in the mirror.

"You do the job, then you leave," he ordered. "And this time, you never come back."

If he'd had a heart, the words would have broken it. Instead, he felt resolved. It was time to stop playing and do the job; before he left—forever.

With a steadying breath, he opened the bathroom door and strode down the hall to the living room. Elle sat on the sofa beside Megan, a chocolate bar in her hand. Her eyes shot straight to him, and the look in them felt like a battering ram against the walls he'd just built. But David was ready for it, and this time, he didn't go to her side. He didn't call her Ellie or Blue, didn't even smile. He simply nodded before turning away.

"Callum's on his way in," Joe said from the window.

The front door opened, then slammed shut, and Callum strode into the room. His gaze went straight to Elle.

"Good. You're alive," he said. "Thanks for letting me know. I just spent hours of my life stuck in a room, answering daft questions from people who clearly had an agenda but weren't willing to share what it was exactly. And then, as they're about to free me, they tell me that Elle's disappeared, and there are three dead bodies in the garage." His frown shifted to David. "Your work, I assume."

David inclined his head but said nothing. It seemed Callum was on a roll and didn't need his input.

When David didn't provide an explanation, Elle jumped to his defense. "A cop handed me over to three of Tommy's guys. He was saving me."

"He could have bloody well done it without the body count!" Callum roared.

The Scotsman was indeed on a roll. David hadn't spent a massive amount of time with Callum, but he knew enough to realize that in situations like this, it was best to stay quiet and let him get it out of his system. Obviously, Elle hadn't gotten that memo. Or she liked to live dangerously. Probably the latter.

"We're in this up to our necks," Callum ranted. "We don't need some hotshot coming in and making things worse." He glared at David. "You're only here because I trust Lake, and he says you've got information we need. If you're going to help us with this shit show, then you will follow orders like everybody else on this team; am I clear?" Apparently, he didn't require a reply, as he kept on going. "That means no more random assassinations. No more covert bullshit. No more secret crap, full stop. Am I clear?" It seemed Callum had run out of steam.

"I can be part of a team when I have to," David said evenly.

"Aye, and that's a half-arsed answer if ever I heard one." Callum stalked over to the coffee pot on the table and poured himself a mug. "Spit it out then. What's this information you have for us?"

The rapt attention of everyone in the room didn't faze David. This, he could easily talk about. It was his area of expertise. "There are several factions after Elle. Her family. The Russian Mob, who thinks she has information that will help them steal her family's operation out from under them. Countless government agencies who want to use her to take down the James Syndicate. A couple of terrorist groups who believe she stole information on them when she ran from her family. There might be more, but those are the ones I know for sure. I checked with my sources on the way here."

He'd been watching Elle carefully as he spoke, and when she paled, he felt the sight like a knife to his gut.

"Being popular is totally overrated," she joked, but it fell flat.

"Add to that, the James Family have people seeded throughout most law enforcement agencies, making it hard to trust even our contacts on the inside. We might know the person we give our information to, but we don't know whose hands it'll end up in."

"You got any good news?" Callum was clearly unimpressed by his intel.

"As far as I can tell, the James Family has a head start on everyone else who wants Elle. If we take them down, we could put an end to this whole thing once and for all. The best way to do that is to escalate tensions between them and the Albanian Mob. They've been nipping at each other's heels for a while now, and it won't take much to make the situation explode. We need a third party, though, to ensure they don't figure out who's to blame for anything that happens. I'm thinking we rope in MC20. They're young, violent, and power-hungry. If we pit all three against each other, that should sort the problem for us."

There was a beat of silence before Callum said, "Your big idea to get Elle off everyone's radar is to start a war?"

"Yeah," David said. "Preferably while *not* getting caught or killed."

"There's one tiny, wee problem with that idea." Callum spread his hands. "All our resources are stuck in the crime scene that used to be our office building. Surveillance equipment, weapons, computers. Hell, we don't even have decent vehicles. All we've got are our crappy junker cars and cheap burner phones. Meanwhile, the people we could call for backup are holed up in Scotland, protecting their families—and ours. The rest of my team, the London team, are out on jobs. They're scattered around the globe and can't exactly walk out on clients, even if they could get back in time to help. This"—he gestured around the room—"is literally everything we have."

David pointed at himself. "One spy." Then he pointed at each of them in turn. "One retired SAS officer, one non-active Marine, one former army ranger, an ex-soldier with skills and experience he doesn't talk about, a first-class project manager who's a savant when it comes to seeing patterns in situations, the best hacker in the world, and whatever Megan is." He took a sip of his coffee. "*This* is everything we need."

They stared at him for a long moment before Ryan spoke. "I'm with the spy. I say we go all A-Team on their arses. I call dibs on Faceman."

"No way," Joe complained. "I'm better looking than any of you, and I've got more charm. *I'm* Faceman."

"Well, I'm not going to be Howling Mad Murdock." Ryan glared at Joe.

"No, that's obviously Megan," Joe said. "You can be B.A."

"Bad Attitude Baracus? Are you nuts? That's Callum!"

From there, things quickly deteriorated into an argument about which A-Team character best suited whom. Meanwhile, David sipped his coffee, keeping his gaze averted from Elle.

8

David was avoiding Elle. The coward. She'd let him get away with it, for now, seeing as they were busy trying to dig her out of her hole. But her generous spirit wouldn't last much longer. Mainly because she was genetically incapable of dealing with other people's mood swings.

The team had worked late into the night, talking with contacts and gathering as much information as possible on everyone's operations before handing it over to Julia for her to organize. Around three a.m., Elle fell asleep on top of the crappy laptop David had bought from an outlet beside the airport—because he was the only one who had untraceable credit cards.

Typical. Bloody spies. Everything about them was secret and untraceable. Which was seriously annoying. Almost as annoying as the distance he'd put between them since they'd hung out in the bathroom. And yeah, that was a weird sentence, but whatever. What the hell was with all that 'I don't matter' crap anyway? That was some seriously screwed up thinking. And one of several topics she'd like to bring up with him if he ever stopped avoiding her. Others included getting him to tell her his full name. Didn't he realize how crazy it made her being kept in the dark? Probably. He had to be doing it deliberately. And *that* conclusion did *not* lighten her mood.

"David's gone out to talk with some of his contacts," Ryan said when she stumbled into the kitchen, wearing yesterday's clothes.

"Did I ask where he'd gone?" She jerked open the fridge and growled. It was full of healthy food.

"Don't blame me for the food options," Ryan said. "Your boyfriend has something against junk food. He cleared it out and replaced it with that crap."

"He's not my boyfriend," Elle snapped in a full-on, head-spinning *Exorcist* voice.

After barely a few hours' sleep, she'd woken with a crick in her neck, a hunger only sugar could satisfy, and a deep desire to stab the first person who spoke to her. Which didn't bode well for Ryan.

"Before you go completely feral on me." Strong survival instincts meant he'd easily read her mood. "You should know I have coffee, and I saved some fresh donuts from the culling. If you're nice, I'll share."

Okay, maybe she wouldn't stab him after all. She stalked to the table and plopped down in a chair, facing Ryan. "Gimme."

"You're usually the unbearably cheery one in the morning. What gives with channeling Megan?"

"Um, let me see." Elle held up a hand and started ticking off on her fingers. "I was shot at by my father's crazy mobster army, my brother wants me dead, or worse, the office was blown up, I was questioned for hours in a police interrogation room, a cop sold me out to three thugs, the thugs tried to kidnap me, I watched David kill the thugs, I'm worried some government agency will find me and make me disappear, David's having mood swings that are doing my head in, I'm stuck in a generic four-bedroom house beside Heathrow Airport, planning to start a war that will probably get us all killed, and I scraped my knee." She took a deep breath. "On top of all that, I had to destroy my baby!"

Ryan hurriedly opened the donut box and thrust one into her hand. "I'm sure your laptop didn't feel a thing when it died."

Elle bit off a chunk of the donut while Ryan poured her a mug of coffee. When he was done, she fell on it as though it were essential for life itself, not even caring that it tasted like mud. She needed the caffeine. There was nowhere near enough of it pumping through her system, especially for a woman who, when asked, gave her blood type as Caffeine-positive.

Feeling marginally better, she continued to munch her way through the carbs. "I need clean clothes," she grumbled around a mouthful of jam-filled sugary goodness.

"Your wish is my command." Ryan jumped up, walked to the corner of the room, picked up a paper carrier bag, and offered it to her. "Julia made me go clothes shopping for everybody—with David's credit card because he had better things to do with his time. Apparently, buying clothes is beneath James Bond."

"Thanks." She grabbed the bag and tipped its contents out onto the table. And promptly choked on her donut. "What is *this*?" She held up a plain black T-shirt between the tips of her index finger and thumb.

"A T-shirt," the fool said.

Elle stared at the pile of clothes in disgust. She had a choice of black or black. No cartoon figures. No sunny colors. No pithy slogans.

"Before you go all Xena on me," Ryan said. "Remember,

it's a disguise. A geeky chick with blue hair is easy to spot, which is why there's a box of hair dye in there too."

Surprise, surprise, it was black.

If Ryan noticed her dismay, he didn't let on. "I got you a pair of black Dr. Martens." To her horror, he actually sounded pleased about that. "There's eyeliner and toiletry stuff in there as well. I figured goth was about as far from fairy-rainbow as you could get, so I even tossed in a tube of black lipstick." He spread his arms, a goofy grin on his face. "Am I a genius or what?"

"Or what," she said as she shoved the clothes away from her. "Wearing this will suck the optimism right out of me."

"While keeping you alive," he pointed out. "You're welcome."

"It doesn't exactly help me to blend with the general populace, though, does it? People are going to remember a goth almost as much as a blue-haired chick." Which left her with a dilemma, as she couldn't go back to her natural brown color either. That would only make her more recognizable to her father's army. "I need to go blonde. I could totally rock a Marilyn Monroe look. What do you think?"

"I think I'm underappreciated," he grumbled.

"Good, you're up." Julia bustled into the room. Unlike Elle, Julia wore a brand-new pair of gray dress pants teamed with a white blouse.

"Why didn't you get a disguise for Julia?" Elle asked the moron.

"I did. She's wearing trousers. When was the last time you saw her in trousers? Never. That's when." His smug self-congratulation was almost comical.

"Don't worry." Julia started a new pot of coffee. "The clothes Ryan bought are only for today. I've ordered more that will be delivered later."

"They deliver, and you still made me go shopping?" Ryan was aghast.

"You were bored," Julia said.

"What she means," Elle translated, "is you were annoying. Which generally goes hand in hand with you being bored."

"We did need clean clothes this morning," Julia muttered, her focus on arranging the boxes of tea bags in alphabetical order. "We're having a briefing in the living room in an hour. If you've learned anything new, could you send it to me before then?"

"Sorry, Julia, I don't have anything else." Elle helped herself to another donut. "I'm not even sure the info I gave you will be any use; most of it is years out of date. They changed how they communicate after I hacked them and took what I found with me when I ran."

"Don't worry." Julia had moved on to organizing the contents of the fridge. "I've been cross-referencing what you gave me with the latest information the rest of the team's getting from their contacts. We won't use anything we can't verify."

"Okay." Elle pushed up from the table, taking the ugly clothes with her. "I'm going to shower."

"Use the one downstairs," Julia said. "Joe's in the upstairs bathroom."

"Our next safe house needs more toilets," Ryan said. "What am I supposed to do if I have to pee while everyone's showering?"

Elle shook her head and pointed at the backyard. "Or you could hold it, you child."

As she left the room, she heard Ryan say, "I don't think the donuts helped her mood any. I'll run to the shop and get some Snickers bars and energy drinks in case we need them."

"Could you pick up a couple of whiteboards while you're at it?" Julia said.

"Yeah." Ryan sounded confused. "Because everybody knows there are whiteboards in the chocolate aisle…"

"Oh," Julia said. "I need a data projector too."

"Guess I'm going to *all* the shops, then," Ryan grumbled as he let himself out of the house. "Good job I've still got super spy's credit card."

Making Elle smile for the first time since waking up.

Elle was back to her perky self by the time the meeting rolled around—despite being dressed top to toe in black. She headed straight for David, who stood by the window and had only lifted his chin to her by way of hello.

Like she'd put up with that crap. The man was talking to her. Whether he liked it or not.

"Look," she told him. "I've got a spy uniform too."

Although, she had to admit, he looked way better in black than she ever would. He also seemed to have an unlimited supply of soft, black sweaters that showed off his lean, muscular physique to perfection.

She cocked her head and considered him. "Do you keep a knitter on retainer to make those for you? Do you vet the wool before she starts? Are there some patterns you just won't consider? Like jacquard, perhaps? Does she make you lightweight sweaters for the summer months?"

"Heard you were off your game this morning." David didn't smile, but his eyes were twinkling. "I see you've bounced back."

"So," Elle mused, "you aren't talking *to* me, but you're still talking *about* me. Interesting…"

"I didn't say off her game," Ryan called from the sofa,

where he wasn't eating for a change. "I said she was channeling Grumpy Smurf."

"His name's Grouchy Smurf," Elle corrected.

"It is deeply disturbing how you know that," Ryan said.

"Is it only me," Megan said from the sofa, "or does your hair look even more luminous now you're wearing black?"

Elle narrowed her eyes at David, just to make it clear she wasn't finished with him, and then flopped onto the sofa beside Ryan. "It isn't you. My hair is suddenly neon."

Ryan snorted. "I hate to break it to you, but this is not sudden."

"Where's my Snickers?" she demanded because, really, there was no dealing with him.

He reached into the pocket of his gray hoodie and came out with half a dozen bars. "Knock yourself out."

"Any energy drinks?"

"The junk-food police already got to those, but he didn't pat me down. Otherwise, the chocolate would be gone too."

Elle narrowed her eyes at an amused David as she bit into a chocolate-and-nut block of heaven. "What have you got against comfort food?" she demanded.

"An operative needs to eat well in order to function at his peak."

"I'm not an operative. A hacker needs caffeine and sugar to stop from killing everyone around her."

David cocked an eyebrow, as if her comment didn't even deserve a full facial expression. It seemed *he* was the main source of her grumpy mood.

"Okay," Callum barked as he strode into the room, wearing yet another gray Henley. "Let's get this show on the road."

Elle elbowed Ryan. "Where are his 'disguise' clothes?"

"Like I have a death wish." With a disgusted shake of his

head, he took back one of the Snickers bars and started eating.

"Julia," Callum said as he stood beside the fireplace, arms folded, "you got everything you need to brief us?"

Julia nodded and got up from the sofa she shared with Joe, her new iPad—again, courtesy of David's credit card—gripped in her hand. Elle couldn't help but notice that David had done a marginally better job of choosing an iPad than he'd done when picking out her new laptop. While she was super grateful for the effort he'd gone to, and the expense, the guy was terrible at buying laptops. It was clear he didn't do any programming because the machine he'd chosen was shiny and pretty but had very little going for it under the hood. The chances of her wearing it out by the weekend were high.

"Ryan picked up a data projector for me," Julia said. "So, if someone will shut the blinds and pull the curtain, I can show you what I have on the back wall. We might need to bring through a couple of chairs from the dining table."

"On it." Dimitri headed out of the room.

With everyone settled into sofas, armchairs, and now kitchen chairs, and the room as dark as they could make it, Julia tapped on her iPad, and a chart appeared on the plain cream-colored wall behind her.

"This is what we know about the three crime organizations we're targeting. The James Family Syndicate is the most traditional of the three, keeping the structure and practices it's used for years. Although, it seems that Marcus and Abasi are trying to modernize things, taking more business online and working in partnership with other groups. There are also rumors that he wants to streamline their interests by getting rid of their more high-risk pursuits—working with terrorists, people trafficking, and drugs." Julia shot Elle a pained smile, as though apologizing for outing her family when everything they did was pretty much public knowledge anyway.

"Don't worry about what you say," Elle told her friend. "I figured out a long time ago that my family is *not* me. What they do is their choice. I'm making my own choices."

Julia's smile was less concerned this time. "Moving on to the Albanian Mafia. They're a different breed of criminals. They prefer the long game rather than immediate profit and slowly built up their network for years before becoming a power player. They've even been in partnership with the James Family in the past, although it was a tense relationship. Their main areas of expertise are drugs and sex. They run a chain of brothels, but it's unclear whether the women are there through choice or have been coerced. They also have a vast network of teens selling drugs." She cleared her throat. "Unlike the James Syndicate, which appears to recruit soldiers who work within their structure, often being promoted to positions with more responsibility, the Albanians tend to use cheap, disposable labor whom they cut off when the police start to show an interest in them."

"It's good to know my family treats their criminal workers better than other crime families," Elle said dryly.

"Then there's MC20," Julia continued. "I thought the MC part was short for motorcycle, but apparently, it's Master Criminals. The twenty part is the age of their founder." Her findings clearly bemused her.

"I'm going to go out on a limb here," Megan said. "And guess that this gang isn't known for their IQ."

"No, they're mainly known for their over-the-top, unprovoked violence." Julia's lip curled in disgust. "Which they often film and share on TikTok and Instagram. As fast as their videos are taken down, they put up another. Meanwhile, someone has already copied the original, which is then shared far too many times to eradicate it from the web.

I honestly don't understand what motivates this group. For the others, it's money and power, but this group…"

"Fame," Megan said. "And respect. Or what they perceive as respect. It's all about emulating cracked-up rappers and American gangbangers. They care more about their reputation for being tough than they do anything else."

Everyone stared at Megan, who shrugged and pointed at her blonde head. "Don't be fooled by the hair. There's a brain in here."

"Okay." Clearly, Julia didn't know what else to say, so she carried on with her presentation. "MC20's main areas of interest are drugs and racketeering. They threaten and abuse the businesses in their neighborhood on a regular basis and are starting to extend their territory. Their drug business is expanding too, and there have been clashes between them and both the Albanians and the James Syndicate. Clashes that ended with MC20 killing some teenage drug dealers who worked for the Albanians. It made the news."

"See? It's all about the reputation," Megan drawled. "Now, how do we take them down?"

Before anyone could answer, the front door opened. Everyone except Julia and Elle had a gun in their hand and was on their feet before the door closed.

"It's just us," Rachel called out as she entered the room.

Their former boss was dressed in a black Chanel pantsuit with a Prada bag hanging from the crook of her arm and the latest iPhone clasped in her red-taloned hand. Her fiancé, Michael "Harvard" Carter, a tall, built African American and former CIA agent, followed her into the room. Unlike Rachel, Harvard liked people and smiled warmly when he saw them.

Until his eyes came to rest on David. Then he rocked back a step.

"David Knight, no way." He strode across the room, beaming at David while he held out his hand. "I thought you were dead, buddy. When you disappeared after that Russian op went belly-up, I didn't even get a chance to say I was sorry about your team. It broke us all up that you lost them. Damn, that was a long time ago. What? Eleven, twelve years? I heard you were freelancing, and then about two years ago, a contact told me you'd taken a bullet to the head. Why the hell didn't you drop by and say hi?"

"Didn't know you were here." David grinned at the taller man as they shook hands. "The freelancing is true, the dead part, not so much. Although, after Russia, I *was* disavowed, which kinda feels like dying. It's good to see you."

Elle gaped at the two men.

Mind *blown*.

Stunned, she got to her feet and pointed at David. "You're CIA? Seriously? After all the weird places I searched, you're plain old CIA? Well, that's disappointing."

"Hey, there's nothing plain or old about the CIA," Harvard said.

"Technically," David added, "since the agency burned me, I'm former CIA."

"That is so not the issue here." She held up a hand to stop him from talking. "I've been hunting you for years, and all along, your *buddy* Harvard was part of my team."

"To be fair"—Harvard spread his hands in a gesture of peace—"I didn't know you were hunting for *this* David."

"Well, duh." Elle glared at him. "I said he was a spy."

Harvard rubbed a hand over his shaven head. "That doesn't narrow it down as much as you think it does. David's a common name, and you said he was exotic-looking. No offense, buddy," he said to David, "but you ain't that."

"Exotic?" Ryan almost choked on his Snickers. "He's

average height, with brown hair, brown eyes, and beige skin. Where's the exotic here?"

"I think it's in the eye of the beholder, dude," Dimitri said with a bemused shake of his head.

Ignoring them, Elle moved on to the other more interesting piece of information Harvard had let slip. "Your name is Knight?"

The expression on his face said, *Really, we're going there?*

Hell, yes. "Knight? As in champion of the king? Savior of damsels in distress? Fighting the good fight, Knight? Armor and jousting? This. Is. Priceless."

Laughter bubbled up inside of her, and before she knew it, she was holding on to Ryan's shoulder while fighting hysterics.

"What am I missing?" Harvard asked, making Elle laugh even harder.

9

———

"Why are you here, Rachel?" Callum faced off against his frenemy, making Elle nostalgic as she fought to remain calm after finally managing to get a grip on herself.

"Honestly, Callum." Rachel tossed her long, straight, dark hair over her shoulder and rolled her eyes at her former partner. "It's hardly rocket science. Elle's secret past life has put all of us on her psychopathic father's radar, and I'd rather not die."

"I've missed this," Ryan whispered, his voice filled with wonder.

"It's good to see the parents back together again," Elle agreed. "Now, if you'll excuse me for a minute, I have a Knight I need to *joust with*."

Barely containing her glee, she bounced across the room to stand directly in front of David while he caught up with Harvard.

"I see you've got someone else who wants to talk to you." Harvard grinned. "Catch you later, bro." His big mitt ruffled Elle's hair. "Go easy on him," he said before heading over to stand sentry at Rachel's side. Not so much to protect her, rather more to protect the team *from* her.

Elle grinned at David, who'd folded his arms as if to defend himself against her. Poor, naïve man. Like that would stop her from getting any closer if she wanted to.

"Do you have a suit of armor?" She batted her eyelashes at him. "Is it shiny?"

"Do you still have those fluffy pink cuffs I gave you? Because I'm beginning to think I should use them on you while I spank the sass out of you."

"Kinky. I like. All this time, I was hunting for you in cyberspace, and all I had to do to find out all your dark, sordid secrets was buy Harvard a beer. I'd be a bit miffed about that if finding out you're a Knight wasn't so entertaining."

"It's a name, not a title."

"Methinks it's a calling, Sir David, knight of the realm. Wanna do some cosplay later? I'll let you rescue me from a dragon. Or maybe you could pillage my village." She waggled her eyebrows at him.

"I'm going to pretend I didn't hear that," Joe muttered as he walked past.

"So," Elle said to her spy, "is it your real name, or did you make it up?"

He managed not to roll his eyes, although, she was pretty sure he wanted to. "Blue, I'm a spy—there's nothing real about me."

"If I keep digging, will I uncover your real name?"

"Only if you want to attract even more attention than you already have."

"No. I think I'm good with the amount of attention I'm getting right now. Guess that means I'll have to think of other ways to *tease* the information out of you."

The heat in his eyes ignited a spontaneous hot flush that made her want to strip to her underwear and fan herself.

"You're playing with fire." His voice came out deeper than usual, making her shiver.

"Funny." She straightened her shoulders and stared him in the eye, issuing a challenge. "I thought I was playing with you."

"Everybody, sit back down," Callum ordered loudly. "We've a meeting to finish."

It seemed intermission was over. Callum and Rachel had come to an understanding—for now. With a saucy wink at David, Elle went back to sit beside Ryan and helped herself to the bag of chips he'd produced out of thin air.

Julia took her position in front of the wall displaying her PowerPoint presentation, and at a nod from Callum, she resumed her talk. "As you can see, the main area where all three organizations overlap is drug dealing. If we undermine their business in that area, there's a very good chance they'll think it's a turf war." She glanced at Joe. "Do people still say turf war?"

"You're doing great," he reassured her.

She smiled at him, making a hot curl of envy unfurl within Elle. Unable to help herself, she glanced over at David, only to find his eyes on her. For a microsecond, the room emptied of everyone but them as Elle's breath hitched in her chest.

Then Julia continued to speak, shattering the moment. "We've managed to gather some information about how each group runs their drug trade, including who supplies them with their product, where it comes into the country, where the low-level dealers work, and the next delivery date for the James Syndicate. Callum?"

She stepped aside for their boss, who was in full-blown

operation mode. You could tell because he was too focused on the task to shout.

"We plan to instigate a campaign of sabotage and escalation," he said. "Starting at the bottom of the power structures, taking out the ground soldiers, before working our way up to higher-value targets if needed."

"Why not blow out a bigger target straight off?" Megan asked.

"Starting small makes it appear more natural," Dimitri said. "Like they're jostling for power, testing each other out. It also reduces the chances of them negotiating their way out of this."

Joe nodded. "If we did something big, it's possible they'd decide to get all the players around a table and knock it on the head that way. Which means they might find out that none of them are behind the trouble. Nipping at their heels isn't worth a sit-down, but it will seed mistrust, anger, and fear. All things you want in a war."

"It's also the approach that'll attract the least attention from the authorities or media," Callum added.

"Okay," Megan said. "How do we do this?"

Callum motioned to Julia, and a new slide appeared on the wall. "These are the targets we've identified. As you can see, there are several, which means we have a lot of ground to cover. We'll split into three teams, each dressing and acting like one of the gangs, then in the gang's persona, we'll take out one of their rivals." He rubbed at the stubble on his chin. "I'd like more time to prepare, but we don't have it. This needs to be done hard and fast, and because of that, we're heading out this evening.

"Julia will coordinate everyone from here. Rachel and Elle will man a mobile post in the field. I'd rather keep you here, Elle, out of harm's way, but we might need your hacking skills."

"I wouldn't want to stay here," she said honestly. "I'm more use to you out there. Don't worry; I'll keep my head down and be the 'man in the van.' Although, I'm going to need better equipment if we're setting up a mobile comms unit."

Rachel looked up from her phone, where she was either checking the stock market or buying something ridiculously expensive—or checking in with her army of demon minions...

"Let me know what you need, and I'll procure it from TayFor."

"By procure," Elle said, "do you mean steal from your family's pharmaceutical company?"

Rachel appeared bored. "Borrow. Requisition. I'm CEO. I don't need to pilfer."

Really, there was nothing to say to that. Elle had been inside the company and knew they were loaded to the gills with state-of-the-art tech. There was no doubt in her mind that whatever Rachel *pilfered,* it would do the job.

"As for the rest of the teams," Callum said, "we've got Dimitri, Joe, and Megan together. Then me and Ryan. That leaves Harvard with David. Anybody got any problems with that?"

There was silence.

"Good. Julia will send everything she has to your new phones. Read up on it and be ready. Then bloody delete everything so we don't have another phone screwup." Callum took a step toward the door, but Rachel stopped him.

"What about weapons and other military gizmos? I can't procure those from TayFor, and I'm assuming the police won't allow us to raid the Benson office armory. How exactly are we going to sabotage things without the right equipment?"

"Gizmos?" Ryan mouthed at Elle, who grinned.

"It's a technical term," she whispered. "You wouldn't understand."

"Don't worry," Callum said. "We'll be well enough equipped to deal with this lot. David and Lake spoke with their contacts this morning, and they're setting us up with whatever we need. Now, get together with your team and prepare as best you can. Ryan"—he was back to barking orders—"get your arse to the kitchen. We'll eat and talk."

"How well he knows you," Elle said as Ryan rushed off. Then her eyes settled on Rachel, and she grinned. Laptop under her arm, she skipped over to Rachel. "High five, partner."

Rachel did not high five; instead, she pointed a red talon at herself. "Me boss." She then pointed at Elle. "You minion."

"Technically, you ain't my boss anymore." Elle sat tailor-style on the kitchen chair beside Rachel and opened her laptop. "I'm sending you a list of all the tech gear I need. Also"—she stopped typing for a second to look at Rachel—"there's a really cool lava lamp on the desk in the IT area, can I have it? The guys wouldn't give it to me when I was working there undercover, even though I asked nicely."

"No."

"Pretty please? You're the boss. You can order them to hand it over. I mean, how professional is it for them to have it on their desk in the first place? Is that the kind of image you want your company to project? Hippy-dippy lava lamps?"

Rachel stared her down until she gave in.

"Fine." Elle started typing again. "But to make up for disappointing me, you can interrogate Harvard on what he knows about David. I'm emailing questions now."

"No," Rachel repeated.

"Seriously? Haven't we discussed this? I know for a fact we went over the girl code with you that time Megan brought pizza to your place. You're supposed to have my back on this. That's what friends do."

Rachel did that dramatic yet bored eye-roll only she could pull off. "We're not friends."

"Yeah, you keep telling yourself that. I'm sending the questions. Make an effort, okay? Remember, girl power. We stick together."

"By gossiping about boys?" If a look could freeze lava, Rachel had it down pat.

"Not gossiping, doing a deep-dive background check on each other's honeys. Haven't you ever had even one female friend? Maybe back in the dark ages of your teens?"

"No." It was Rachel's favorite word.

"I'm deeply disturbed by this news. I mean, I was raised by a psychopathic gangster, and I still managed to have a girl gang in my teens. Sure, I didn't see them that often, but they still had my back when it came to boys, homework, and teen drama." Honestly, there were times when she wondered exactly what Rachel had done during her teen years. Then again, she wasn't sure she wanted to know.

Rachel frowned at Elle's head. "Did you know that your hair is more Fraggle than usual?"

"Did you know that you turn mean when cornered?"

They stared at each other until Elle blinked.

What? Rachel was scary!

"It's obviously time you learned some more about the girl code," Elle started sending Rachel links to helpful websites while she talked, pleased when she heard her phone ping repeatedly. "When you have female friends, you have responsibilities—checking out their dates, supplying chocolate when things go wrong, and helping to bury any bodies they might *accidentally* leave in their wake. I checked out Harvard for you."

That had the Queen of Darkness sitting up straight in her chair. "You did *what*?"

Elle waved off her thanks. "I check up on everybody who gets near our team. FYI, Harvard's one of the good guys." She patted Rachel's knee. "You fell on your feet with him. Well done."

"Okay, I'm finished here." Rachel got to her feet and headed for the door.

Elle followed. "I'm more than happy to walk while we chat," she said cheerily.

"Oh, for the love of Prada." Rachel spun around to glare at her. "What do I have to do to get you to stop talking and go away?"

"Talk to Harvard. Get the skinny on David." Elle wanted to pat Rachel on the head for catching up with the conversation. "Otherwise, I can talk all day. After all, your education in the girl code is seriously lacking, and we have a lot to cover. Let's start with Princess Leia. When things get particularly complicated in my life, I like to ask myself, WWLD— what would Leia do? I find the answer usually sets me on the right track. You have seen *Star Wars*, right?"

There was silence. It was *not* reassuring.

"Rach, you've seen *Star Wars*, right?" Surely everybody had seen at least one *Star Wars* movie?

Rachel pointed a talon toward the door. "Go away. Now."

"No, not until we've established your position on *Star Wars*. This is serious. If you haven't seen it, I'm setting up a screening at your place. We can watch the movies in story order or in release-date order. I know"—she beamed— "we'll do both."

If looks could kill, Elle would have been vaporized. "I'll

talk to Harvard." Rachel gritted the words between her teeth.

"And then tell me in detail what he said." Elle wanted to ensure Rachel got the fine print.

"If I have to."

"Yes, Rachel, you do have to."

"Then fine." Rachel pointed to the door.

"Thank you. We'll schedule our *Star Wars* summer school for a later date. But, right now, I have lost the need to chat, so I'm going to have a nap." After giving Rachel a cheery wave, Elle headed upstairs to find an unclaimed bed.

10

The streets of North London were as busy after sundown as they were during daylight hours. The only difference was in the type of people out and about. Of course, you had the run-of-the-mill activity you'd expect on a weeknight—couples on dates, students clubbing on the cheaper nights, families eating out, and shift workers going about their business. But if you looked in the darker corners, the out-of-the-way places that the average city dweller didn't spend too much time peering into, you saw the other side of London's nightlife.

Scantily clad women loitering on street corners. Guys wearing hoodies huddled together in dark alleys. Teens congregating around a park bench that sat under a conveniently broken streetlight. The steroid-induced musclemen with bulges under their jackets where a shoulder holster sat. And the furtive groups skulking in doorways or idling in places they shouldn't.

These people congregated where the light was the worst and the smell of rot the strongest. They gravitated toward the places that were crumbling, broken, forgotten. The places with graffiti-covered walls and garbage-strewn floors.

But no matter where they gathered, they were invisible. Mainly because if there were residents around, they were the kind who chose what they saw or heard.

"My skin's crawling," Rachel said from the driver's seat of the van as she checked the locks were secure for the millionth time. "How do people live like this? Don't they have any pride in their environment? Wouldn't they be happier if they took care of where they lived and worked?"

"I know you won't get this," Elle said from the back of the van, where she was monitoring what surveillance cameras were working in the area in the hope of being able to warn their teams if trouble approached. "But generally, poor people don't have the money, time, or energy to take care of their environment. It's hard to pay for a pot of paint when you can't afford to feed your kids."

Rachel, the multi-millionaire, oozed her usual compassion. "They could at least clean up the rubbish."

"You know that feeling when you get home after a hard day, and you don't have the energy to hang up your clothes, so you throw them over a chair and promise yourself you'll deal with them later?"

"Or the maid deals with them," Rachel said, as though everyone had a maid.

"Imagine you don't have a maid. Now imagine you've worked fourteen hours in a fast-food restaurant, earning minimum wage. Imagine coming home smelling of grease and burgers, and you still have to feed the kids and figure out how to pay your bills. Would you even see the street outside your house? That's assuming you have a job. Sometimes, just surviving day-to-day can take all of your energy. There's nothing left for anything else."

There was no judgment in Elle's tone. She knew from experience that Rachel was way more soft-hearted than she let people see. Also, if you had the patience, she could be reeducated too.

"I wonder what programs the government runs here?" Rachel mused. "If they can spend billions on the latest nuclear submarine, surely they have money to spare to clean up the city. I'm going to have a word with Boris next time I see him."

Only Rachel could casually mention that she planned to rake the prime minister over the coals. It made Elle grin. "While you're at it, you might want to talk to him about the underfunded charities and the lack of apprenticeship schemes or decent housing."

"I might just do that," Rachel muttered before clearing her throat and raising her voice. "At the very least, he must realize areas like this are an eyesore. What must the neighbors think?"

"The neighbors?"

"France, Germany, Holland. I bet the Scandinavians have this sort of thing sorted already. I wonder who I know in Sweden that I could have a chat with. Surely Mother must know someone. If I remember correctly, I'm pretty sure she's distantly related to their royal family."

Yeah, Rachel was something else entirely.

"This is Command One." Julia's voice came over the speakers of the computer set up in front of Elle. "Teams are in position. Handing over to Mobile One."

"This is Mobile One." Elle felt silly using their call name, as there was only one van, so it wasn't like they had to number them. But—military. The guys couldn't turn off their training. It was stamped into their genetic code. "Teams, sound off, please. I'm going to need a status report."

"Alpha Team." Callum's rough brogue came over the speaker. "We're in position and ready to go."

"Gamma Team," Harvard rumbled. "We are good to go."

"Delta Team," Joe said. "Waiting for the all clear."

Elle glanced at Rachel. "I'm sick with nerves, and these guys sound like they're about to go for a Sunday afternoon stroll." She scanned the monitors in front of her, searching for any reason at all that their op couldn't go ahead as planned.

"They're better trained and have more experience than anyone they're dealing with tonight," Rachel reminded her. "Their targets sit at the bottom of the food chain."

"Even the bottom-feeders can still wield a knife."

"If a teenager stabs Harvard, I'll eat my favorite Prada handbag—with a fine Chianti."

That was the thing about Rachel: her heart was soft and her sense of humor dark. It was the reason the women on the team insisted on being her friend, even when she clearly didn't know what to do with them.

"Okay," Elle said. "Alpha, Delta, and Gamma, you are good to go. Repeat, proceed with the operation as planned." She hated that they were working with phones instead of the throat mics and body cams that made it easier to keep tabs on everyone.

"Roger that," each team leader replied.

Once they'd checked in, there was nothing for Elle to do but monitor the screens. If things went south, she'd pull the teams out. If things got really bad, she'd call in every enforcement agency in London for help and hope it didn't backfire on them later.

"Rach, get back here. I need another set of eyes." On the screens displaying the footage from the street cameras she'd hacked into, the three teams were making their way toward their targets.

Rachel climbed into the back. "I really hope no one tries to steal the tires while we're parked here. That would *not* make me happy." And she was usually so chipper.

"Watch the four screens on the left," Elle told her. "I'll watch the rest. Do you know what you're looking for?"

"Bad guys doing bad things."

"Then we're as ready as we can be. You know, if I was here with Megan instead of you, we'd take this opportunity to decide which of the guys has the best backside."

"Yet you wonder why I would rather not have female friends." Rachel stared at the screens in front of her. "Of course, the answer is Harvard," she said at last. "Nobody has a better backside than him."

Elle was grinning as Callum and Ryan strode onto the top left-hand screen, showing a dilapidated park.

It had begun.

11

ALPHA TEAM
TARGET: Teen drug dealers working for the Albanians
Mason Park
North London

They'd worn suits in an attempt to make the baby drug dealers think they were part of the James Syndicate. Ryan kinda liked his suit. It fit like a glove and was a deep blue that brought out his eyes. Megan had told him so. With a matching shirt and polished shoes, Ryan was pretty sure he could *GQ* with the best of them.

"You know what to do," Callum muttered as they strode toward the teen thugs who worked the territory for the Albanians. Callum's suit was gray and nowhere near as nice as Ryan's.

"I've got this." Ryan wasn't being cocky, just honest.

They'd decided that Callum's Scottish accent was too distinctive for him to take point. The teens would remember it, and then there would be questions about who in the

James Family was from north of the border. Ryan, on the other hand, was born and bred in London, which meant his accent was perfect.

"Bloody hell," Callum muttered, "that kid can't be more than twelve years old."

Ryan heard it in his voice, the same distaste for confronting the kids that he felt. They'd both joined the military to protect and serve their country, not to take on lanky tweens making shitty decisions when they were barely out of nappies.

Sometimes, life really sucked.

As they neared the group, the boys huddled closer. Their chatter ceased as wary eyes, betraying suspicion beyond their years, focused on the two strange men approaching them in the dark. The fact that none of them ran meant they'd already figured out that Callum and Ryan weren't cops. From their expressions, they assumed they were being approached by the James Syndicate, and they were wary. So much so that one of the kids pulled a knife.

Barely in his teens and already carrying.

It made Ryan sick, but it didn't surprise him. Very little did anymore.

"Boys," Ryan called out to them. "We're closing you down. Put everything on the bench behind you and clear out. You can tell your handler this park is now James' territory."

The biggest kid stepped forward, pulling his own knife from the pocket of his hoodie. "Who the fuck are you?"

"Did I stutter?" Ryan swept back his jacket to reveal his gun. "James Family Syndicate. Now piss off out of here."

"You won't shoot a kid," a boy at the back of the group called out, obviously feeling brave because his mates stood between him and Ryan. "You don't want the cops after you any more than we do."

Callum casually drew his pistol and shot the bench. The sound reverberated around the silent park.

"We own the cops," Ryan said evenly.

Three of the seven boys dropped their stash and ran for the trees behind them. The ones left behind paled as they visibly broke out in a nervous sweat. All except for their fearless leader. He stepped toward Ryan, knife in hand.

"Don't do it," Ryan warned, although it was obvious his advice was falling on deaf ears.

His hand shaking, the clearly terrified baby criminal kept coming at Ryan. Until, with a stream of curses, the boy lunged. And Ryan took him down. The entire altercation lasted mere seconds. Once he had the boy immobilized by holding his arm out behind him at an angle that made it impossible to move or his wrist would break, Ryan faced the rest of the gang.

"Money. Drugs. Weapons. All of it on the bench now, or my associate starts shooting kneecaps. I've run out of patience with you boys."

They rushed to do as Ryan ordered while the boy in his hold whimpered.

"Now," Ryan said, "tell the Albanians that we run this park. We see you here again, we won't care how old you are. You get me?"

He shoved the boy toward his friends and watched as they ran off together, feeling disgusted with himself for what he'd had to do. The teen's arm hung limply at his side; his shoulder dislocated. Injuring the boy in a way that was serious but easily fixed had been a deliberate move. It was either that or allow himself to get stabbed. Sometimes all the choices life threw at you sucked equally.

A hand clasped his shoulder. "He would have had no problem stabbing you," Callum said.

"That's supposed to make me feel better about hurting a kid?"

"No. That's supposed to remind you that the kids around here grow up helluva fast, and maybe a dislocated shoulder will be the encouragement he needs to make better choices in the future."

Ryan didn't believe that any more than Callum did. Around that neighborhood, there weren't many choices that one could make. "This plan is beyond shitty," he said as they gathered up everything the boys had left behind. There was quite a collection of drugs, money, and knives. Along with one very expensive cell phone.

"This might be useful." Ryan held it up for Callum to see.

"Aye." He scanned the area to make sure no one was watching or waiting for them. "Like taking candy from a baby."

"Drugs, not candy."

"Come on." Callum turned toward the road, where they'd parked their car. "One down, two to go."

Ryan's lip curled in disgust as he followed his boss out of the park.

12

———

GAMMA TEAM
TARGET: MC20 drug dealers
Islington
North London

Harvard and David were also masquerading as James Family members. Unlike the kids Callum and Ryan had targeted, their dealers were young men who'd already developed a taste for violence. Also unlike their teammates, only Harvard wore a suit. David was dressed in his usual black sweater and jeans. Not because he had anything against wearing a suit. Purely because Elle had been so proud of having her own "spy uniform" that he'd felt the need to keep his on.

And, yeah, he wasn't about to look too closely at his reasoning.

"Three at the end of the alley," David said as they walked toward them.

"Two behind them, farther up," Harvard said. "And

looks like they've got another two on the opposite side of the street."

"That's a lot of gang members for a low-level dealer."

"I'm thinking our intel might have been a bit off on this one. I don't see any of the members named in Julia's dossier, but this clearly isn't the two-guy setup they've got elsewhere." Harvard paused to scan the area. "My guess is the smaller teams report to hubs like this one. They probably keep a bigger stash here too."

"And more weapons. Do we move on or take them out?" David carried on walking, aware that they now had the attention of every single MC20 member standing at the end of the dark street.

Harvard grunted. "We're already here, so might as well get on with it."

"Last time you said that to me, I took a bullet in the leg."

"You still bitching about that? Buddy, you need to let it go. That was well over a decade ago."

"It still aches when it rains."

"That's 'cause you're old," Harvard muttered as they rounded the cars and came to a halt in front of a group of three gangster wannabes.

A tall black kid broke away from his friends, showing all the swagger of a B-grade rap star. "You buying?" he asked.

"We're taking," Harvard replied.

"Business is over, *boys*." David assessed each threat level with clinical precision as he spoke to their leader. "The James Syndicate owns this street now."

"The fuck?" Mr. Swagger held out his hands. "You got any idea who you dealing with, *boy*? Nobody fucks with MC20. This is our turf, and we ain't moving over for nobody."

"Sounds like you think you have a choice in the matter," Harvard said. "You'd be wrong."

The two guys behind the leader and the two in the alley came to stand beside their brother. All but Mr. Swagger held a knife in their hand. David casually glanced over his shoulder and noted that the duo on the other side of the street were heading their way too.

"We gonna slice you two up good," the leader sneered. "Teach you who rules these streets."

David caught Harvard's eye and nodded once. As though synchronized, they each pulled a silenced gun from their person—Harvard from his shoulder holster and David from the back of his jeans.

They didn't hesitate. They were outnumbered, and they'd seen what the gang was capable of. MC20 liked to make people bleed. It was a matter of pride to them.

Harvard spun around and fired, hitting the two gang members running toward them in the leg. They went down loudly. The rest of their friends didn't have time to react because David shot four of them in the leg before Harvard did the same to the last guy.

While Harvard went around disarming each of the moaning gang members and relieving them of their stash and cash, David crouched beside Mr. Swagger.

"Never bring a knife to a gunfight," he said. "Now, repeat after me, this territory doesn't belong to MC20. It belongs to the James Family."

"Fuck you!" Mr. Swagger spat at him.

David shot him in the other leg.

"Repeat after me," he said when the guy had stopped screaming, "this territory doesn't belong to MC20. It belongs to the James Family."

With pure hatred burning in his eyes, Mr. Swagger forced out the words.

David stood and surveyed the mess. The wannabe gangbangers writhed on the dirty ground, clutching their wounds while cursing and whining.

"These are only flesh wounds," David told their leader. "Next time, we aim for the head. Make sure there isn't a next time."

With that, Harvard and David turned and strode back down the street.

"I've got a whacked-out assortment of highs here," Harvard said as they walked away, careful to keep an eye on their surroundings for further threats. "We've got everything from coke to oxy. Who the hell is supplying these guys?"

"We don't know for sure yet, although Julia has some ideas she's following up." David pulled out his phone and called Elle. "Gamma Team moving on to next target. You might want to send a couple of buses to this location. We had to expend some bullets."

"Anybody dead?" Elle said. "By buses, you mean ambulances, don't you? You're just too cool to say the word, right?"

"Way too cool," David answered. "And no fatalities."

"Tell her we've got half a dozen cell phones for her to hack," Harvard said.

"You hear that?" David climbed into their car.

"Yep, I get presents."

He hung up on the smile in her voice.

13

Dressed from head to toe in black, Joe, Dimitri, and Megan wore tactical vests containing everything they needed for their mission. Well, everything David could rustle up from his contact, or they could source at a local store. Unlike the other teams, their mission was to get in and out without attracting too much attention. They wanted the James Family to wonder who'd attacked them—until the other two gangs retaliated for the hits on them. Or until the following night, when Benson Security would go out pretending to be the Albanians and strike at the other gangs. But for Delta Team's mission, it was all about stealth.

"Ready?" Joe asked his team.

Megan nodded. "I'm beyond disgusted that they're selling drugs out of a strip club. It's such a cliché. You see that guy?" She pointed at the image on her phone. "He's lounging in the corner booth, in his cheap suit, holding court like he's a Mafia don instead of some two-bob drug dealer."

"It's two-bit," Dimitri corrected.

"This is England. It's bob." Megan was still staring at the live feed from the club's security cameras, which they'd tapped into courtesy of their pet hacker.

They were sitting in their car, up the street from the strip club, waiting for confirmation it was time to go in.

"You ready, Elle?" Joe asked into his phone, which was on speaker.

"One more minute." He could hear her typing furiously. "Power will only be out for about ten minutes at most before the company finds the problem and fixes it. It's the best I can do without attracting too much attention."

"Will the James Family figure out you're behind the power cut?" It was always a worry when the enemy had a clear understanding of Elle's skills.

"No. I've botched the whole thing. It looks like a monkey did the hack while wearing ski gloves and drinking martinis. There's no way they'd know this was me. It's amateur hour."

While Joe and Dimitri chuckled at the visual image, Megan said, "Monkeys wouldn't drink martinis. They're more cocktail hour. Something with paper umbrellas."

Dimitri shot Joe a grin, and he shook his head. He'd take Julia's brand of crazy over Megan's any day of the week.

"Okay, guys," Elle said. "Lights going out in thirty seconds."

Joe signaled for them to get out of the car and shut down the call with Elle. Without throat mics, the team was going in with no way of communicating covertly, other than hand gestures, and Megan hadn't been trained in most of those.

All they could do was follow the plan and rely on experience to get them through.

Sticking to the shadows, the three of them strolled up the street toward the strip club. No one gave them a second glance. It wasn't the kind of area where people went out of their way to notice strangers. They were nearly at the door when the streetlights cut, and the neon signs blinked out.

With black beanies pulled down over their foreheads and guns in hand, they slipped through the side door of the club. As expected, people were using the flashlights on their phones to see what was happening. Beams of light crosscrossed the room, illuminating it more than enough for Joe's team to see where they were going but also making it easier for them to blend with the crowd.

Their voices raised in confusion, people milled around as though they weren't sure whether to head for the exits or wait where they were. It was good cover, but Joe wanted chaos.

He nudged Megan, who shouted, "Stop groping me! Get your hands off me! Help!"

"Hands off the talent," a male voice roared.

Lights swung toward the stage, where strippers ran for the back rooms, and bouncers ran toward the clientele.

Perfect.

Someone threw a punch. Someone else cursed loudly. A woman screamed. And then it turned into a massive free-for-all as drunken men threw themselves into the fight.

Ignoring all of it, Joe and his team made their way to the booth in the back corner of the room, where the dealer and his two backup men were in the process of clearing out. Megan walked straight up to the suit-wearing dealer and pressed her gun to his forehead.

"Give me a reason to pull the trigger," she said with a cheery smile.

The bodyguards rushed forward, but they were no match for Dimitri and Joe. Two choke holds and a few seconds later, both men were on the floor. Delta Team patted them down, confiscating everything they could find. Meanwhile, the drug dealer stared at Megan with a tough attitude that fooled no one. That man absolutely wanted to pee his pants.

Joe gave Megan a nod, and she dropped her gun. A second later, Dimitri's right hook connected with the guy's jaw, sending him back into the booth. With quick hands, Dimitri patted the guy down and relieved him of his phone, money, weapon, and several small bags of white.

Leaning in to whisper in the dealer's ear, Joe said, "Spread the word. This turf ain't yours any longer. You're out of business as of now." As English accents went, it wasn't the best, which is why he'd whispered. It was easier to hide his American accent that way.

The guy's eyes blazed. "You got no fucking idea who you're dealing with. You're dead. The three of you. Dead men walking. Tommy James is gonna skin you alive for this."

"Excuse me." Megan rose from where she'd crouched, out of the gangster's line of sight, to tape a cell phone to the underside of the table. She frowned at the dealer while pointing to her chest. "See these? They're tits. Which means it's dead *people* walking, you sexist pig."

"Finish it," Joe ordered, and Dimitri let out a stream of Russian before knocking the guy out.

"Really hoping that guy doesn't speak Russian," Dimitri said. "Otherwise, they'll think the Russians hit them instead of the Albanians."

Megan scoffed. "I don't think you need to worry. He could barely speak English."

As one, Delta Team walked through the room and out

the side door. As they headed along the street toward their car, the lights flickered back on.

"You couldn't stop yourself from pointing out you weren't a guy, could you?" Dimitri shook his head at his wife.

"What?" Megan held up her hands. "It was offensive. Like only a guy could take him down." She snorted.

"Get in the car, you two," Joe said.

As soon as Dimitri was behind the wheel, Joe dialed Elle. "You got the signal?"

"Yep. The cell phone you placed is on speaker, and we're getting every word. Your guy is pissed and looking for someone to blame."

"Shouldn't take him too long to find a target." Dimitri was talking about the phone he'd "accidentally" dropped under the bench seat for easy discovery. It was broken and couldn't be hacked for information—not that there was any on it. What it did have, though, was a lock-screen photo of two MC20 gang members.

"Heading to the next target," Joe said. "Delta Team out."

"Is this drug dealer in a strip club too?" Megan asked. "Because I find that offensive."

"If I remember rightly, you made me watch that stripper movie about ten times because you wanted to be Jennifer Lopez," Dimitri pointed out.

"I wasn't talking about the stripping. I was talking about these criminals' sheer lack of imagination. It's pathetic."

Joe and Dimitri shared a grin as they drove on to their next target.

14

James Family Home
North London

"I heard," Marcus said as he prowled into his father's study.

It was 4 a.m., and Marcus had pulled on jeans and a T-shirt when the call came through. Tommy, meanwhile, had taken the time to get dressed in one of his many three-piece suits.

"They've declared war," Tommy raged. "On *me*. Doesn't the James name mean anything anymore? Who the hell do they think they are? I'm Tommy Fucking James. I've ruled this city since before they were born, and I deserve some fucking respect." He swiped a hand across the credenza behind his desk, sending photos and memorabilia crashing to the floor. "Little shits ain't got no respect. It's time we taught them some."

Marcus stood on the other side of the desk, his arms folded and his eyes on his father rather than the mess he'd wrought. "What we need is to have a sit-down with them before this situation gets out of hand."

"It's already out of hand," Tommy roared, making his bodyguard poke his head into the room to check on them. "They hit three locations tonight. *Three.* There once was a time when people would have been too scared to tangle with even one, but no, they hit three. Where's the respect?" He pointed at his chest. "I earned my place in this business. Worked my way up by doing the hard graft. Not like these little shits, thinking respect is something you get on the internet."

"Let me set up a meeting, see if we sort this out like gentlemen first."

"Gentlemen?" Tommy's rage narrowed in on Marcus as he made his way around the desk. Nothing made Tommy feel better than inflicting pain, and who better to take the brunt than his son.

Marcus knew the drill. Tommy needed an outlet. And it wasn't going to be him. Reaching behind him, he curled his hand around the grip of the gun tucked into the back of his jeans. He was sure his eyes were just as cold as Tommy's when he spoke. "Take a deep breath before you make me put a bullet in your head."

Tommy considered him. A predator sizing up his prey only to find it might be something worse waiting for him in the shadows. His smile was razor-sharp. "You'd do it, wouldn't you?"

"In a heartbeat." And enjoy every second of the experience.

"See? That's why you're my choice to replace me, not Cutter. He wouldn't have the balls to say that to my face. He might think it, but he wouldn't say it. Only family would have enough guts to be honest with me." Tommy perched against the edge of the desk behind him, brimming with parental pride. "You think we should set up this meeting?"

"I think we go cautious." Marcus returned the gun to the back of his jeans and folded his arms again, but he didn't take his eyes off his father. "Direct retribution would attract too much attention right now, and we can't risk that, not when we're this close to getting Elle back. Let me call the Albanians to set up a meet for the morning."

"Why the hell would I want to talk to the Albanians?" Tommy exploded.

Marcus was beginning to wonder whether his father was still fit to lead the business. "Because they hit three of our prime dealers tonight."

"The Albanians? It was that TV gangster mob, MC20, that hit the clubs."

Marcus shook his head as he tugged his phone out of his pocket. "Abasi said they were overheard talking Albanian, or at least that's what our guy thought it was. It sure as hell wasn't English. They were older too, dressed all in black with none of that crappy jewelry MC20 wears."

Tommy was shaking his head. "No. Terry's crew found a phone that one of them dropped, and it belonged to someone from MC20."

"That makes no sense," Marcus said.

"Get everybody in here." Tommy adjusted his tie. "I want to know what's going on and who attacked us. Then I'm taking them apart."

With a nod, Marcus sent a message to their captains, telling them there was an urgent meeting. He didn't bother informing his father's advisor. Cutter was never far from Tommy's side. Something Marcus would very much like to change, but he'd never found the opportunity. But, as Elle used to say, even Peter Pan managed to lose his shadow. It was only a matter of time.

Once back in his bedroom, which was scanned three times a day for listening devices, he called Abasi. "Any news?" he asked as he walked over to his desk to open his laptop.

"Nothing yet." His best friend knew he wasn't talking about the hits on the business. "Her whole team has disappeared off the grid. My guess? They're holed up in a safe house somewhere. Either that or they're on their way to Scotland."

"Have we sent a man to the Scottish office, see if they've turned up there?"

"Are you kidding?" Abasi barked out a laugh. "Benson Security's got that town locked up tight. Remember years ago, that Russian Mob nut who tried to kidnap some woman in Scotland?"

"The fight in the castle? That was Benson Security?"

"Hell no, that was the town's women! Benson's boys came in and cleaned up after them. I'm telling you, man, they're nuts up there. If Elle's gone to Scotland, we don't have a hope in hell of cracking that town to find her."

"If Tommy thinks she's in Scotland, he'll send everything we have after her."

"Suicide," Abasi muttered. "We need to play this smart."

"Then we'd better hope she's still in London. What do our contacts in the force say?"

"Nothing. They're scrambling to find her, same as us."

Marcus opened a folder on his laptop and clicked on a photo. It showed Elle, blue-haired and shouting at him from the London office. She barely resembled the sister he'd known. In fact, he would have walked straight past her if he'd seen her on the street; she'd changed that much...

Or had she?

She'd stood in that doorway and ordered him not to shoot because she was protecting her friends. The Elle he knew would never let someone or something she cared about get hurt when she could stop it. "We need to draw her out, bring her to us. The people she cares about? Who's the most vulnerable?"

Abasi sighed. "Dunno. They locked down pretty tight once word went out she was made."

"There has to be someone. Find that person and use them to bring Elle to me."

"On it." Abasi hung up, leaving Marcus to change into a suit for the meeting.

Somebody had to be there to stop Tommy from losing his temper and killing their crew.

15

The team debriefed over pizza and soft drinks. Megan had wanted beer, but Callum pointed out that they were on alert and might still need to shoot somebody, and as he'd much rather it wasn't him, he'd vetoed the beer. Although, he'd said it in a more technical and whole lot less tactful way than Elle would have done.

With food filling their bellies and the adrenaline working its way out of their systems, tiredness soon set in. Slowly, everyone drifted off to bed, leaving Elle with the mountain of cell phones they'd confiscated during their raids. She could have left them until the morning, gotten some sleep before she started breaking into them, but her nature wouldn't let her. Which meant a long night working with her crappy laptop. The machine was the computer equivalent of a drunken snail, zigzagging slowly across the garden and likely to die from overconsumption at any minute.

As Elle wiped down the phones with antibacterial spray —because: dirty gangbangers—silence descended on the house. The world outside didn't slow any, though. This was London, and they were right beside one of the busiest airports in the world; there was no division between day and night at Heathrow. In truth, Elle found the hum of activity soothing. It meant she didn't feel alone.

"You need help with that?" David asked, making her startle.

"I'm going to put a bell around your neck," she threatened. "Out of all the men, you're the quietest, and that's saying something." Even with two prosthetic legs, Callum could be pretty damn silent if he wanted. "I thought you'd gone off on some secret spy mission. You know, to avoid me."

"The secret spy mission was for intel; avoiding you was just a side benefit." He grinned at her.

"And yet, here you are, back with me." She tried to cock an eyebrow at him, but they both went up. How did people do that? "Ever get the feeling you're fighting the inevitable?"

"Do you want help or not?" he grumbled.

"Well, I was going to make the best of some alone time, but you can stay. I can be alone with you in the room."

"Not sure how to take that." David sat on the arm of the sofa beside her. "You should be sleeping."

"So should you." She bit her lip to stop herself from asking about his bruises. They seemed worse than ever. But he'd made it clear they were none of her business... Of course, she'd never been much good at minding her own business. It was how she'd gotten into trouble with her family in the first place.

"Are you in pain?" she asked.

"No more than I can handle."

Even though his tone was light, Elle caught a worrying undertone to his words. One that suggested he was well versed in pain and had been for a very long time. Well, either that or she was seriously overtired and hearing things.

"How much can you handle?" she said.

His dark eyes captured hers. "You shouldn't ask me questions like that."

"David." She rolled her eyes. "I've been asking you nothing but questions like that since we first met."

He rubbed his chin, seemingly perplexed. "I shouldn't have allowed it."

That made her laugh. "Like you could have stopped me. Anyway, you like answering; you just don't think you should." A little flex of his jaw was his only reaction. It was enough. "Now you don't like that I know that about you."

"I swear you're part witch," he muttered.

"And don't you forget it." She pointed at the phones sitting in the disconnected microwave she'd had brought in to store them. "Do you know how to crack these?"

How one raised eyebrow could come across that sardonic, she didn't know. David leaned over and opened the microwave door to grab a phone. Giving Elle a first-rate view of his backside. Of course, she looked. It was right there. It would have been rude not to.

"I forgot, you're a superspy. A super *CIA* spy. The question is, are you more or less super than Harvard? I mean, he's bigger for a start, and he can speak like a gazillion languages. How can you top that?"

"Quand tu me regardes ainsi, ça me donne envie d'être un homme meilleur." His French accent was perfect, and the look in his eyes...

Holy Hotness, Batman.

"I think I just got pregnant," Elle whispered.

"Walan 'urid 'ann 'uqbilaka."

"I have to warn you." Her gaze flitted between his dark, sensuous eyes and his oh-so-kissable lips. "I think we've stumbled on a fetish I didn't know I had. It's possible that if you keep speaking in languages I don't understand, I *will* be forced to jump you."

"Vy vvoditye cheloveka v grekh." His dark gaze held hers for what felt like an eternity before he cleared his throat and moved to the armchair beside her. "Then I'd better stick to English."

"What happened to all those *threats* you made in Scotland and in that alley in Chinatown? Weren't you going to show me pleasure beyond my wildest dreams? Or were you just talking yourself up?"

"Ellie, do I seem like a man who needs to talk himself up?"

No, he really didn't. "So, the flirting was just you being a tease? I don't think so. The kisses felt pretty genuine to me. The *two* kisses. I mean, once you can excuse, but you, my man, are a serial offender."

"Can you call twice serial?" David's eyes sparkled with amusement. Further proof that he enjoyed this dance between them at least as much as she did.

"You can when they were that hot. I mean, one with me in pink handcuffs and one pressed up against a wall. Although, I'm not sure that one counts because you ruined it by stealing my laptop. Which, by the way, wasn't cool, and the only reason you're still alive is that you returned it."

"It was tagged with a tracker. I was protecting you by removing it."

"Yeah, right, and you couldn't just tell me that so I could remove it myself?" Elle narrowed her eyes at him. "Stop trying to derail this conversation. I'm not one of those women who enjoy trying to figure out what a guy's thinking. I'd rather just ask and get an honest answer. So, what's with the sudden distance?"

He stared at her for long enough that she wondered if she should start squirming. *Hell no.* He'd kissed her. Both times. *He* could bloody well squirm.

"Why is there a microwave oven full of phones in the

middle of the floor?" Callum asked as he prowled into the room, followed closely by Joe.

"This isn't finished," Elle hissed at David before answering her boss. "Makeshift Faraday cage, which is basically a metal structure that stops signals going in or out. I've turned off all the phones and taken out the batteries where they weren't sealed in. Unfortunately, even when a phone's turned off, someone can still hack it—if they have the right tech. Hence, the microwave."

"That works?" Joe was clearly skeptical.

"Mostly. However, don't be fooled—not all microwaves are created equal. This model has a better cage. Until I've hacked each phone, it's safer for us if they're in there. Plus, I wiped them down, but I don't like the look of some of them, so I'm treating this as a phone quarantine." She held up the antibacterial spray. "Each time I open the door, I spray some of this inside and hope it kills anything that could kill me."

Callum was all business. "Have you accessed any phones yet?"

"I've done a couple so far. One had nothing but cheap porn and texts that were ninety percent emojis." She reached for the iPhone with a cracked screen sitting on the coffee table in front of her. "This one might have some good stuff. They're using a popular encrypted chat app to talk, and if I can hack his password, I'll be able to access his conversations. I don't think it'll be too hard. The password for his phone was MC2oRULZ."

Joe burst out laughing as he sat on the sofa facing her. Callum, as usual, stood. She'd once thought he chose to stand more often than sit because it was more comfortable on his prosthetic legs. Now she knew he did it because it made it easier to walk out when he grew tired of everyone around him.

"You holding up okay, Elle?" Joe leaned forward, his face a mask of concern.

Suddenly, their late-night chat made a whole lot of sense. Callum wanted to check in on her emotional state and had brought along as backup someone who was more capable of doing that than he was. *Bless his wee grumpy heart.*

"I'm doing fine. I mean, I'm in my happy place." She pointed at her laptop and the phones. "It also feels kinda nostalgic. Here we are, dealing with my family, and I'm back to hacking phones. Seems apropos, considering the first thing I hacked was a phone."

"Yeah?" Joe encouraged her to keep talking, like a big, combat-trained counselor. "What brought that on? Curiosity?"

Callum, meanwhile, studied her as though trying to ascertain whether the stress of the situation would make her crack.

"My family used purpose-built cell phones to communicate, and I wanted to know what was on them," she told them. "The phones were designed to be completely secure. All they had on them was an encrypted messaging platform. No cameras, no GPS, nothing. Only this unhackable communications app."

"Which, of course, you had to crack." Callum sighed.

"Which I *did* crack."

"Tough job?" Joe asked.

Elle shrugged. "I had to borrow my brother's phone to do it. And let me tell you, that wasn't easy. He practically slept with the thing in his hand. Once I got it, I set up a program to infiltrate the messaging app and send copies of every communication sent by everyone using it to me." She fiddled with the trackpad on her laptop and spoke more to the screen than the men in the room. "That's how I found out my father killed my mother for having an affair with a cop."

There was cursing, some of it quite creative. Elle sat quietly, feeling somewhat detached from their reactions. As though she was talking about someone else's life instead of her own. To shake off the feeling, she reached for a slice of cold pizza covered in appetizing congealed cheese.

"Not gonna happen." David took it from her hand. "Don't move. I'll be back."

Confused, she watched him leave the room.

"Must have been hard"—Joe drew her attention back to him—"finding out about your mom like that."

"It's okay, guys. You don't need to be upset on my behalf. It was a long time ago, and I pretty much suspected something like that by the time I hacked the phones. It wasn't really news." Although, having her suspicions confirmed had destroyed her. All hope that her mother would return for her one day had been wiped away. She'd hidden in the back of her closet, curled up on the floor, and wept until she couldn't weep anymore. Then she'd started planning her escape from Tommy.

A hand rested on her shoulder as David set a plate on the cushion beside her laptop. On it was sliced apple and banana and a handful of almonds. He took her hand and placed a glass of milk in it. A glass of *warm* milk.

"What's this?" Elle stared at the plate and the milk.

"We, in the trade, like to call it food."

"I wanted pizza." She didn't. Not really. What she wanted was chocolate cake, David naked and pressed against her, and a father who wasn't trying to kill her—although not necessarily in that order.

"I know, but somebody has to do something about all the junk you eat. If you have a heart attack while we're trying to save your life, the irony will kill me."

"Back to you hacking your family business," Callum said.

"What he means to say is he's sorry about your mom." Joe shot their boss a pointed glare.

It didn't faze Callum at all. "Elle knows I'm sorry; I don't need to say it. What I will say, though, is that I'd like to put a bullet in the bastard who killed her. Although, I'm thinking you'd be a wee bit conflicted about that, seeing as he's your father." The scary expression on Callum's face was one of the reasons she loved him, that and his fierce need to protect anyone he considered family. In many ways, he was the father she'd never really had.

"I'm not conflicted." Reluctantly, she picked up a slice of banana. "Tommy James is a psychopath. Seriously, I even spoke to a psychiatrist about this once. He's textbook material. He delights in making people suffer purely for his own pleasure. It's only the fact he's smart as well as ruthless that lets him get away with it. Trust me. The world would be a much better place without him."

There was no argument to the contrary from the men.

"So, when you hacked their phones," Joe said, "other than what happened to your mom, what else did you discover?"

"Everything." She took a sip of the milk and had to fight not to tear up. It'd been a long time since someone had cared enough to think about such a trivial aspect of her comfort. Man, she must be exhausted if warm milk was making her emotional. "I was thirteen at the time. My dad had been using my programing talent for years, getting me to hack things for him or write apps and malware that he'd sell to his partners or use to destroy them. Of course, I didn't know any of that at the time; the truth of the family business had pretty much been hidden from me. Probably because I'm a girl. On top of everything else, Tommy's a chauvinist."

David shifted in his seat, making her aware that his full attention was focused on her. "More likely it was because he knew how smart you were and that you'd become a threat to him."

Yeah, that sounded more like wishful thinking than fact. "I was a young kid when he asked me to code for him. I thought if I did a good job, he'd be proud of me. Plus, honestly, I was bored and enjoyed the challenge. Up until then, he'd only ever approved of me if I wore pretty dresses and talked about horse riding. I think he wanted a society daughter, and he ended up with a geek.

"Anyway, that's what I thought until one day I saw something on the news about a group of DEA agents who'd died in Mexico when their communications were compromised. There was an interview with a tech expert who said it all came down to one little piece of malware. That's when I knew what I'd done. That malware was something I'd written. Those men died because of something I'd done."

She swallowed hard but squared her shoulders. It hurt, but there was no hiding from the truth. Nor would she want to. "Guess you could say I killed for the first time when I was twelve. If you kill a bunch of people, does that make you a mass murderer or a serial killer? I've always been too scared to Google it."

A hand curved around hers. "What it makes you is a kid who was used," David said. "Those deaths aren't on you. They're on your father. You're innocent in this."

Elle's smile was mirthless as she stared at his hand. "You sure about that? It's not the worst thing I've done." Not by a long shot. "You don't know all of it."

To make matters worse, every day she'd learned of some new atrocity that her coding had caused. Even if she tried to make amends for the rest of her life, she'd never make up for the damage she'd done. Unwittingly or not, she was still responsible for all those lost and broken lives.

"You were a kid," David repeated. "He's to blame, not you."

Elle shook her head and decided to let him have all of it. The story she'd discovered the night before. The one she was still trying to get her head around before figuring out a way to explain it to him. But listening to him now, she realized there would never be a right way to tell him what she'd done.

To tell him she was the one who'd ruined his life.

Elle swallowed through a throat so tight it hurt. "Yesterday, Harvard mentioned an operation in Russia eleven years ago that went bad on you. It set off alarm bells for me, so I looked it up." She took a shaky breath as she slid her hand out from under his. "It was my fault. You were the victim of some malware I wrote to corrupt a comm system. I didn't know."

Her voice broke, and she cleared her throat. "Now I do. I know you were working with a group of operatives from several agencies to bring down a terrorist cell financed by organized crime. I know you had all the intel you needed to put an end to their violence. And I know that right before you moved in on the group, your system was corrupted, and your comms knocked out. You went in blind, and it was a bloodbath. According to the news site, only one person made it out alive. I guess that person was you."

She leaned toward David and whispered, "Am I still innocent now?"

16

———

No one moved as the air in the room grew oppressively heavy. Elle tucked her hair behind her ear, wishing she'd confessed her sins to David privately. Wishing she'd managed to hide her shame from her team, solely because she wanted them to think the best of her for just a little while longer. She took a deep breath. It was better they knew who she really was before things got a whole lot worse for all of them.

And David...

She was the reason his mission had been a disaster.

She was the reason his teammates were dead.

And she was the reason he'd lost the career he'd loved. She wasn't dumb; it hadn't taken her long to join the dots between what happened in Russia and his freelance work now. His whole life had been turned upside down—by her.

"I'm sorry," she whispered to him. "I'm so sorry."

"How old were you?" David's voice was rough, making her blink several times until the question sank in.

"Thirteen." She found it hard to meet his eyes.

"A baby," he muttered.

Elle shook her head. "I knew what the malware did by

then, but I just hadn't figured out how to get Tommy to stop making me hack things. I'd scour the news, searching for hints about the damage I'd caused. I even kept note of them in the hope that one day, I could somehow make it up to people. It wasn't until just before my fourteenth birthday that I figured out all I needed to do was make a mistake in my coding, and the hack or malware would be useless. Unfortunately for you, for your team, I didn't work that out until it was too late."

Her eyes closed against the memory of her father's rage when she'd suddenly started screwing up her jobs. Marcus had been the one to save her from the blows Tommy rained down on her. She'd spent weeks in bed after that, recovering from the damage he'd caused. Lying in pain while her mind raced to find a way to fix everything.

Only to realize there was no fixing any of it.

From that moment on, she'd been picky about which jobs she sabotaged. By then, she'd hacked their cell phones so knew how Tommy intended to use the code he demanded she write. If it was impossible for her to screw it up without raising his suspicions, she'd tipped off the cops and tried to stop things that way. Only if the situation was life or death; otherwise, Tommy would have become suspicious, and she hadn't thought she'd survive a second beating.

Even then, the jobs that went wrong had drawn Tommy's wrath—a slap or a kick, being locked in a closet for days, humiliated in front of his men, threatened with acts that had made her vomit. It was only Marcus, hovering around, that had given her some measure of protection. Of course, that was before Marcus got sucked so far into the James business that he couldn't see anything outside of it.

David's hand covered hers again, the warmth of his

touch seeping into her cold, weary bones. "What happened when you screwed up the code, Blue?"

Elle shook her head, lips pressed tightly together. There were some things she wouldn't—*couldn't*—say.

Fingers wove through hers, making her stare at their hands. "You. Are. Innocent. In. This," he repeated.

Her eyes closed, and she shook her head again, in protest this time.

Not innocent.

Never innocent.

"You were a child," David whispered. "You were used. And you *are* innocent."

No. Just no. The protest was loud in her head, even though the words wouldn't come out of her mouth.

Gentle fingers wiped her cheek, making her realize she was crying. Damn exhaustion. It had eroded her bravado, exposing her fear and regret to those she cared about most.

"It's been a tough couple of days," David murmured. "You need to sleep, Ellie Blue. We'll talk more tomorrow."

That got her voice working. "I need to finish cracking these phones."

"It can wait." There was no give in his voice.

He stood and, without asking, lifted her into his arms. Elle couldn't stop herself from curling into him. Ashamed of what she'd done. Ashamed that she felt the need to hide from Callum and Joe—two people she loved very much. Silent tears streamed down her face, soaking David's sweater. Tears for the child she'd been. For the lives that she'd taken. For the damage she'd caused. Tears for the little girl who'd desperately wanted her father to love her— enough to willfully ignore the warning bells going off all around him.

David pushed open the door to a bedroom and placed

her in the middle of a soft bed. The lights were off, and the room was cool.

"Sleep," he ordered before turning away.

"Whose room is this?" Surely someone had already claimed it. She'd fallen asleep on the sofa the night before and thought she'd do the same again that night.

"Doesn't matter. Go to sleep." In other words, it was his.

Elle's hand snapped out to curl around his wrist. "I know the words don't mean much, but I'm really sorry about your team."

"Blue, you need to let it go. It's in the past, and it wasn't your fault." His deep voice, with its weirdly generic accent, was filled with understanding. With forgiveness. Which made her feel worse because she didn't deserve either.

"Please don't go." She grasped his wrist tighter.

David ran his other hand through his hair. "You don't know what you're asking of me."

"I do. I'm asking you to pretend that I didn't just tell you I'm responsible for you losing your team in Russia, and I'm asking you to hold me for a little while because I'm too worn out to hide that I'm terrified my father will get me." She blinked back yet more stupid tears. "I know you probably want to get as far from me as possible, but if you can stand it, I'd really like to have you near...me. I promise I won't try to jump your bones. Tonight, you totally get a reprieve. I swear I'll behave."

"You're impossible," he grumbled as he reluctantly stretched out beside her on the bed.

Elle hesitated to move closer, but David took the worry out of the situation for her. He wrapped around her, curling her into his side. They were two long-lost jigsaw pieces, fitting together perfectly on the first try. With a shiver, Elle pressed closer, wanting his heat to warm her chilled soul as she inhaled his fresh ocean scent deep within her.

"I hate being weak," she confessed. The night, the dark, the emotion—all of it worked together to loosen her tongue.

"You're far from weak." He sounded serious. Not at all like he was trying to appease her so she'd shut up.

So, she carried on. "I hate being this tired too. I feel sore in my bones."

"Then sleep."

"I'm trying to, but there are thoughts in my head."

"I'm scared to ask," David muttered.

"I've killed a lot of people." The words tumbled out, falling over each other in their rush to escape.

The names of her victims haunted Elle's soul. Not that she knew all of them, even though she'd tried hard to find out. She'd wanted to know who they were. To mourn them even if they were awful, cruel people. No matter what they'd done, they were someone's child. Surely that alone deserved her regret.

"I've killed more," David said. Unlike her, he didn't sound like it bothered him too much.

"How do you live with it? All that death. The families who miss them. The knowledge it's all on you."

His cheek pressed against her hair before he answered. "I'm not like you, Ellie. I was trained to kill people. Bad people. And I've never once regretted it or thought those lives didn't need to be taken. I don't think about their families or the people they've left behind. Mainly I think about the people who won't suffer or die because they're gone."

"I can't do that."

"I know, but you can try to forgive yourself for what happened when you were a child. If you hadn't trusted the person who gave you those jobs, you wouldn't have done them."

Elle took a deep breath and confessed to one of the worst things she'd ever done: "I killed three of Tommy's men. The night before I started working with Benson Security, three syndicate members found out where I was living, and I killed them with booby traps I'd rigged to protect myself."

Once the adrenaline had worked its way out of her system, she'd spent hours shaking and vomiting. The following day, she'd emptied her bank accounts, sending everything she had to their families, knowing full well money wouldn't make up for what she'd taken from them. But it was all she had to give.

"Were they good men?" David asked, and something about the way he said it made her think he already knew the answer. "Was it self-defense?"

She'd known at the time that Tommy had ordered anyone who found her to hurt her. And there'd been no doubt in her mind that those men would have abused her before returning her to her father. One of them had threatened to rape her when she was a teenager and would have done so if given a chance. The other two were brutal to their families and cruel to anyone who got in their way. They were vile men. Evil and twisted and sick. Men who enjoyed making women suffer.

But that didn't change the fact she was neither judge nor executioner.

"It was self-defense," David said with finality when she didn't answer. "Now go to sleep."

"I can't. My brain isn't tired."

"I know I'm going to regret this, but is there anything we can do that will make it tired?"

"We could snuggle naked?" She was pretty sure that having David naked would eliminate the possibility of her having any more thoughts—ever.

"I walked straight into that one," he muttered. "Anything other than naked snuggling?"

"Have you gone off me? Is that what it is?" Yeah, in that moment, her mouth definitely had a mind of its own. One that needed to be silenced.

"It's a bad idea, me and you." His tone was gentle but firm. "It would be a mistake."

Her stomach clenched, and she had to fight the urge to push away from him. "Because of what I did to you when you were in Russia?"

He was quiet for so long that she wasn't sure he would answer. "I've known for years that your hack was used to bring down my team." His voice was so soft it took a long moment to register what he'd said.

Elle tensed, ready to put some distance between them. But his arm tightened, holding her closer still.

"You've known for years?" Her dulled, sleep-deprived mind struggled to comprehend what he was telling her.

"About a year or so before you started working for Benson Security, a woman at MI6 stumbled across your new identity and location. Don't ask me how; I don't know. She hired me as an outside contractor to keep an eye on you until she was ready to use you against your family."

Holy Subterfuge, Batman!

Elle wouldn't have believed anything—other than Naked David—could render her unable to think. She'd been wrong. There were absolutely no thoughts in her head. None. Nada. Zip. The feeling was strange...and unwelcome. All she could do was lie there, frozen, as David carried on talking.

"My contact suspected there was at least one MI6 operative on the James' payroll and wanted to keep you a secret. Which is why she brought me in. And when she did, she handed over every piece of information she had on you—including the hacking you unwittingly did as a child."

Elle scrambled into a seated position. "You knew all

about me? You were following me? For over a year before I met you?"

"Not all the time, but enough." He didn't take his eyes from hers. "I saw what you had to do to survive and not be caught."

The muted shadows of the room seemed to lengthen, feeling ominous for the first time since they'd entered it. "You were there the night I killed those three men?"

David reached up to brush a stray hair from her face. "I'd been ordered not to break cover. Told that you couldn't know you were being watched. Hanging back that night was one of the hardest things I've ever done. Even then, I followed them to the warehouse. I was prepared to end them, if you didn't. They weren't good men, Ellie Blue. I heard what they planned to do with you. None of it was good. And there was no way I'd have let them carry out their plans."

"You would have broken your cover for me?"

"In a second." He smiled. "But you dealt with the situation before I had to."

Wow. Talk about a plot twist. He'd been in her life all this time? "And Peru? You already knew me? I was your...asset?"

"I knew about you, but you weren't my asset. The job ended when my contact at MI6 was killed."

Memories of the past few years flashed through Elle's mind, and a pattern began to emerge. Things falling into place suddenly or near misses that saved her life and identity. Never once had she even suspected someone was behind the scenes, pulling strings.

"It didn't though, did it? Your job didn't end then. You've been looking out for me for years—even after I joined Benson Security." It wasn't a question because she knew in her gut that it was absolutely true. Now that she knew to look for it, she could see his hand in everything—even her job. "Did you talk Lake into merging with Harry's cybersecurity company?"

"You don't talk Lake Benson into anything, Ellie Blue. You can, however, present him with an opportunity that would be beneficial to him and let him come to the right conclusion."

"You wanted me working for him." A warm feeling started deep in her stomach.

"I couldn't watch over you all the time; I wanted you safe. And Lake's one of the few people I could trust to do that."

He said it as though it wasn't the most amazing thing anyone had ever done for her.

"You knew my hacking caused you to lose your team, your career, and you still looked out for me."

"It was a job, Elle. You were a job."

"A job you stopped getting paid for what—at least three years ago, right?"

Superspy rolled his eyes at her and tugged her back down to his side. "You're deliberately ignoring the truth of what I did. I spied on you. I followed you. I investigated you, and I manipulated your life. I'd say that makes us more than even for any perceived mistake you made as a kid."

She wasn't so sure about that. In her own way, Elle had been atoning for all the wrongs she'd done as a child ever since realizing her part in them. But it would never be enough. Each life she'd helped to snuff out was a scar engraved on her soul for all eternity.

"Other women would probably be annoyed you were spying on them for years." Elle snuggled closer. "But it makes me feel safer knowing you were watching out for me. It's like Buffy and Angel. Before she knew about him, he was lurking in the background, backing her up from the shadows, making the world a safer place for her."

David's low groan rumbled through her body. "I tell you I was paid to stalk you, and you tell me you feel good about it. Seriously, Blue, that's not normal."

"I told you I was behind an ambush that almost got you killed and cost you your team, and you said it wasn't my fault. In what way is that normal?"

He groaned again. "How about we stop talking and go to sleep?"

Elle wrapped her arm around his waist and hugged him tight. "Don't worry; all couples have their problems."

"We're not a couple."

"We've kissed and we're in bed together," she said through an evil grin. "Face it, you find me irresistible. It's Angel and Buffy all over again. He couldn't resist his attraction to her, and it pulled him out of the shadows and into her heart. Admit it—you find me irresistible."

"Go to sleep, woman," David grumbled. "We're not a couple. We'll never be a couple. Let it go."

"Hmm, I don't see you rushing to get out of bed and away from me. I wonder why that is... Oh yeah. You're hot for me."

"I'm comfortable and tired. I'll deal with your delusions tomorrow."

"It's already tomorrow." She snuggled closer, breathing him in.

"Go to sleep," he ordered again.

As she felt sleep take her under, Elle could have sworn she heard him say, "Who the hell are Buffy and Angel?"

17

The coward was gone when Elle woke the next morning. Typical. So much for being the big, fearless spy. As if ignoring what was between them would make it go away. One way or another, he'd have to face the fact he was crazy about her. And if he couldn't do it on his own, she'd just have to hit him over the head with the truth until he got it.

"Why are men so dumb?" she asked Megan and Dimitri when she walked into the kitchen. The rest of the team were elsewhere; otherwise, she'd have included them too because, honestly, she really wanted to know.

"Tiny brains." Megan waved her cereal spoon for emphasis. "Also, what gray matter they do have is floating around in a sea of testosterone. Makes it hard for them to process anything that isn't football, aggression, or sex."

"Hey!" Dimitri swiveled in his seat to glare at his wife. "Do you even know how offensive that is?"

"Fine." Megan put down the spoon and folded her arms over her black T-shirt emblazoned with a white skull. "What are the three main things that occupy your mind? Let me see—football games or fantasy football league, planning missions or taking part in dangerous missions, and jumping me whenever you can or thinking about ways to jump me when you can't. Am I wrong?"

He stared at her for a moment before his shoulders slumped and he turned to Elle. "I can't argue with that. I wish I could, but I can't."

Megan smiled smugly at Elle. "I rest my case."

"Okay..." Elle made herself a massive mug of coffee. "Here's a better question, Dimitri. Why are men so scared of relationships?"

"Wait? Was that Callum shouting for me? Sorry, gotta go." Dimitri pushed back his chair and practically ran from the room.

"Seems the expert's too scared to answer," Megan said with a wry smile. "Problems with your spy?"

"He's an idiot." Elle sat down at the table, facing Megan. "He says we can't have a relationship because...actually, I don't know why. There was something about it being a bad idea. It was too vague to be anything other than an excuse. Maybe I misread the spark between us."

"Well, if you did, we all did. Because..." Megan mimed touching something and being burned. "Hot," she said when Elle stared at her blankly.

"Why would it be a bad idea? I'm a catch." She waved a hand. "Not right now, obviously. I mean, when there aren't people out to question, capture, or kill me. When things are quiet, I am awesome to be around. I'm funny. I know lots of cool facts. I can get you free movie downloads. And I'm fantastic in bed. What's not to love?"

"I'll get something to eat later," Ryan said from the doorway, where he stood frozen with a horrified expression on his face. "I'll come back when you aren't talking about sex." He disappeared. Almost as fast as Dimitri had done.

"Men," Elle grumbled.

"Maybe the complications that make it a bad idea for you two to get together are something so gruesome he can't even talk about it," Megan said. "Like he's dying from something. Or he's really your brother. Or he's already signed up to become a monk."

Elle considered Megan's theories for a second before shaking her head. "Naw, he's just a pathetic coward. One who keeps giving off mixed signals. They're giving me whiplash. He doesn't want to be with me, but he rushed right here to protect me. He doesn't want to get naked, but it's okay to flirt. He thinks a relationship is a bad idea, but he hasn't been able to keep away from me for years. Then there are the handcuffs. What man brings fluffy pink handcuffs to the bedroom of a woman he isn't interested in? Huh?"

"Nope," a voice said from the door, and they turned to see Harvard pivot and walk away.

Rachel strode into the room instead. "Why are you talking about relationships when it would be smarter to talk about ways to keep you from getting sliced and diced by your father? Have I taught you nothing? I didn't get to be CEO of a major pharmaceutical company by sitting around chatting about boys with my friends. Woman up. Get the job done. Prove you're the superior sex. *Then* the man will fall at your feet and beg you to take him on. Now, somebody make me a coffee." She took a seat at the table, dressed in a pristine Prada pantsuit and sporting a perfect manicure and expertly styled hair.

Elle looked down at the Princess Leia nightshirt Julia had bought her to sleep in, but she'd decided it should be worn during the day, when people could better appreciate it. Unlike Rachel, Elle hadn't even brushed her hair yet that morning, and she couldn't remember ever having her nails done. Typing would have ruined a manicure anyway. It was as if Rachel came from a completely different planet. One where clothes were pressed and makeup flawless. On Elle's planet, makeup didn't exist, and clothes were only bought if they didn't require pressing.

"I don't even know where to start with that little speech," Elle said to Megan.

"How about with the fact Rachel became CEO because her family owns the company and not because she worked her arse off?"

Elle inclined her head, as though considering the merits of Megan's suggestion. "Or we could discuss how she got jiggy with Harvard while someone was trying to blackmail her. Because, you know, priorities during a mission."

"True. Oh, I know, let's discuss the weird imagery of Rachel talking about boys with her gal pals."

"Or Rachel even having gal pals," Elle added. "According to her, we aren't friends, even though we totally are, and last time I checked"—she glanced down at her boobs—"yeah, still a girl."

"Is the coffee happening anytime soon?" Rachel asked, sounding bored.

"She's right about one thing, though," Elle said to Megan. "This isn't the time to start anything romantic with anyone. David and I could both be dead by the end of the week."

"For the love of Prada, somebody make me coffee," Rachel said.

"On the other hand," Megan said to Elle, "it is a very good time to jump into bed with him and work off some of that sexual tension you two have going on. Just so you're clearheaded for whatever comes next. Plus, what better excuse for getting jiggy than it might be your last ever chance?"

"Fine. I'll get my own coffee." Rachel made no effort to move from her seat. Instead, she tapped at her phone.

Elle sat up straighter and grinned at Megan. "You're totally right. I've been looking at this all wrong. We don't need to throw ourselves into something heavy. I mean, I did just learn his name. There are other ways for us to work out our issues."

"In bed, right?" Megan appeared confused.

Elle sighed. "Why am I even asking you for advice?"

"It's anybody's guess." Megan sat back in her chair as Ryan strode into the room.

"I got your urgent text," he said to Rachel. "What do you need?"

"Thank heavens. I need coffee." She pointed to the pot. "Make it strong. I've developed a headache from listening to these two."

Ryan put his hands on his hips and glared at her. "You sent for me because you want me to make you a coffee."

"I'm sorry, wasn't I clear?" Rachel stared at him coolly. "Should I have texted the instruction instead? Perhaps a coffee emoji would have made it easier to understand."

Ryan's hands came up to form claw shapes in the air, as though he was getting ready to wring Rachel's neck. For a second, Elle could have sworn she saw smoke coming out of his ears. Thankfully, Rachel was saved by the bell. Or, in this case, Ryan's phone.

"If this is another text from you, I'm going to strangle you." He checked the screen. "You are so lucky," he told Rachel before saying, "Hey, Granddad, what's up?" into the phone.

Ryan's smile faded as he listened to his granddad, and suddenly, the women in the room were all very much focused on his phone call. His gaze found Elle and darkened. His jaw clenched as his body became visibly tense. He tapped the screen, then held out the phone to Elle, his face a mask of utter fury. "Your brother wants a word."

Feeling as though she were stepping into an alternate dimension, Elle took the phone. In her peripheral vision, she could see Rachel tapping furiously at her phone screen. A second later, the team started streaming through the door.

"Elle?" Marcus said from the phone, louder than expected, making her realize Ryan had switched it to speaker before handing it over.

"Marcus," she said, her heart racing and her palms sweating. "What have you done?"

"I didn't want it to come to this, little sister." Marcus was speaking when David slipped into the crowded room and made his way straight to Elle's side, hating the pain and shock on her face. "But you gave me no choice. I have Granger's family, and unless you surrender to me, I'll start putting bullets in them."

"Don't listen to him," an older male voice shouted in the background. "We can take a couple of bullets. Run, Elle, run!"

Ryan made a deep growling sound, and Callum slapped a hand on his shoulder.

"Can you take a bullet to your head?" Marcus asked the old man casually. "Could your wife?"

"If this is the way we go out," the old man said, "then so be it. It's been a good life."

"Are you happy with their lives ending today, Elle?" Marcus asked, sounding like it didn't matter to him either way.

Her tear-filled eyes met Ryan's, and she mouthed "I'm sorry" before answering her brother. "You know the answer to that, Marcus. I don't want anyone else to die. You really have turned into him, haven't you?" Her voice trembled, and David took a step closer, wanting to hold her tight while she dealt with her brother but forcing himself not to. "You swore you'd never end up like Tommy. You swore."

"You've got an hour to get to the Granger house."

"Not possible. The drive takes more than an hour from here," Ryan said. "An hour twenty, maybe, if the traffic cooperates."

"Then an hour twenty it is," Marcus said. "Come alone, Elle, or someone dies."

"No," David snapped. That was not going to happen. He plucked the phone out of Elle's hand and held it close to his mouth. "This is David Knight. Your family set up an ambush for me in Amsterdam."

Elle gaped at him, horrified, and his fingers tingled with the need to touch her. Which he didn't.

"You aren't running this show, Knight. I am," Marcus said. "Put my sister back on the phone."

Elle made a grab for the phone, but David moved it out of her reach, earning himself a glare and a quick kick to his shin. He was glad she was barefoot.

"Not going to happen," he told Marcus. "We can do the exchange, but Elle won't be alone. You take her; you take me. I'd like some payback for Amsterdam. How about you be a man and face me yourself this time?"

Marcus gave a bark of laughter. "Is that supposed to intimidate me? I'm happy to have you too, Knight. There are several parties who'd bend over backward to take you off my hands. You try anything, pull any tricks, and everyone dies. Am I clear?"

"We'll be there in an hour twenty," David said and hung up.

There was a moment of utter silence before Elle shouted, "Are you insane?"

Probably, but he wasn't about to share that with the group.

"Knight," Callum rumbled. "What did I say about working as a team? That means you don't take over an op by making unilateral decisions. You've painted us into a corner, boy, and I am bloody furious. I should have kicked your arse out after that first debrief."

"We can still salvage this." Ryan clasped his hands on top of his head. "I know the layout of my granddad's house like the back of my hand. We can storm the place and take them down."

"Marcus would shoot your grandparents at the first sign of trouble," Elle said softly.

His jaw tightened. "Then we go in covert and sneak them out."

"Normally, I'd agree," Joe said. "But we don't have the time. Maybe if we'd said we were three hours away, we could have sneaked up on them. Right now, there's very little wiggle room between when we'll arrive at the house and when Marcus expects to see Elle. We can't stage a rescue in under five minutes."

"I shouldn't have mentioned the drive time." Ryan was clearly pissed at himself.

"It doesn't matter," David told him. "There was only ever one option in this situation. He wants Elle, and we need to give her to him in order to save your family. I'll make sure she gets out in one piece."

"That wasn't your decision to make," Callum snapped. "This isn't a bloody movie. You aren't James Bond. We're a team. And you just undermined all of us."

"It was the only choice." David wasn't intimidated. He might be the smallest man in the room by a couple of inches and some body mass, but he was definitely the most danger-ous. And he'd faced off against far worse than Callum

McKay. "Marcus wouldn't have let anybody else go with Elle, and she can't go in there alone, so that leaves me as the only logical choice. None of you have a price on your heads. I'm worth something to him."

"So what?" Elle exploded. "You're just going to sacrifice yourself for me? How is that smart? How does that help?"

"I have skills that will help us get out of whatever we're walking into."

She nodded, a little frantically. "I forgot. You're a one-man army. You can take on the whole James Syndicate on your own. What was I thinking? You don't need backup. You're bulletproof."

Rachel stood, sighed loudly, and strode to the middle of the room. "Argue later, children. We're cutting it fine with drive time. David has chosen the plan. It's stupid and will probably get him killed, but we're stuck with it. I suggest we use the next couple of minutes to come up with a way to protect Elle as best we can before we have to be on the road."

As the men continued to glare at David, Julia turned to Elle. "How can we track the two of you? We don't have any tracking equipment, except for phones, which are easy to detect."

"Harvard?" Elle said. "Is that a smartwatch you're wearing?"

"Yeah, why?"

"I need it."

Without another question, he unstrapped it and handed it over.

"Come on," she said to Julia. "We have work to do."

As soon as the two women left the testosterone-ridden room, Callum loomed over David. "Once this is over, I want you gone. Understood?"

David glanced around at the implacable faces of the

Benson Security team, seeing they all agreed with their boss. Not that he would have argued anyway. The last thing he wanted was to divide their team.

"Understood," he said before striding out of the kitchen to find Elle.

Deep inside, a strange sense of loss reared its head. Frowning, David examined his reaction. Could it be that he wanted to be a part of the team? He shook off the feeling. In his line of work, there was no space for wishing things were different. There was no space for feelings of any kind.

18

———

Elle managed to nurture her anger toward David for a whole fifteen minutes. What could she say? It took way too much effort to hold a grudge when your personality wasn't tuned that way. No, she preferred other methods for torturing the morons who annoyed her— like talking endlessly, or spamming their email, or...well, she'd think of something else just as soon as she was done dealing with her psychotic family.

"We probably should have taken the M25," she said, breaking the tense fifteen-minute silence. Well, tense for *her*. "It's the long way round, for sure. But driving through the city center means we're more likely to get stuck in traffic. I'm not sure this route was the right decision. Did you know that the M25 was the inspiration for Chris Rea's song, 'The Road to Hell'?"

David's jaw clenched and unclenched.

"I've never liked Chris Rea; he gives me the creeps. Not sure why." Elle stared back out the window at the crowded city streets.

According to Rachel's GPS, at that time of the day, the fastest route from Heathrow Airport to Fish Island in East

London took them straight past the Victoria and Albert Museum, Buckingham Palace, and the Tower of London.

"Have you ever done the tourist thing in London?" she asked.

David's hands flexed on the wheel. She'd wanted to drive, but he seemed genetically incapable of letting her do so.

"We need to talk about how we're going to handle this situation with your brother, not whether I've visited Buckingham Palace or what songs were inspired by a motorway."

Seemed David wasn't in his happy place and hadn't been since Marcus' phone call. Why he was grumpy, she didn't know. She also thought it was a bit of a cheek, considering he'd been the one to insert himself into the situation. If it'd been up to Elle, she would have dealt with her brother on her own.

As much as that thought terrified her, Elle was pragmatic enough to know she couldn't run forever. This meeting with her brother—and then her father—had always been inevitable. Along with the chance that she wouldn't survive either.

"Elle, we need to make sure we're on the same page when we get to our destination."

"Oh, don't worry about that; we're totally on the same page. You have a death wish, so you included yourself in this exchange. Congrats. Your wish will probably be granted."

He did that jaw-clench thing again. "Nobody is going to die today."

"That sounds like something Dean Winchester in *Supernatural* would say—right before everybody dies."

"Elle..." he warned.

"Fifteen seasons of that show, and every season, Dean Winchester would say nobody is going to die today, which meant somebody was definitely going to die. Most likely a character you'd grown to love. The writers of *Supernatural* were cruel, evil masterminds."

"We're heading into a volatile situation," David said. "Is this really what you want to talk about?"

"No. I'd like to talk about why you keep avoiding me or why you think you're bad for me. Or we could discuss the mixed messages you've been throwing in my direction. One minute you're flirting, and the next, you avoid eye contact. It's making me dizzy. That's what I'd like to talk about. So? Got any ideas?" She twisted in her seat to give him her full attention and smiled brightly.

"This won't work, Elle," he said as they crawled to a halt for a red light. "You can't put off talking about Marcus."

"Tell you what, I'll answer your questions when you answer mine."

"It just wouldn't work out between us. Can't we leave it at that?"

"We could if I thought for one second that you didn't want me as much as I want you. Tell me you don't crave me. Tell me you aren't desperate to get naked and see what will happen. Tell me you don't dream about me and wake covered in sweat, desperate to see what your dream would be like in reality. Tell me any of that, and I'll stop asking and we can discuss my brother instead."

"You need to stop talking," he growled.

She inched across the seat, leaning into him, staring into his dark eyes while she called him on all the crap he was telling himself. "I will once you admit that you dream about having me at your mercy, fluffy pink handcuffs around my wrists while you tease and taste and—"

His palm clasped her nape, and his mouth was on hers before she could finish speaking. Elle didn't care that she could taste frustration in his kiss. She was angry with him too. Threading her fingers through his hair, she clutched him to her as she took what she wanted. What he wanted to give. Lips. Teeth. Tongues. Desperate, hungry need swirled around them, sucking them down together. A wild, hot tornado of lust, desire, frustration, anger, and...longing.

A car horn blasted.

The light had turned green. David broke the kiss, swiveled in his seat, and put the car in gear.

"Damn it, Ellie." His voice was rough, his lips swollen. "There are reasons we can't keep doing this."

Elle cleared her throat, blinked at her surroundings several times, and resisted the urge to take her pulse. Because: *hot damn.*

"Are you listening to me?" David said. "We can't do this. There are reasons."

She flapped the bottom of her T-shirt to get some air circulating before she passed out. "Unless those reasons include you being my long-lost brother, I'm not interested. We definitely need to do that again. And again. And again. Then do more. Way more. In fact, we need to do *everything.*"

His expression morphed from exasperation to clinically cold. "We have chemistry, and we're both horny as hell, but that's all there is between us. If you expect more from me, you won't get it." He shrugged. "I didn't want to hurt you by laying it on the line. I thought if I told you there were serious issues that prevented us from getting together, you'd get the message. Obviously, I need to be clearer. Truth is, baby, I'm just not that into you."

Elle burst out laughing.

"I'm serious." He scowled with irritation.

Elle laughed harder.

"Uh," the phone on the dash said, "is this a good time to point out that we're still on a group call?" Megan snorted.

"And FYI, spy man, the only one you're fooling is yourself. You are so into our girl you can hardly see straight."

"I hate your team," David muttered.

"Aye," Callum said. "Well, we're no' too happy with you either."

"Because he's messing with Elle?" Megan asked.

"No." Callum's voice was filled with despair. "Because he went rogue on us and took over the op without consultation."

"I knew that," Megan said.

"Can we talk about what we're walking into?" Callum said. "I mean, if the two of you aren't too upset over the state of your relationship to focus on actual, bloody work."

"Oh, I'm not upset," Elle told Callum while looking at David. "I'm furious. I'd quite like to put David in my degausser machine, just to see what it would do to that screwed-up brain of his."

"Elle—" he said, a warning in his tone.

"Nope." She held up a hand. "I've had enough cowardly man-logic for one day." She stared out the window again. "Callum, tell us what you want us to do."

COWARDLY?

The word rang in David's head. Repeating on an endless loop that wouldn't quit.

Cowardly?

Had anybody ever called him that and lived? Was she right? He believed he was sacrificing himself to protect her but was he only protecting himself? And why the hell was he thinking about this instead of what they might face with her brother?

"This is why relationships don't work in the field," he

told her. "Instead of discussing the mission, we're fighting over our future. It could get us killed."

"Future? What future? We've had three kisses and some fun flirting. As you pointed out, that doesn't even make a relationship, let alone a future." She rolled her eyes at him. "You keep talking, but all I hear is 'blah, blah, blah, I'm a big scaredy-cat with commitment issues and a deep fear of crawling into bed with Elle.'"

"I've been sayin' this for years," Callum barked through the phone, reminding David yet again that they weren't alone. That was twice now he'd forgotten. Elle would get them both killed. "Less girly chitchat and more profession-alism, people."

"Again, with the girly," Megan said. "Stop being such a sexist old man."

"Yeah," Elle said. "Try being a whiny man-child, like David instead."

David took a deep breath before focusing on the mission. "Ryan, run us through it again."

The rest of the team were in vehicles behind and in front of them—except for Julia and Rachel, who were back at the safe house.

"My grandparents live in a standard seventies-built semi-detached house in a small estate near Victoria Park," Ryan said. "They share the house with my great-uncle and his wife. This time of day, it would only be the women who're home. Granddad should have been at work—he's on retainer with Benson Security and is building something in Callum's house right now. So, the police shutting down the office shouldn't have stopped him from going to work. I don't understand why he's home."

David recognized the clipped, hard tone of Ryan's voice. It was the tone of a man who was mad and had the training to do something about it. "What about the neighbors? Would they notice something going on at the house?"

"Absolutely. It's a tight community. They're all older and in each other's business. I'm surprised somebody hasn't called the cops by now."

"The James Family must have gone in quiet," Callum said. "Wouldn't be surprised if they picked up your granddad while he was working and took him back home."

"That's how I would have done it," David agreed. "A stranger walking up to a door in a tight-knit community can attract a lot of attention, especially if they seem out of place anyway. But somebody the homeowner brought home? They wouldn't warrant so much as a second glance."

"Wish we knew how many we were up against," Callum said.

"I never should have let Granddad talk me out of installing security cameras," Ryan said. "As soon as this is over, that house will be wired with everything I can throw at it, whether they like it or not."

Nobody pointed out that was a case of closing the stable door after the horse had already bolted.

"That's our exit," Elle said coolly from the passenger seat.

David wanted to hit something. They were heading into a dangerous situation, and she was mad at him. *That would help.*

Ryan and Callum's car took the exit she'd pointed to, and David followed.

"I'll do a loop of the area first," Ryan said. "Get an idea what we're up against. You hang back."

"We don't have much time to spare," David reminded him.

"I know," was his terse reply.

The area was classic London—a mixture of building

types interspersed with the greenery of public parks. There were tall apartment blocks overshadowing Victorian terrace houses and a whole bunch of newer builds that were smaller and tweaked to appear less uniform. Ryan's grandparents lived in one of the newer builds: a caramel-colored brick semi with small windows and a postcard-sized garden, sitting at the end of a cul-de-sac. Hertford Union Canal ran behind the house, and beyond that, Victoria Park Green Belt. There was no doubt that Ryan's grandparents had managed to secure one of the coveted spots in a very built-up area.

Unfortunately, the things that made their location attractive also made it hard to surveil their house without Elle's brother noticing.

"Can you get to the canal from their house?" David asked.

"There's a gate at the end of their garden," Ryan answered. "You think Marcus came in by boat?"

"I don't know." David parked, engine running, at the end of the street, behind a large white plumber's van that obscured their view somewhat. Callum and Ryan were driving the cul-de-sac road to get an idea of what was happening in the house. The rest of the team sat in another vacant spot farther up the street.

"Any cars in the drive?" David said.

"They don't have a driveway," Ryan replied. "But there's nothing out of the ordinary parked on the street, and the garage door's closed. Curtains are drawn too. If I didn't know better, I'd say no one was home."

"Any neighbors out and about?" David said.

"No, it's a ghost town."

"We have to assume he's in there," Callum said.

"Wait," Ryan said. "My cell's ringing. Everybody, stay

silent; I'm answering it while I keep the other phone on speaker." There was a pause. "Marcus?"

"No, it's your granddad." And he was clearly angry.

As David listened to the call, he scanned his surroundings, and the hairs on the back of his neck stood on end. Suddenly, the back of the plumber's van opened, and Marcus and Abasi jumped out—guns in their hands, pointed at him and Elle.

"They're here," David snapped.

He put the car in gear, intending to drive right into them. A bullet hole appeared in the top of the windshield, and he let the engine idle.

"We're coming," Callum barked.

"Who's here?" Ryan's granddad shouted. "What's going on? That gangster told me to phone you at twenty past the hour and not a minute later, or someone would die. Did I do something wrong?"

"No," Ryan said. "You haven't done anything wrong."

Marcus and Abasi wrenched open the rear passenger doors and climbed in.

"Drive." Marcus pressed his gun to the back of David's head.

"Do not drive," Callum bellowed.

"Drive, or Abasi puts a bullet in Elle's leg," Marcus said evenly.

David put the car in gear while Elle gaped at her brother in horror. As they took off down the street, the rest of their team came running toward them.

"Floor it," Marcus ordered.

"Sorry, guys," David said as he accelerated toward the team, making them scatter.

"Elle, throw the phone out the window," Marcus ordered. "Throw *all* phones out the window. We're having this conversation in private."

Still stunned, she did as instructed.

Once she'd closed the window again, Abasi handed her two sets of handcuffs. "Cuff both his hands to the steering wheel."

"How will he change gears, genius?" Elle had clearly gotten over her initial shock.

"You can do it for him." Abasi was unfazed.

"Get it done, Elle. My trigger finger's getting itchy." Marcus pushed David's head with his gun.

Glowering at them, Elle leaned over David and secured his hands to the wheel, using one set of cuffs for each hand.

"Not as much fun as we had with the pink ones," he whispered to her, trying to reassure her somehow.

"Don't talk to me. I'm still seriously annoyed with you." She turned toward the back seat. "But not as annoyed as I am with you, Marcus, or you, Abasi. Shoot me in the leg? Really? You should aim for my head instead because I will beat you to death with my bloody leg if you put a bullet in it."

19

Marcus looked pained. "That doesn't even make sense, Elle. If you're going to threaten somebody, at least try to make it sound credible."

David focused in on the arguing siblings. Marcus didn't sound like a man who was out to hurt his sister. Interesting...

Elle glared at her brother before focusing her attention on Abasi.

"Could you do it?" she demanded of one of the most feared men in London. "Could you shoot me in the leg and not feel anything when you did it? Just because he told you to?"

"Fuck." Abasi slumped back into his seat, his gun lowering. "Don't blame me; the threat was his idea."

Every instinct David possessed screamed at him. What the hell was going on? This wasn't the conversation he'd expected. Nor the reaction he'd prepared for. Right now, Elle seemed to be engaged in a stare-down with her brother.

David cleared his throat. "Where am I heading?"

"South. Not far. Hit the A12, and I'll tell you when you get off," Marcus replied, his eyes still on Elle. "Tommy lost the plot when he saw the blue hair." He cocked his head, considering her. "I think it suits you."

"And I don't give a crap what you think," Elle said. "Put down the gun, right now."

"I don't think so. Your man might be attached to the steering wheel, but that doesn't mean he hasn't got a trick or two up his sleeve. I think we're all safer if I keep the gun on him."

Elle threw up her hands in exasperation. "Are you kidding me? He can't move! What exactly do you think he'll do?"

Hoping he'd read the situation correctly, David spoke up and told the truth. "I could use the heel of my foot to press the lever and shove the seat back into your brother. The steering wheel in this car's fitted with a quick-release hub, which means that once I've slammed the seat into Marcus, I could remove the steering wheel and use it to disable him. Then I'd grab his gun and shoot Abasi."

Elle blinked at him several times. "This car has a quick-release steering wheel? Is that standard?"

Abasi burst out laughing. "I have missed you, girl."

"No," David told her. "It isn't standard. The car's been modified. There's more power under the hood and weapons stashed in the frame."

"This isn't a Benson Security junker, is it?" It seemed that, in a fit of curiosity, Elle had completely forgotten they were being held at gunpoint by her blood-thirsty family.

She also seemed to be waiting for an answer.

"I borrowed the car from an acquaintance."

She cocked her head—using the exact same mannerism as her brother. "Of the spy kind?"

"Yep."

"Next left," Marcus ordered.

Which shifted Elle's attention back to her brother.

"What are you doing? If you take me to Tommy, he'll kill me. You know that, right? This isn't about the information I stole or him wanting me to hack for him again. All he wants is to prove that no one can run from the great, psychopathic Tommy James."

"I know," Marcus said. "Next right. Third garage down. It'll be open, so drive on in."

They turned into an alley with a row of garages at the end of the gardens belonging to some old terraced housing. The third garage was open, and David parked inside. The metal door closed behind them, but no one got out of the car.

"So, even knowing what Tommy's going to do with me, you're still taking me to him?" Elle sounded incredulous, making David wonder if she'd read the news reports about her brother over the past few years. David had. None of it was good.

"Chill," Abasi drawled. "Marcus knows what he's doing."

"I'm so reassured. Where are we, anyway?" Elle asked as the garage's dim light filtered in through the windows of the car.

"Nowhere you know," Marcus said. "And, more importantly, nowhere Tommy knows." He took a deep breath. "We need to talk, and we're going to do it in here, where your boyfriend is somewhat controlled."

"He isn't my boyfriend." Elle lifted her chin. "He's too chicken to take me on. Keeps making up sad little excuses to justify him running away. It's pathetic."

David cocked an eyebrow at her. "Really? You're complaining about me to the guy who has a gun to my head?"

"Whatever." She rolled her eyes. "He's annoying me, but I don't want him dead, which means I'd appreciate it if you didn't pull the trigger. As for talking, I don't care where it happens, Marcus. I'd just like you to get to the point. Are you going to shoot me or take me to Tommy?"

"Neither," he said before catching David's eye in the mirror. "I'm lowering my gun. Hear me out, or Abasi puts a bullet in you."

Abasi smiled at David. "Just so you know, I don't think of you as my sister, so I won't have a problem shooting you."

"Understood," David said.

"What's going on?" Elle had obviously used up her reserve of patience. "Why am I here? What do you want?"

Marcus' cold eyes met his sister's furious gaze. "You're here because everybody on the planet is out to get you. And what I want, what I've always wanted, is for you to be safe."

"You want me to be safe? I'm sorry. I think I must have misheard. You? Want *me* to be safe?" Great, now she looked like she might explode.

"It's not that hard to understand," Marcus said, proving he was the one with a death wish. "I want you safe."

"And you thought the best way to achieve that was by terrifying Ryan's elderly relatives and then kidnapping me?"

David caught Abasi's eye in the mirror. "Maybe we should step outside and let them discuss this on their own," he said.

"Word," Abasi answered but didn't stop aiming at David's chest.

"Elle," Marcus said, "nobody can keep you safe from Tommy the way I can. You need to give me a minute to explain. Trust me, I only want what's best for you."

"Trust you?" There was a long pause before Elle added, "Thanks, but I'll pass. Instead, I'm going to trust the only person who's never let me down—Princess Leia. And do you know what she'd do in this situation? She'd say buh-bye and then go sort the problem herself. I'm done dealing with crazy. I'm especially done dealing with men who think they know what's best for me yet manage to demonstrate their greater wisdom in the world's weirdest ways." She threw her door open. "You can keep David. You two have a lot in common."

With that, she stalked toward the garage door—a tiny black silhouette buzzing with fury and topped with luminous blue hair.

"Is anybody going to stop her?" David asked. "She can't go out there on her own."

The two James men shared a look before Marcus sighed heavily. He handed David the keys to his cuffs.

"Maybe you'll have more luck getting through to her," Marcus said. "But, Knight, don't wander off. We need to talk —for Elle's sake. I'm not working with or for Tommy. Everything I've done, everything I am, it's all to keep her safe. I've spent my entire life keeping that crazy woman safe. I can't stop now when she's in more danger than ever."

With a nod, David undid the cuffs and climbed out of the car, wondering how he'd managed to become Marcus James' ally that fast.

"WHERE THE HELL IS THE HANDLE FOR THIS DOOR?" ELLE muttered as she searched for a way out of the garage. Shouldn't there be some sort of mechanism to open it from the inside? Wasn't it illegal not to have one? What if a child got trapped in there? Or a kidnapped hacker who wanted to get as far away as possible from the men in her life?

"Elle." David came to stand beside her. "You need to come back to the car. We have to hear them out."

"Nope. I don't have to do anything I don't want to do. Can you see the button that opens this door?"

Of course, he made no effort to help her find it. "You can't leave; it's too dangerous out there on your own."

Elle threw back her head and laughed. It was a brittle sound. "Yeah, because it's super safe in here." She crouched and tried yanking up the door. It didn't budge. She glanced around. There was another, smaller, door at the far end of the garage, which she assumed led to the garden. It would do. Anything to get her out of there. Seriously. She was two minutes away from hijacking the car and making her own exit. "Never mind, I'll go the long way round." She stomped past David, the car, and the idiots inside it.

David strode around the other side of the car to block her exit. Behind her, the car doors opened. Great. The boys were ganging up on her.

"I would kill for a Taser right about now," she muttered.

"We need to talk," Marcus called out to her.

"No, we don't," she called back while glaring at David. "Get out of my way."

"I can't do that. We need to hear what your brother has to say. If he's broken cover to help you, this is more serious than any of us realized."

Oh, now she was seeing red. As in, literally. The garage was flooded with it. "More serious than half the world being out to arrest me? More serious than the other half wanting to kill me? More serious than that?"

"I don't know." He folded his arms.

Ooo, intimidating—not.

"What I do know," he continued, "is that Marcus isn't behaving like a man who's out to use or hurt you. He's behaving like a brother protecting his sister."

"Protecting me? By abandoning me? By becoming like Tommy? By letting me think they were working together to hurt me?"

"It was the only way I could keep you safe." Marcus'

deep voice echoed through the garage. "I had to keep my distance. It was for your own good."

"Now, that sounds familiar." Elle wanted to scream. "Are you two working from the same playbook? *How to Deal with Elle*? You're both these big, bad, brooding men who feel the need to lurk in the shadows to protect the poor defenseless woman. Yet neither of you have the guts to actually speak to her and ask what she wants. Or have a relationship with her. You're both cowards."

She cocked a thumb over her shoulder at Marcus. "And if my brother spent ten minutes thinking things through, he might have realized that I'd rather have him in my life than skulking around the edges of it. Do you know who you both are? You're Batman. Do you hear me? Both of you are Batman—the suckiest, most pathetic of all superheroes. He's ninety percent angst and ten percent gadgets, and he's too damn scared to show his true self to anyone who cares about him."

"Guess that makes me Robin," Abasi drawled.

"You wish," Elle snapped as she narrowed her eyes at David. "Let. Me. Pass."

His jaw firmed. "No. You know you can't win in a fight with me, so calm down and be reasonable."

She leaned into him, taunting him. "I don't need to win in a fight with you. I just need to mention relationships, and you'll run away."

"Marcus," Callum's voice called out. "We've got the garage surrounded. Send out Elle and David, and no one gets hurt."

All at once, Marcus and Abasi held guns in their hands.

"How did they find us?" Abasi hissed. "No one followed us."

Elle dug into her cleavage and came out with part of an Apple Watch. She tossed it on the floor in front of Abasi.

"They found you because I put the battery back in that, and it triggered the GPS. Shouldn't have bothered removing it in the first place, but I foolishly thought you might scan us for signal. I forgot how low tech you are." She raised her voice and called to her boss, "I'm coming out. Feel free to shoot all of the men in here—David included."

She moved to push past David, but he wrapped an arm around her and held her to his side.

"Callum." David raised his voice. "Marcus and Abasi aren't a threat. They only want to talk. Come on in." He stared her brother down. "I'll be annoyed if you shoot anyone."

"Yeah, and we wouldn't want to annoy you, Knight," he drawled. "Don't know if you noticed, but we were trying to keep this meeting to the three of us when you crashed it. Don't need more ears."

"And yet, you're getting them."

"Callum," Elle shouted. "Send in Megan. Tell her to shoot at will. I'm done here."

"Yes!" Megan whooped with genuine excitement.

Marcus and Abasi lowered their guns as the door at the back of the garage opened, and Callum stepped inside, his gun aimed at her brother. "Drop your weapons," he ordered.

The men put them on the floor.

"We just want to talk," Marcus said.

"Weird way of setting up a meeting," Callum replied. "The only reason I haven't already put a bullet in your forehead is that Ryan's family is unharmed. That's not to say I won't still do it. I'm a wee teensy bit pissed off with you two."

"How about we go up to the house and talk?" Marcus suggested. "More comfortable than standing around in the garage."

Callum didn't move. "You got any more surprises waiting for us up there?"

"None I can think of," Marcus replied.

"Elle?" Callum said. "What do you want?"

What she wanted was to kiss him for even thinking to ask her. She was fed up with men moving her around as if she were a pawn in their ego-driven game of chess. "I would very much like you to Taser all of them," she said.

"Don't have a Taser on me."

Well, that was disappointing. "Fine, tell David to release me, and we can go hear what my moron brother has to say."

"David," Callum rumbled.

"This isn't over," David whispered against her ear before letting her go.

Elle ignored him as she stomped out into the immaculate backyard.

"You okay?" Joe asked.

"No. I'm fed up with men." She stalked past all of them toward the terraced house.

Behind her, she heard a thud.

Megan fell in at her side. "Ryan punched your brother." She glanced over her shoulder. "And Abasi."

"If we're really lucky, he'll punch David too," Elle grumbled.

Megan draped an arm around her shoulders. "Let's see if we can find you some sugar," she said as they walked together up the path.

Elle leaned into her friend. "This is very stressful."

"I know." Megan patted her shoulder.

"If I had my laptop, I wouldn't feel so helpless. I still can't believe I killed my baby. I designed and built her from scratch. She was everything I ever wanted in a machine. Every tool I'd ever come across that was of any use, I'd installed on her. Every piece of code I'd written to shortcut a job. All the virtual machines I'd set up to align with the operating systems of the computers I hacked. I even had my favorite stickers on the casing." She sniffed. Stupid tears.

"It's going to be okay," Megan cooed. "After all this is over, we'll get you everything you need to build a bigger and better baby."

"I just feel lost right now without a laptop under my fingers. I can't think without one. I don't even need a top-of-the-line machine or to build my own setup again. All I need is something with a good amount of RAM and a screen that doesn't hurt my eyes. To that, I can add the Kali Linux OS, a few of my favorite hacking tools, and Tor to hide my IP. I don't need all the bells and whistles to get the job done; everything I need is up here." She tapped her head. "If I had a few uninterrupted hours in front of a screen, I know I could figure out the best way to deal with this whole situation. Without Dumb and Dumber getting in my way." She gestured back toward her brother and David.

"You are the second smartest person I know," Megan said. "You can totally figure this out."

"Harry, right?" Elle guessed the first smartest.

"Yeah, but he's only smart when it comes to computers. You're smart with people too. That's why you'll always do better under pressure than my cousin ever could. Trust me, if my life was on the line, I'd rather have you at my back than Harry."

"Honest?" Elle sniffed again.

"Would I lie to you?"

Elle thought it best not to answer that.

20

―――――――

James Family Home
North London

Arnold "Cutter" Matthews entered Tommy's home with a spring in his step. Ten long years he'd waited for this moment, and he planned to enjoy every single second. With a nod at the guard positioned in the entrance, he headed to the back of the house and Tommy's study.

It'd always been the two of them—Tommy and him. As far back as he could remember, it'd been them against the world. They'd built the James Family Syndicate together, with the unwritten agreement that when Tommy decided he'd had enough, Cutter would step in to take the helm.

At least, that had been the plan until Tommy's boy grew a pair.

One day, he'd been whining about wanting to go to college, and the next, he'd been acting as an enforcer for his father. It came out of nowhere, his sudden dedication to the business. And the worst part was that the little shit showed a flair for it. He was a natural, just like his father.

Cutter should have smothered him in his crib when he was a baby. The thought had crossed his mind at the time. It was one of the few occasions in his life where he'd exercised restraint, and look where that had got him—he'd been replaced as king-in-waiting by a pampered dickhead who didn't know what it meant to fight his way to the top.

It was a fucking insult. That's what it was. Cutter had proven his loyalty time and again, yet he was supposed to sit back and let Tommy hand over everything they'd built together to his kid? All because blood was important, and Marcus would carry on the James Family legacy? Bullshit!

Tommy had knocked up the wrong woman to begin with. Rebecca had been too soft for the business. Always whining at Tommy to go legit—like that would earn enough to provide her with all the luxuries she enjoyed. Cutter had hated her on sight. The way she always looked down her nose at him had made his fingers itch to choke the smug superiority right out of her.

The day Tommy had ended her ranked as one of his best days ever.

But this day, this news, might top it all.

"Boss in?" he asked the guy standing outside Tommy's door.

The guy nodded and held open the door for Cutter to go through. Respect. Like it should be.

Tommy sat behind his desk, his chair turned to the side, and the woman who gave him his facials kneeling between his spread legs, giving him something else entirely. Cutter smirked at the sight.

"Want me to come back, boss?" he said.

"Nah, gimme a minute." Tommy grabbed handfuls of the slut's hair and forced her to finish up to his schedule.

Cutter heard her scared whimpers and watched her struggle as Tommy took what he wanted with no care as to whether she liked it or not. With an approving chuckle, Cutter sat in the guest seat on the other side of the desk.

Tommy grunted as he finished, then pushed the woman away. "Get the fuck out of here," he told her as he zipped up his pants.

She crawled away before staggering to her feet and running for the door.

"Be back next week," Tommy shouted after her.

Cutter caught her sob as the door closed behind her.

"What you got for me?" Tommy said as he rested his elbows on his wide leather-topped desk.

Cutter crossed his legs. "We hit the Albanians and that shit street gang, the MCs, and made sure they learned their lesson. I don't think there was any misunderstanding."

"Good." Tommy reached for the box of cigars on his desk, opened the lid, and offered one to Cutter, who refused. "What about Elle? Marcus found her yet?"

"You're not going to like what I have to tell you about that," Cutter said. "You sure you want to know?"

Tommy's eyes were shark-like. "What?"

"Had one of my men follow Abasi, figured he was the weak link. Marcus and Abasi cornered a couple of people your girl knows and used them to flush her out."

"What's not to like about that?"

Cutter sat up straighter, looking his oldest friend in the eye. "They left the people alive when they were done. Then they took off with Elle and some other guy—not sure who he is yet, but I'm digging. My guy lost them. I can see there's no sign of them here, and they haven't surfaced in any of our other locations."

The air in the room thickened as Tommy reached for his

phone. "No messages," he said as he peered at the screen. "How long ago was this?"

"Couple of hours," Cutter said.

"You think he's playing me?" His words were encased in ice.

Cutter spread his hands. "I'm just telling you what I know. Marcus and Abasi have the girl, and they've disappeared. Maybe he's questioning her, and he'll turn up later to tell you what he found out."

"He should have called," Tommy said.

"I would have, but kids these days..." He shrugged.

Tommy stabbed at his phone before putting it to his ear. His eyes turned to flint when he spoke. "Marcus, call me as soon as you get this. I want an update on your sister."

"Maybe you should tell him we know he found her?" Cutter suggested, knowing full well that would be the last thing Tommy would do.

"No. We wait. Let's see what the boy has to say when he finally turns up."

"It's your call, boss." He reached toward the desk. "You know, I think I will have a cigar," he said as he helped himself.

"Does your father know about this place?" Callum asked as his team took position throughout the living area of the terraced house.

Marcus glanced over at him as he opened the fridge. "You've got your safe houses. I've got mine. Beer?" He held up a bottle.

"Think I'll pass," Callum said in reply.

"Suit yourself." Marcus popped the cap from his bottle and drank deeply. "Elle? You want one?"

"I hate beer." Elle sat at the breakfast bar, studiously ignoring David, who stood by the back door, staring at her. "Do you have any laptops?"

"Last time I checked, you couldn't drink those. And no, I don't keep computers here." Marcus grinned at her. "Same old Elle, coping with life by looking at it through a screen."

Oh no, he wasn't playing the nostalgia card. "You don't know who I am or what I do anymore. I haven't even set eyes on you, let alone talked to you, in years."

His lips thinned. "It was for your own good."

"People keep telling me that, but no one ever asks what I

think." She shot David a pointed glare. "Except for Callum, which is why he's now my favorite."

The room felt chilly. It could have been the vast open-plan area or the company. Either way, Elle was shivering. She looked around for a blanket, but all she could see was high-end décor in chrome, black, and white. Maybe it was the cold, clinical feel of the place that made her want to wrap herself up in a thick, fluffy blanket.

A black sweater materialized in front of her. "Put it on," David said, now wearing only a black T-shirt. "You're bluer than usual."

"I don't want it." It would smell like him and would probably still hold the heat of his body.

"I know. Put it on anyway. Otherwise, I'll do it for you."

She snatched the jumper and shrugged into it. It was an oversized woolen dress on her. Worse, it felt like David was hugging her. His warmth and scent engulfed her, making her glare at him. He just did that eyebrow thing of his and sauntered back to his position by the door. Elle stuck her nose in the air and tried to pretend he didn't exist. Or at least tried to look like that was what she was doing.

"I'll make some coffee." Joe made himself at home in the kitchen. "Who wants one?"

Those who wanted it answered from where they'd positioned themselves around the room. Elle noted that not one member of her team had relaxed. They all kept their hands close to their weapons and an eye on the windows and doors. In fact, she was the only one sitting. Everyone else either stood sentry or paced. Except for Megan and Dimitri, who were nowhere in sight. Elle glanced toward the stairs in the corner. No doubt they'd gone to scope out the rest of the building—and been distracted by the sight of a bed.

Elle forced herself to deal with her brother. "Why did

you go to so much trouble to capture me if you aren't taking me to Tommy?"

Marcus rested his forearms on the other side of the kitchen island. "I didn't capture you. I rescued you. You have no idea what's coming for you, Elle. It isn't only Tommy; there are groups who think you sold them out, and they want to make you pay. I had to make sure you were safe, and it was clear Benson Security wasn't doing the job."

"That's a load of crap, and you know it," Callum said. "We didn't even know what we were up against until your guys hacked our system. Now we do, and we have this covered."

"You might think you have things covered," Marcus said. "But thinking don't make it so."

Elle was still stuck on something else he'd said. "Wait a minute. How did you know I was with Benson Security?" She clutched the edge of the bench, feeling a little hysterical.

"I have my own men, people I trust, and they'd been searching for you on the lowdown since you left. They spotted you on security footage outside Abramovich's house a few years ago while you were working an operation to find Dimitri Raast's sister. We had to hide your trail before one of Tommy's people discovered you were involved in the Abramovich mess. Did you honestly believe tangling with a guy who ran a sex-trade business *in London* wouldn't blow your cover? Tommy knows every crook, crime organization, and mob wannabe in the city."

"I was in disguise, and I wasn't in the field." She'd been careful. She wasn't an idiot.

"You drove your own car to a known mobster's house and kept the engine running for one of your teammates until she fled the premises."

Okay, when you put it like that, it didn't sound that

careful. "If you've known where to find me for that long, why did you wait until this week to come in with guns blazing to get me? Why didn't you just take me for a coffee?"

"Because," he said slowly, as though she were a dullard, "I was keeping Tommy away from you. But that all went to hell when he hired a bunch of Russian hackers to follow your online trail. Didn't even know he'd done it until he ordered me to take a team and come get you. Since I didn't want him to shoot me between the eyes for playing him all this time, I took the team Tommy handpicked and came to get you—James Syndicate style."

Suddenly, Marcus and Abasi leaving their men for the cops made a whole lot more sense. "That's why you let the cops clean up your team," Elle said. "They were Tommy's men."

"Bingo."

"And you came to get me because you're trying to protect me?"

"I'm always trying to protect you. It's a full-time job."

"It's also one I didn't know you had until this week."

Marcus sighed heavily. "Elle, I've been watching over you since the day you were born. I'm your brother. I just stepped it up some when Tommy started asking you to hack for him." He tipped back the cold bottle, gulping it down. "You were nine, and all he could see was another tool to use. You were so excited about him taking an interest in you, and there was no way to explain what Tommy's interest meant without putting you in more danger." He shook his head, his smile wistful. "Back then, you couldn't keep a secret to save yourself."

"We were both different back then," Elle told him. "You kept out of Tommy's sight; all you did was study."

He inclined his head. "I wanted to be a vet."

"Big animals," she said softly. "Not people's pampered pets."

"No guinea pigs or pet rats." He shuddered. "It was a dumb plan. Tommy would never have let me become a vet."

She hated seeing him shrug off the dreams of his childhood. "He agreed to you studying business. You could have gotten out. Away from him, once and for all."

"No, I couldn't, Elle." Marcus took another long drink, ending that line of discussion. "You know, I kept a close eye on what Tommy asked you to do when you were a kid." He cocked his head toward Abasi. "He helped."

Elle blinked in surprise at Abasi, who was leaning against the wall beside the kitchen area, keeping an eye on her team. "I thought you liked to talk about code."

"Ellie," he said with a smile, "I only understood about every tenth word that came out of your mouth. I'm just very good at acting."

"Huh," she said. She'd missed that entirely.

"When you were about twelve," Marcus continued, "something changed. Tommy started looking at you differently. Took me a while to realize he was trying to figure out ways to maximize your skills for the business. Suddenly, the code you wrote and the sites you cracked weren't only about stealing money or secrets; they were about ending people and starting wars."

"I know," Elle said. "I figured it out after watching the news one night."

"I always wondered how you found out," he muttered before taking a deep breath. "It was at that point, when the jobs Tommy gave you changed, I realized he was never going to let you go. You were worth too much to him—not only financially but also in terms of power. No secret stayed hidden when he had you; no enemy could feel safe. You were his ace in the hole, and he would have used you until there was nothing left. I knew the only way to protect you was to be on the inside, so I quit school and went to work for Tommy." He waved his bottle at Abasi. "This idiot came with me."

"Couldn't let him go in there without somebody to watch his back," Abasi said absently.

"You joined the syndicate for *me*?" Her stomach lurched, and the room spun. Lightheaded, she searched for an exit. Any exit. She had to get out of there. She had to get some air.

"Head between your knees," David ordered as he gently pressed a hand to the back of her neck. "Give her a minute," he told Marcus. "Breathe through it, Ellie Blue. It'll pass."

Elle felt far too disorientated to snap at him for using that nickname. All she could do was concentrate on breathing slowly while hoping her breakfast didn't take an encore.

"She okay?" Marcus said.

"Looked like she was going to faint," David said. "She's done it before. It's okay; she'll be fine in a minute."

Sure enough, the room stopped moving, and her stomach ceased trying to climb out of her throat. Slowly, carefully, she sat back up. Joe put a glass of orange juice in front of her before returning to stand beside the coffee machine.

Elle frowned at David as she lifted the glass. "How do you know I faint sometimes?"

"Secret stalker, remember?" Before she could tell him to back off, he retreated. But he didn't go as far as the back door this time.

Taking a deep breath, Elle confronted her brother. "I can't believe you joined the syndicate because of me."

"Elle"—Marcus' voice softened—"think about it for a second. Tommy would never have let me do anything else.

He might have allowed me to study business because that would work in his favor, but he wouldn't have let me turn my back on the family business. I was always going into the syndicate; there was never any other choice for me."

She shook her head furiously, making herself light-headed again. "No, we could have run away. We could—"

"Tell her," Abasi said. "She deserves to know everything."

Her eyes shot to her brother's best friend. His face was blank. She turned back to her brother, aware that everyone in the room was listening to their conversation. Bearing witness to the complete and utter mess that was her life.

"Tell me what?" she asked Marcus.

He cast Abasi an angry glance before answering. "I lied to you when we were kids. I told you I didn't know what the family business was. Truth is, I always knew. Tommy started taking me on jobs when I was barely in my teens. He was grooming me to take over from him. There was never any way out for me."

"You knew this?" she asked Abasi.

"My dad was one of Tommy's soldiers. I grew up in the life, just like Marcus." He glared at her brother. "Tell her the rest, or I will."

Elle pressed her fists into her stomach, unsure how much more truth she could take. There was a warm presence at her back, and she knew David had taken a step closer. Protecting her. Caring for her. Worrying about her.

Yeah, he really wasn't *that into her.*

"Crap." Marcus turned away from her and clutched the edge of the sink, his arms straight, his head lowered.

"Abasi?" Elle's voice trembled.

He didn't reply; he was too busy staring at Marcus.

Her brother took a breath and turned to the room, his

face a storm. "Would it be asking too fucking much to have a minute alone with my sister?" he growled.

Callum motioned for Ryan, Harvard, and Joe to step out into the back garden before he headed to the front hallway. Abasi hovered beside Marcus.

"You too," Marcus told him. "Take Knight with you."

Abasi shook his head. "Not going to happen."

The two men locked eyes in a death-stare contest until David interrupted. "We'll move to the sitting area. That's as good as you'll get from either of us. I'm not letting Elle out of my sight, and your man here won't do anything less with you."

"Fine." Marcus spat out the word, and they moved to the other end of the open-plan room.

With a stream of curses, Marcus pushed away from the sink and paced the area between the counter and the island. It was clear that whatever he had to tell her was ripping him apart.

He rubbed his jaw again. "You were four when my father found out your mother was having an affair with a cop. It'd been going on for years."

If that was the bombshell he was worried about, he shouldn't have been. "I know," she told him.

"No." His dark eyes were pools of agony. "You don't. Think about what I just said."

Elle went over his words, but nothing stood out. "You need to be clearer... Oh!" He'd said *your* mother, not *our* mother. "We had different mothers?"

His jaw clenched.

Then the other part registered. *My* father. Not *our* father. "Tommy isn't my father?"

He nodded sharply.

Shock, closely followed by elation, stole through her body, and she shot to her feet. "I'm not related to Tommy?"

And then it hit her. "I'm not related to you either." She swallowed hard, her throat suddenly tight. "Why am I still alive? Why didn't Tommy kill me when he killed my mother and her boyfriend?" She blinked. "Was the cop my father?"

Marcus gave a terse nod. "Yeah. Tommy ran your DNA."

She was very much afraid that the full truth of the matter was beginning to fall into place for her. "He wanted to kill me when he killed them, but you stopped him, didn't you?"

"You're my sister, Elle. I was the first person to hold you after Tommy and your mother brought you home. You were tiny and purple and sort of prune-like. But you were *my* baby sister. Blood never meant much to me."

"It means everything to Tommy," she whispered.

Marcus nodded slowly. "We made a deal—I got to keep you; he got to train me."

"You were thirteen when he killed my mother. That's when he started taking you out on jobs, isn't it?"

"He would have done it anyway, Elle. He wanted an heir and didn't give a shit if I planned on doing something else with my life."

"I know Tommy; he'd have made your hands as dirty as possible as soon as he could, just to make sure you never got out." She blinked away tears. "You were only thirteen. What did he make you do in exchange for saving my life?"

"It doesn't matter. I was never getting out anyway, no matter what happened to you."

"No, you would have found a way." She knew it absolutely. "You'd have run as soon as you could, but instead, I kept you there. Damn it, Marcus. You've ruined your whole life to save mine."

He stepped around the corner of the island to cup her cheek. "I'd do it again if I had to."

The tears spilled down her cheeks. "I am *so* angry with you."

"I know," he said softly.

"I never stopped loving you," she confessed.

"I know that too, Ellie. Otherwise, I'd be in jail. You've always had more than enough information on us to put me away for a long, long time."

"I couldn't," she whispered. "You're my brother."

"See?" His eyes shone with barely controlled emotion as he smiled at her. "You're just as dumb as I am."

"Nobody's that dumb." Elle wrapped her arms around the only family she'd ever truly had and held on tight as she wept. Shedding tears for everything she'd lost and for everything Marcus had just given her back.

Damn, she was so fed up with crying.

22

"I'm just not that into you?" Harvard mocked as they watched Elle laugh with her brother.

"Shut up." David kept his eyes on Elle. They'd been in Marcus' house much longer than he would have liked, especially when every extra minute increased the chances of one of Tommy's men knowing where to look for his son.

"Hey, believe it or not, that line's still a step up from you having mysterious reasons why you couldn't get together. Have you met Elle? She lives for mysteries she can crack. You basically handed her catnip."

"You know, normal people would have mentioned the phone was still live way earlier, instead of listening in. Benson Security's had a bad effect on you. Which is my way of saying, I don't believe this is any of your business, buddy."

"And yet, I still have an opinion." Harvard grinned at him. "Not only that, but I'm happy to share it."

"Thanks, but think I'll pass." He watched Abasi check his watch for the third time in five minutes, letting David know he wasn't the only uneasy one in the room.

"Nice try, but I don't remember giving you that option." Harvard clasped his hands in front of him, looking every inch the relaxed spy who could take everyone in the room—except David. "You're screwing up," he said.

David waited for more, but it didn't materialize. "That's it? That's your big insight?"

"I figured it was enough, but if you need me to expand on it, try this: you're hurting a woman who has at least ten combat-trained men in her corner. All of whom consider themselves her honorary big brothers. Not to mention those two." He jerked his chin toward Marcus and Abasi. "Who, I'm pretty sure, kill people for fun. Which makes me think you either have a death wish, or you're totally clueless. I'm going to give you the benefit of the doubt and assume clueless."

"Thin ice, my friend, thin ice," David warned.

"Don't worry; I can skate." The big man was every bit as fearless as David remembered. It had been years since he'd seen Harvard, and yet he still sauntered right into the middle of David's personal business. That took balls.

Which he used to carry on speaking. "You ever considered your skills are just what that woman needs to protect her from all the crap swirling around her? You might think you're putting her in more danger by being with her, but I don't think that's possible. She has her own enemies, and they are never going away. Even if we take Tommy out of the equation, there's still the terrorist groups, the Russian Mob, the various agencies—all with an interest in your girl. It's gonna be one long race to see who gets the prize first. My guess? It won't be any of your enemies who win. Elle doesn't need you to walk away to save her. She needs you to dig in and build a fortress around her."

"You about done giving me unwanted advice?" Especially when each word struck a little too close to home.

"For now." Harvard grinned.

"Did it ever occur to you that I'd figure that out on my own?"

Harvard's eyebrows shot up his forehead. "Not in a million years."

David was wondering which pressure point to hit on Harvard's body when Abasi raised his voice. "Marcus, you've got a job you need to do."

"I know." Marcus stood and buttoned his suit jacket as he spoke to Callum. "You've convinced me you can take care of Elle, for the most part. I didn't realize you had Knight on your team, which makes a difference. Plus, I might have overreacted when things hit the fan. You have to understand, I'm used to being my sister's first line of defense when it comes to Tommy."

"Next time," Callum said, "pick up a phone instead of a gun if you have questions."

"Or maybe don't give me a reason to have questions," Marcus answered. "You left her too exposed."

"It would have helped if we'd known there was a threat to begin with," Callum growled.

Before it could descend into another argument between two men who were both used to being in charge, Joe stepped in. "We've got this, but you know it's time the threat was removed permanently, right? Are you gonna be okay with that?"

"More than okay. The only reason I haven't done it before now is that Tommy has powerful allies—both inside and outside the syndicate." He glanced at Abasi. "We've slowly been dealing with them while we work on our own exit strategy. I had thought to keep hold of the organization and slowly bring it out of the murkier waters. Maybe even go completely legit one day. Now I see that was a pipe dream. There's nothing in the syndicate that can be salvaged. The only thing to do is burn it all to the ground."

"Then we're in agreement," Joe pressed.

"We'll talk more tomorrow." Marcus inclined his head. "I need to deal with syndicate business, or Tommy will become suspicious. I'm leaving Abasi with you as extra insurance."

"Not happening," Abasi said. "I'm coming with you."

"Aye, take him," Callum added. "We don't need extra insurance."

"Humor me." Marcus was implacable. "I'd stay myself, but there has to be a high-level presence in the street tonight. We've got some business issues that need to be dealt with quickly."

David bet they did. The team's latest intel suggested that their efforts to start a war between the James Syndicate and the other two crime organizations had been a roaring success. The situation between them had already been precarious, and it hadn't taken much to tip it over the edge. However, the team wasn't taking any chances that the tension would fizzle out. They had more targets planned for that night.

"Use the house," Marcus said. "Only Abasi and I know about it. You'll be safe here."

"We'll stay in our own safe house for now, thanks." Callum crossed his arms. "And he isn't coming with us. It would compromise our security. You might talk a good game, but I'm no' sure we can trust you yet."

"He's right," Abasi said. "I don't trust him either. It's best all-round if I just come with you."

Marcus stared him down. "I want you with Elle until I feel secure with this arrangement."

Abasi gestured around the room. "She's got an army at her back."

"Abasi," Marcus said, his voice lowering, turning to flint.

For the first time since David met him, he sounded like a man who'd earned his reputation. Marcus James might not have wanted to go into the family business, but he'd taken to it like the proverbial duck.

Abasi let his head fall back with a sigh. "Get your arse out of here; I'll stay with Elle." He grimaced at Callum. "We'll work something out."

Callum's grim expression made it clear he thought that unlikely.

Marcus, meanwhile, went to his sister. "I'll see you tomorrow." He clasped the back of her head and pressed a kiss to her forehead. Elle lit up under her brother's affection, leaning into his touch. "Stay out of trouble until then, okay?"

"I make no promises." She beamed up at him.

With a shake of his head, Marcus strode out the front door and down the path to where a parked car waited for him.

Once the door had closed behind him, Callum turned to Abasi. "You're not coming to our safe house, and we're not staying here."

Abasi sighed again. "Hotel it is then. Got any preference?"

"Who's paying?" Elle bounced eagerly.

"Oh, definitely your brother," Abasi drawled.

"Then I vote the Savoy!" she sang cheerfully.

To Elle's great disappointment, there was no fancy hotel. Abasi didn't pay because, as Callum told her, Benson Security wasn't funded by criminals. In the end, David's credit cards furnished them with a room, and he didn't stretch to the Savoy. Instead, they ended up in a mid-range tourist hotel on Glasshouse Street, off Piccadilly Circus.

The next time she was on the run, Elle would make sure she had her own untraceable credit card and a suite booked at the Savoy.

Elle had been around military men long enough to recognize the reasons for their choice of hotel—all of them being security related. Shaped like a pie wedge, the hotel had several exits onto different streets. There was an Underground station a few feet away, and thanks to the masses of tourists, the area was well-lit, regularly patrolled, and unclaimed by any gang.

They asked for a three-bedroom suite to accommodate all seven of them—Joe and Harvard had returned to the safe house and their wives—but the hotel didn't do suites. The best they could offer was what they called their "family room."

This turned out to be one long, narrow room, divided by a tiny bathroom and a flimsy sliding door that separated it into two bedrooms—or, more accurately, closets with beds. One room had a queen-size bed squeezed into it, and the other had three single beds lined up in a row along the wall —with barely enough space to walk between them.

On the wall opposite the beds was a small flat-screen TV, a tall cubby with coat hangers, a desk with one drawer, and a dining chair. Everything was made of MDF with a blonde wood veneer. Sturdy, it was not. On the wall above the beds, two cheap prints showed London attractions. Neither hung straight.

"We should have taken separate rooms on the same floor." Ryan stared at the three beds in horror. "Where the hell are we all going to sleep?"

"Not all of us are going to sleep," Callum said. "We'll

take shifts, keeping an eye out for trouble. And to watch him." He pointed at Abasi, who saluted him.

"It could be worse," Elle said, trying to lighten the mood. "The place is clean, there's free Wi-Fi and internal parking, and Megan bought me a laptop." She patted the machine Megan and Dimitri had handed her before they left Marcus' safe house. When Elle had thought they were upstairs, going at it on every bed they could find, they were actually out buying her a laptop.

"We got the memory upgrade," Megan said cheerily. "And we picked the one that's easiest to customize. That way, if you like it, you can add bits or upgrade crap to make it more like your baby."

"It's perfect, thanks. Waaaaay better than the last one. It was already glitching on me."

"Technically, you should be thanking David," Megan said. "His credit card paid for it."

"I'll pay you back," she told David from the other side of the room. She'd been trying to keep as much distance as possible between them, which was kinda hard in a room that barely fit three beds, a dresser and a mini-fridge. "The last one wasn't a bad choice. It just wasn't suited to what I wanted to do with it. I appreciated it though."

His jaw clenched, but he didn't reply, which was fine with Elle.

"Okay," she said. "Looks like the girls are bunking together tonight." She turned toward the other room, which was even smaller than the one they stood in.

"Guess that means I'm sleeping on the floor through there, then." Abasi followed her.

Dimitri went from laid-back American to full-on predator within a fraction of a second. "You're not sharing a room with my wife."

Abasi appeared unfazed by Dimitri's threatening demeanor. "Marcus ordered me to watch over his sister. If Elle's in there, so am I."

"Then so am I," Dimitri said with finality.

"Uh..." Elle held up her hand to speak. "One question. If you and Megan are in the same room, what are the chances of you being able to keep your hands off each other?"

"Slim." Megan snapped the bubblegum she was chewing. "We're exhibitionists. We can't help it. Also, we can totally multi-task. We can have sex and guard you at the same time."

"Technically," Dimitri said with a despairing shake of his head, "she's the exhibitionist. I'm the enabler."

Ryan scrunched up his face in the universal expression for TMI. "You two need boatloads of therapy. You know that, right?"

"Okay," Callum snapped, clearly exasperated. "Megan and Dimitri in the private room. The rest of us out here, where we can all keep an eye on Abasi while he keeps an eye on Elle."

Elle stared at the three beds. "That isn't going to work."

"I tell you what isn't going to work," Megan said as she came out of the bathroom. "One toilet and one shower for seven people. There aren't enough towels to go around either. I pity the family that gets stuck in here. There's no space to move, the only person who'll comfortably fit in the shower is Elle because she's tiny, and I suspect the walls are made of cardboard. You can hear everything through them."

"Maybe we should go back to reception and ask for more rooms," Ryan said, his gaze also on the three beds.

"Suck it up," Callum told him. "You were in the army; you've suffered worse."

"Don't know if you've noticed, boss, but I left the army because of this crap. Sleeping on shitty beds, feeling cold all the time, getting blisters from all that bloody marching. That's why I went private, so I could sleep in a decent bed, wear shoes that didn't hurt my feet, and eat meals that didn't come liquidized in a metallic pouch."

"I've figured out how we can make this work," Elle said in an effort to keep the peace. "I'll sleep on the floor. I'm small and can make a pallet out of the pillows. That leaves three beds and four men. One of you will always be awake, so you can rotate. How's that?"

"Not going to happen," David said. "I'll sleep on the floor. You get the bed."

"What he said," Callum agreed, eyeing Ryan. "Elle can have the bed farthest from the door. You want to check the other two beds to make sure they're soft enough for you?"

Ryan gave his boss the one-finger salute.

"Or," Megan said, "you could shove all the beds together and sleep in a big puppy pile."

Callum pinched the bridge of his nose and muttered something about how much he suffered. Once done with his pity party, he pointed at Ryan. "Go get food, drinks, and toothbrushes."

"I need a hairbrush," Megan said.

"I wouldn't mind another T-shirt to sleep in," Elle said. "I feel like I live in mourning clothes." She looked down at all that black and shuddered, wishing she'd kept her Princess Leia nightshirt on for the prisoner exchange. Somehow, that hadn't seemed appropriate at the time.

"I'd kill for some new underpants," Megan chipped in.

"When did I turn into everybody's personal shopper?" Ryan asked anyone who would listen.

"Don't forget deodorant," Elle added, then shrugged when the men looked askance at her. "It's not like I packed for the hostage exchange." She considered the idea. "I should have though. I've never thought about it before, but in the movies, they only ever exchange the people. Never their luggage. It would make more sense to supply them with a bag of essentials, don't you think?"

Callum stared at Elle for a second before turning back to Ryan. "Add earplugs to the list."

23

Dinner was pizza. Again. Ryan had returned armed with bags full of shopping. Toothbrushes and toothpaste for everyone, an assortment of deodorants, a multipack of women's underpants, and two oversized T-shirts declaring *I <3 London*. He'd forgotten the hairbrush.

The T-shirts came in pink or lemon. Megan had taken one glance at them and declared she'd rather sleep naked. Which meant Elle got both, and she'd never been happier to have two big, cheap, ugly shirts.

As soon as the bathroom was free, Elle showered and dressed in a new pair of underpants and a T-shirt long enough to be a dress on her. Teeth brushed, hair in a messy bun, she climbed onto the bed farthest from the door, which someone had pushed flush against the wall to make more floor space between the beds. With a pillow on her lap and her new computer perched on top of it, she felt more herself than she had since this whole mess started. Really, she was as close to being in her happy place as possible. She was clean, she wasn't wearing black, and she had internet access.

All was well with the world. And she'd work through all

the heavy stuff her brother had revealed later. Maybe when people weren't out to kill her. Right now, she wanted to hold the knowledge that she had her brother back close to her and just let it sit for a while.

"Elle," Callum barked at her, as he was wont to do.

She tore her attention from setting up her new laptop to find him pointing into the bathroom.

"What the hell is that?" he demanded.

It took her a second to figure out what he meant. "It's a bra, Callum. I'm pretty sure Isobel wears them too." Especially seeing as she'd gone lingerie shopping with Isobel on numerous occasions.

His face turning luminous red, he blustered. "This is a mission. On this mission, there are no men and no women. That means you don't hang your bloody underwear from the shower rail. Does this look like a college dorm room?"

"I don't mind if you move it out the way." Elle honestly couldn't see what the big deal was.

"I will *not* touch your unmentionables," he told her, still pointing at the bathroom.

"Did he just say unmentionables?" Abasi asked from where he was lounging on the bed nearest the door, scrolling on his phone—but only after Elle had made sure he'd disabled the GPS.

"Callum hasn't quite made it to the twenty-first century yet." She considered her boss. "Or possibly the twentieth."

David sauntered past Callum from the direction of the bathroom, Elle's lacy underwear in his hand. "The bathroom has been secured, sir," he reported to Callum.

"Why do I bother?" Callum muttered as he stalked into the bathroom.

Meanwhile, David held up her lilac-colored and very lacy bra, along with its matching French-cut boy shorts.

"Cute." He flashed the smile that usually made her brain melt.

Usually being the operative word.

Now that she knew he'd never admit to there being anything more between them than rampant hormones and teasing, she was immune to him. He smiled wider, but she stood firm against his charms. If he wanted to be an idiot and pass up on all that was her, so be it. She'd moved on with her life. His thick lashes lowered, and a butterfly tried to take off in her stomach. She squashed that bug dead. He'd been only a passing fascination. His eyes smoldered at her. Unable to stop herself, she licked her lips. No! Firm.

Elle made a show of wiping the back of her hand over her mouth. *No entry here, buster.* Now, where was she? Yes! Puzzle. He was nothing more than a puzzle. He turned, grabbed a hanger for her lingerie, dropped her bra and bent to pick it up...

Holy Backside, Batman.

What was she saying, again?

He hung her underwear in the open cubby that passed for a wardrobe. For some reason, seeing his hands on her lace made her mind go blank. He had such strong hands—lean and elegant, and...he was doing it to her again!

She pointed at him. "Stop flirting with me."

"I wasn't."

"Are you trying to gaslight me?"

"Just say the word, little sis," Abasi drawled, his attention on his phone, "and I'll put a bullet in this clown for you."

David crossed his arms and cocked an eyebrow at Abasi. "I wasn't flirting," he said to Elle. "I was playing. That's what we do, isn't it? Play?"

Damn it, he knew exactly what to say to make her heart melt.

"Not anymore." She forced out the words and went back to staring at her screen.

What had she been doing? Oh yeah, downloading Linux. She tapped keys and pretended her full attention was on the screen in front of her when, really, she was aware of every move David made around the room.

What would Leia do in this situation?

Leia would jump him and force him to admit he was an idiot.

Sometimes, Princess Leia was no help at all.

There was a three-two tap at the door before it opened and Ryan slipped in. "Spoke to the olds," he said as he sat on the single chair. "They're driving down to Cornwall to visit my parents. Like I told them to after the office was shot up."

Guilt made Elle's stomach clench, which made the pizza repeat on her. Yeah, she was *never* eating pizza again. Ever. From now on, she'd always associate pizza with being on the run. And congealed cheese.

"I'm so sorry about your grandparents, Ryan," she said. "Are they okay?"

"Physically, they're fine. Mentally, they're freaked out. Don't apologize; you have nothing to be sorry about. It wasn't you who held them hostage in their own home. That was this arsehole's fault." He cocked a thumb at Abasi. "You deserve a beating for what you did."

"You only get one free punch," Abasi said. "You had yours. Next time, I hit back."

"Right." Callum stalked back into the room. "Bedtime. Ryan, you're on first watch. David can take second, and I'll take third. Abasi doesn't get a watch. He gets watched. I'll take the middle bed. Elle, you stay where you are. David, you can sleep on the floor between our beds."

Elle considered the space between the beds. It wasn't

very wide, and David's feet would stick out beyond the end of the bed. Surely that was a tripping hazard.

"I'm shorter," she said. "I think I should sleep on the floor."

"No," was all David said as he took the blankets Callum handed him and spread them out in the narrow space.

Elle looked at Callum's bed—there was no way David could share it. Callum's shoulders barely fit in it as it was. She glanced at Abasi, who was much slenderer.

"Don't even think about it," he said when he caught her eye. "I ain't sharing a bed with nobody."

"I'm fine." David toed off his shoes. "This isn't the first time I've slept on the floor."

She noted that all the men had done to prepare for bed was take off their shoes, guns, and jackets. In fact, neither Abasi nor Callum had even bothered getting under the bedding. They lay on top of their beds, ready for action at any second. Even though they were tired. All of them. It'd been a heavy couple of days, and it wasn't over yet.

"Hit the lights, Ryan." David crawled between the blankets on the floor.

The room went dark, with only slivers of light from around the curtains and the light from Ryan's phone to see by. Elle lay on her nice soft bed, which was plenty spacious for her small frame, and listened to everyone's breathing. It sounded like Abasi and Callum were already asleep.

She quietly rolled over to peer down at David. Lying flat on his back, he had his hands clasped on his chest and his eyes closed. If he rolled over, he'd smack into one of the beds. That floor couldn't be comfortable. And how clean was it really? There was no way to tell because the carpet was all red and brown swirls. Like they were trying to hide the dirt. It wasn't reassuring.

Stifling a groan, she lay back down and stared at the ceiling. He'd be fine. He was trained to sleep anywhere. Right?

Her hands slid out until they hit the edges of the bed. For some reason, all she could see was images from the movie *Titanic*. The end scene played on a loop in her head —Rose lying on the board, floating in the ocean, while the man she loved froze in the water. All Rose had to do was roll over to make space for Jack. There had absolutely been room on that board for both of them.

Elle scrunched her eyes shut tight, trying to keep the logical conclusion out of her head.

Like that ever worked.

There was no getting around it: there was definitely room in her bed for David too. Mentally slapping herself for being so soft, she rolled back over and poked his shoulder.

"You can share my bed," she hissed at him, sounding completely begrudging.

"I'm okay here."

"I feel guilty and won't be able to sleep. This isn't about you. It's about me. I need to sleep. So, get your backside in this bed right now."

Rolling over to flatten herself against the wall, Elle told herself she was making space for David. She wasn't attempting to distance herself from him in the tiny bed. Because that would be pathetic. She was an adult. Mature. Totally sensible. And completely capable of sharing a bed with someone who needed one.

She was totally going to hell for all the lies she told.

The bed dipped as David lay down beside her—on top of the blankets. It was a tight fit, but he somehow managed to keep a sliver of space between them. Elle lay there, stiff as a board, hyperaware of the man lying close to her. Was he on his back? Was he facing her? And why was the room so eerily silent when there were four huge men in it?

"I'm an asshole." The whisper was a barely-there breath of air over her ear.

Elle stilled, her heart racing as she tried to process what she'd heard.

"Yes," she whispered back, not being bitchy, just giving him the truth. "You are."

"I don't know what to do with you." He sounded lost and bewildered, with an undertone of longing that she could be imagining.

Elle had to bite her bottom lip to stop from listing all the things he could do with her. There was a long list. She'd spent a lot of time thinking about it.

"My instincts tell me the only way to protect you is to walk away," David continued to whisper. "But logic tells me that you're in trouble anyway and could use someone like me in your corner."

Hope surged within her. Stupid emotion. It would be the death of her.

"What does your heart tell you?" she asked, against her better judgment.

"It's telling me to hold on to you and never let go."

Her breath hitched as her stomach clenched. "What are you going to listen to?"

"I figured the loudest voice should win."

Was he deliberately trying to drive her insane? Wriggling around to face him, she hissed, "Give me a straight answer, or you can get back on the floor."

It was just possible to make out his smile in the darkness. "You couldn't cope with me on the floor. Your heart's too soft to allow it."

"My temper is happy to overrule any misguided feelings of guilt I might have."

David's smile widened before he sobered. "You've been on my mind since the first day MI6 gave me your file. Can't get you out of there. Not sure I want to." His hand came up slowly and brushed her hair from her face. "Blue's my favorite color," he whispered.

Elle didn't dare move or speak as she willed him to keep talking.

"I'm screwed up," he said. "Right to the core."

"So am I." She gave him the truth.

"I don't know what the future will bring." He continued to play with her hair, as if fascinated. "I'm not sure I'm worth anybody's time, and I've no idea what this thing between us is or where it's going. But if you want me, I'm in."

"You're in?" The air had been sucked out of the room, making it impossible to breathe.

"All the way." It sounded like a promise. "For however long it lasts."

"No more being a coward and telling me you're bad for me?"

"Oh, I'm bad for you, Ellie Blue." His smile turned her into a puddle on the mattress. "I said I'm in, all the way, no more needing to use the C-word."

Laughter, hope, relief bubbled up inside of her, which wasn't reassuring. When it came to David Knight, she was so freaking easy. "No more mixed messages? No more teasing? No more stupid macho crap?"

His lips twitched, and she would bet his dark eyes were sparkling. "I can't promise there won't be any more stupid macho crap or the good kind of teasing. But I can stop giving out mixed signals."

"This is your last chance." Her heart couldn't take any more confusion. She'd built so much of her life on the insecurity of not knowing where she stood.

David leaned into her, closing the scant gap between them. "I'm sorry I hurt you, Ellie Blue," he whispered against her lips.

The whisper turned to gentle teasing, then tasting, and Elle found herself sinking into him. The world faded away as David gently kissed her, his hand cupping her cheek.

Don't break my heart. Don't break my heart. Don't break my heart...

The chanting in her head faded to nothing as David's lips silenced her always busy mind.

"If you two start going at it on that bed," Abasi drawled, "I'm gonna shoot you both."

"Amen to that," Ryan grumbled.

"I'm with the criminal," Callum said. "Knock it off. We all need sleep."

"Come on, Ellie Blue." David snuggled closer until her head nestled in the crook of his neck. "The guys are right."

She breathed deep, taking his ocean scent inside of her, making him a part of her in some small way. All the while wondering how many pieces she'd end up in if he walked away.

The silence and the warm strength of David's embrace lulled her to sleep.

At least until the moaning started in the adjoining room.

As Callum exploded, Elle pressed her face into David's shoulder and laughed until she ached.

24

———

James Family Home
North London

Tommy James sat at the head of his mahogany dining table, sipping brandy while he waited for his son to arrive. On the table in front of him were the remains of the late-night snack his chef had prepared, and to his right sat Cutter. Unlike Tommy, he'd only ordered coffee from the kitchen.

"He's finishing up with the Albanians, right?" Tommy said.

"Yeah." Cutter's eyes went to the two men who stood guard at the entrance to the room. They were soldiers on the rise, big men who'd proven their loyalty time and again. "You sure you want to talk with ears in the room?"

"Those boys don't hear anything unless I tell them to, ain't that right?" he asked the men.

"Yes, sir," they said without breaking expression or moving position. They knew their job, constantly scanning the large room for threats while pretending to be invisible. They also knew that if either of them ever uttered a word about Tommy or his business, it would be the last thing they ever did.

"We did two hits on each gang," Cutter continued. "Woulda done more, but your boy was adamant we needed to get the message across without going overboard."

Tommy didn't like that at all. "How're they supposed to learn their lesson if we go easy on them?"

Cutter shrugged. "Exactly what I said, but Marcus overruled me. Said they had to get the message without us attracting the cops' attention too."

He hated to admit it, but Marcus had a point. "I can see that." He placed his brandy glass on the table. "Any fallout from the attacks?"

"Not yet, but we're prepared if they decide to take it further." Cutter's smile was slow and hard. "I made sure our message to the MCs was hard to miss—by slicing it into the little shit's chest. Marcus said it was overkill." His eyes narrowed. "You ever wonder if he's going soft?"

"He's a different generation," Tommy said. "Wants to be smart about what we do. He tells me that technology and surveillance make it harder for families like ours to carry out the bigger statements. I gotta trust he knows what we're dealing with. Times have changed, Cutter. Not for the better, either."

Cutter's face became carefully blank. "True, boss, true." He hesitated, as though weighing his words. "You asked him about the girl yet?"

"He's due to report back to me any minute; we'll see what he says then." Tommy frowned at the door, impatience beginning to set in. "He was right behind you, wasn't he?"

"Yeah, a few minutes at most."

There was a rumble of voices in the hallway before the dining room doors opened and Marcus strode in.

"Just a coffee for me," he told the hovering maid.

Tommy couldn't remember her name, only that she gave shitty blow jobs. Might be time to get some new staff.

"Been thinking we need to change things up around here," he told Cutter, his eyes on the hastily retreating woman.

Cutter's cold gaze followed his. "I'll deal with it."

Tommy knew he would. Cutter had been "retiring" his staff for years. Those still useful were sent to a brothel on the continent. Those that weren't...well, they were retired permanently.

"What you got for me?" he asked as Marcus took a seat farther down the table.

"I'm sure Cutter's already brought you up to speed." Marcus lifted his chin at Cutter. "We took over some territory and made sure the other gangs understood their place in the food chain. Nobody's dead; the message was relayed. I don't expect any kickback. We made it clear that next time, we wouldn't leave witnesses."

Tommy nodded slowly as he toyed with a silver butter knife. "Any word on the girl?" he asked casually, watching his son to see how he reacted to the question.

Nothing about Marcus' demeanor changed. He seemed relaxed, at ease, maybe a little tired. For a second, Tommy expected Marcus would fill him in. And then he opened his mouth.

"Nothing yet," he lied.

Cutter stirred beside Tommy.

"Nothing?" Tommy spread his hands in a questioning gesture. "You shake down her connections? Lean on the people important to her?"

"They've all gone to ground." Marcus accepted a cup of coffee from the maid.

Deep inside, the feral beast that drove Tommy uncoiled from its lazy sleep. "Cutter tells me there're some old people, relatives of one of her friends. Seems like they'd be a good place to apply pressure, make her come to you."

"Dead end," Marcus said. "Everybody connected with Elle has been warned to keep their heads down. The only ones still showing their faces in public are the Collins family, and they're too high profile to touch."

"Always liked Libby Collins," Tommy said. "Great actress. A British treasure."

Nobody replied.

"You sure you haven't heard anything about the girl?" Tommy pressed.

"No." Marcus put down his coffee. "She's in the wind. But don't worry; I've got everybody out looking for her. She can't hide forever."

"That's my boy." Tommy stood and casually fastened the buttons on his waistcoat. "I got an appointment. Walk me out?" he said to Cutter.

Cutter pushed back his chair and followed Tommy. As he reached his son, Tommy jerked his head to the two men on the door, signaling for them to come forward. Then he placed his hand on Marcus' shoulder. "Glad you've got things in hand."

His words were a signal. Hearing them, the guards grabbed Marcus' arms and pressed his palms to the table in front of him.

"What the fuck?" Marcus spat out, pushing back in his chair as he struggled against the two men holding him. "Tommy? What the hell are you doing?"

The men had a foot each wedged against the chair's back legs, keeping him in place. Trapping him against the table. Tommy took the knife Cutter held out to him and leaned over his son. With one powerful swing, he stabbed it through the back of Marcus' hand, wedging it deep into the table. Marcus roared just as Cutter did the same to his other hand. Now he was pinned, unable to reach for his gun.

While Tommy turned to perch beside his boy, one of his men grabbed Marcus' hair to hold his head up, making him look his father in the eye. The other soldier made sure the chair didn't move an inch—not that Marcus was pushing against it anymore. Cutter stood close, watching Marcus' every move while repeatedly tossing his knife in the air, making it spin with each throw.

Casually, Tommy reached down and helped himself to Marcus' coffee. He sipped it before shuddering. "Not enough sugar. Now, let's start again." He placed the cup back on the table. "Where's the girl?"

"How the fuck should I know?" Marcus spat out as blood poured from his hands, pooling on the table in front of him.

Tommy backhanded his son, the ring on his finger slicing his son's cheek. "Don't lie to me. You were spotted."

Sweat dotted Marcus' brow, his skin flushed as his gaze darted between his impaled hands and Tommy's face. Shock, disbelief, fear: it was all there for anyone to read. Tommy shook his head in disgust. Too much fucking emotion, that was Marcus' problem. The boy was ruled by it, had let it corrupt him until he couldn't make the right decisions for the syndicate or himself.

Tommy had never had that problem. Even when his old man had beaten and cut him, he'd just waited, biding his time until he was able to slit the dickhead's throat and walk away—after making him suffer, of course. Cutter had been there that day too. Two twelve-year-olds, learning their craft together. He never should have favored Marcus over Cutter. Forty years and he'd never once betrayed him.

"I don't know what Cutter's been telling you." Marcus fought to keep his voice even. He failed. Each word was drenched in pain. "This is a setup. I don't know where she is. I'm telling the truth."

"No, you ain't." Tommy thrust his hands into his pockets and sauntered around the table to stare at Marcus from the opposite side. "You are a huge fucking disappointment to me, you know that? I groomed you to take over the business. Taught you everything I know. Let you represent me in deals. And what do I get? Your loyalty? No." He spat out the word. "You gave it to that slut's kid, even though she was nothing but the by-blow of a betrayal against *your father*." He jabbed at his chest. "She betrayed me, producing some cop's bastard instead of my kid. And you, you begged for that kid's life. Told me you felt like she was your real sister. Told me to let her live, that I wouldn't regret it. That you'd do anything if I spared her." He pressed his palms to the table and leaned forward. "Anything except choose me over her."

"This is bullshit." Marcus squeezed out the words. His eyes had glazed over, and it was clear he was struggling to concentrate on their conversation. "I'm being set up. Cutter's always hated me. Hated that you picked me over him."

Tommy lifted his chin at Cutter, and a phone dropped onto the table between Marcus' bloody hands. It showed a video taken from a camera in somebody's doorbell a few houses down from where Elle's weak links lived. Cutter tapped the screen, and Marcus watched himself and Abasi jump into the car with Elle and another guy.

Realization spread across Marcus' face, followed swiftly by acceptance. He'd been around Tommy long enough to know he wouldn't leave this room alive.

Eyes filled with hatred met Tommy's. "You'll never find her," Marcus said.

Tommy sighed. "I don't get it. I'm your father. I've given you everything, taught you the business, stood up for you when others thought you worthless. What's she ever done for you? Nothing. That's what. Not a damn thing."

Marcus stared him down, the color fading from his face as shock set in. "She loves me."

It was a punch to the gut. "That's it? Love?" He shook his head in disbelief. "You tore down everything you built because some tart who isn't even blood related loves you? Guess I didn't teach you anything after all. It doesn't matter now. All I care about is where you stashed the girl. If you tell me, I'll make it quick."

"Go to hell," Marcus told him.

Tommy slammed his fist down onto the table, making it shudder and Marcus grimace in pain. "You were a waste of my fucking time." He pointed at his son while looking at Cutter. "He's all yours. If you can get him to talk, great. If not, dump his body for his sister to find. I'm done here. And buy a new fucking table."

With that, he strode from the room. Marcus' screams ringing in his ears.

25

"David," Callum hissed.

Just like that, he was wide awake. Elle was snuggled into him, her face in the crook of his neck. It was reflex to hold her tighter when he saw the grim expression on Callum's face.

"What?" he whispered.

Callum jerked his head to the other end of the room before striding over to say something to a grim-faced Ryan. There was no sign of Abasi, but water was running in the bathroom. Ryan strode silently through the door to the adjoining room, no doubt to wake Megan and Dimitri, as David gently moved Elle off him and slipped out of the bed. He took a second to pull on his boots before joining Callum.

"We've got a situation," Callum whispered. "You need to deal with Elle." He jerked his chin toward the rest of the team who were coming into the room. Even Megan was wide awake, which meant this was far more serious than he'd hoped.

"Turned the TV on a couple of minutes ago." Callum glanced at Elle, his face pained. "BBC breakfast was interrupted with breaking news." He rubbed a hand over his jaw. "Marcus James' body was dumped on the steps of Benson Security. Checked my phone, cops haven't even had time to call Lake yet. They're only now arriving on the scene. Some arsehole saw the dump and posted it online, with close ups of the damage done to Marcus."

"Not some asshole." David was certain. "Tommy ordered it done."

"Likely. He'd want the news out there as a warning. For Elle."

"Shit." David shook his head as he watched her sleep. "She just got him back." This news would devastate her. "Abasi?"

"He doesn't know yet." Callum jerked his chin toward the team. "They're on containment."

Yeah, because Abasi was going to lose his mind at the news.

"Tommy found out Marcus had Elle," David said. "He'd see it as betrayal, and Tommy kills those who betray him."

"Aye." Callum pinched the bridge of his nose. "We've got seconds before Abasi comes out of the bathroom. How do you want to play this?"

"I'll tell her now." David walked back to the bed and sat on the edge. "Elle." He gently shook her shoulder. "You need to wake up."

She blinked several times before focusing on his face. He hated how the smile curling around her luscious lips faded as soon as she saw his expression. She sat up quickly, shoving her wild blue hair from her face.

"What happened?" Her gaze scanned her team then came back to rest on him.

"There's no easy way to tell you this, Blue, so I'm just going to say it." Damn, he wanted to stall because he didn't want to cause her pain. Never wanted to cause her any pain. He took a deep breath and held her hands in his. "Marcus was killed last night."

"What?" She frowned at him as though his words made no sense. "I don't understand."

"We think Tommy killed him. They dumped his body on the front steps of Benson Security."

The color drained from her face, and she shoved him away before scrambling out of bed to stand beside it. "He's dead? How can he be dead? I was talking to him last night."

David's hands itched to hold her, but it was clear from the tension in her body that she wasn't ready to be touched. "I'm sorry, Blue."

"Benson Security? Our office?" she asked Callum, who nodded tersely. "A warning then...to me... Why would Tommy do that? Unless... Oh no!" Her palms flew to cover her mouth, to cover the wail that started to escape. Panic, horror, realization—it was all there in her face. Questioning eyes pleaded with David for answers.

"Tommy had to know Marcus found you." David's stomach was a knot inside of him.

Her hands stayed pressed to her mouth as her eyes welled with tears—although none of them fell. David couldn't take the distance between them any longer and pulled her into his embrace, wrapping around her as though he could shield her from the pain. As Elle stood stiffly, not making a sound, David cast a worried glance at Callum, who stared at them with a mixture of pain and fury.

The bathroom door opened, and Abasi sauntered out. Instantly, everyone's attention focused on him. He scanned the room, taking in everything before his gaze lingered on Elle.

"What happened?" he demanded.

"You need to keep your cool," Ryan told him.

His eyes turned to steel. "What. Happened?"

Dimitri took a step closer to the man, ready to shut down his reaction if it turned violent.

"Tommy killed Marcus," Callum said with compassion.

For a second, it felt as if the walls moved in and out as Abasi stood motionless. "Details," he snapped at last.

Elle raised her head, her eyes red. "I want to know too."

Callum's head fell back, and he stared at the ceiling for a second. "You don't want to know," he said to Elle when he looked back at them. "And you don't want her seeing that," he said to Abasi.

"Seeing?" Abasi spotted the TV remote in Callum's hand. "It's on the news?" He strode to the TV and turned it on manually.

"Elle shouldn't see this," Callum repeated.

"No," Elle said. "I want to know what that monster did to my brother."

With a curse, Callum tossed the remote on the nearest bed as the volume from the TV filled the room.

"It is believed that the body is that of Marcus James, thirty-two-year-old son of infamous mobster Tommy James," the news anchor said from her clinical studio, far removed from the brutality of her report. "Witnesses at the scene report that the victim was tossed from a car shortly after six this morning. One of the witnesses filmed the event and sent us their footage. I must warn you, this may not be suitable for sensitive viewers."

"And yet, they show it anyway," Megan muttered in disgust.

Standing between David's knees, Elle clung to his shoulders, nails digging in while she stared at the screen in absolute horror. Shaky footage showed a car screeching to a halt, then two men climbed out, their faces conveniently averted from the camera. They opened the trunk and removed Marcus' body, which they unceremoniously tossed in front of Benson Security before speeding away.

"Hell, man, the guy's been totally fucked up," the person holding the phone shouted as they ran toward Marcus. "Is he alive? Fuck, there's a lot of blood. Check for a pulse."

A hand came into view, pressing against Marcus' neck, and in doing so, turning his face straight toward the camera.

Elle gasped but couldn't tear her eyes away. David held her tighter. Wishing it would end—the broadcast, the danger to her, the pain she suffered, all of it.

"His face..." she whispered at the sight of the gashes covering Marcus' face, rendering him almost unrecognizable.

"Cutter." Abasi was cold as ice. "That's his trademark."

"Don't look, Blue," David begged her. "Remember him the way he was yesterday. Not like this."

"Shit, man," the guy filming it said. "That's Marcus James from the James Syndicate. We need to get outta here. The cops are gonna be crawling all over this."

"He's definitely dead," said the other voice. "Tortured too, poor bastard. Look at his—"

The TV screen went mercifully blank.

Slowly, Abasi turned to Elle. It didn't take a genius to recognize the fury emanating from him. It was written in every taut muscle. The team hovered around him like catchers at a game, ready to deal with whatever came their way. Their caution was unnecessary. Abasi kept it contained.

With precise movements, he reached into the neck of his shirt and pulled out a set of silver dog tags. Not bothering to unhook the chain, he yanked the tags from his neck he strode the few steps to Elle.

He held them out to her. "Marcus would have wanted you to have these. You'll know what to do with them."

With a trembling hand, Elle took them from him. "What are you going to do?"

"Take down as many of those fuckers as I can before they get me." He grabbed his jacket from the bed he'd slept on and shrugged into it.

Elle freed herself with a jerk and rushed over to Abasi. She hugged him tight from behind. "Don't do it. Don't give them anyone else." Tears streamed down her face now. "Marcus wouldn't want you to die for him. He wouldn't. You know that."

"Marcus was an idiot." Abasi twisted around to hold her. "If he'd listened to me in the first place, he'd still be alive."

"Please don't go," Elle begged. "Please."

Abasi stepped back and cupped her cheek. "You do you, little sister, and I'll do me." He looked over at David. "She's yours now."

David closed the distance between them and tugged Elle from Abasi. "You don't need to do this. You can work with us, and we'll take him down together."

"Maybe. But right now, I need my own payback." With a nod to Callum, Abasi strode from the room.

Leaving Elle sobbing in David's arms.

David worried that Elle would need sedation to get her to stop crying and make her rest, but in the end, she'd worn herself out and fallen asleep in the car on the way across London. She'd been fast asleep for hours and showed no signs of waking anytime soon.

Callum spent most of the day on the phone to Lake, who

was running point for Benson Security with the police. Tessa Sharp, their main police contact, wasn't happy that the London part of the business had gone into hiding and was threatening all sorts of retribution if they didn't surface soon.

Ryan, Megan, Dimitri, and Joe hit the streets, talking with their contacts in the hope of getting a better idea of what was happening in the James camp. Word was the Albanians had taken out Marcus, and Tommy was gearing for war. In other words, Tommy killed his son and was using his death as an excuse for a power grab. It was ironic that the war David had hoped to start was actually going to happen, but instead of taking down Tommy, it would make him more powerful. And to make matters worse, Tommy had gone to ground. Hiding from the coming violence and from Abasi, because even Tommy had to realize Marcus' loyal friend would want revenge.

As for Marcus' death itself, one of David's contacts leaked the initial coroner's report to him, and it read like a how-to manual on mutilation. There wasn't an inch on Marcus' body that'd escaped Cutter's knife, and several parts had been cut off entirely. Elle's brother hadn't died quickly. Or easily. But he had died without saying a word. David knew this because there wasn't even a murmur about Elle on the streets. He also knew it because, according to the coroner, the last thing removed from Marcus was his tongue.

"You okay?" Harvard asked quietly as he came up beside him in the hallway, where he was peering in on Elle.

There was no stopping himself from checking on her frequently. He closed the door quietly before answering. "I'm pissed," he said, jerking his head toward the stairs.

"I get that." Harvard followed him downstairs. "All signs point to Tommy hiding in his bunker while his soldiers go to war. Kinda hard to kill a man when you can't get at him."

No kidding. David entered the kitchen, opened the fridge, and took out two beers. He handed one to Harvard.

"We need some way to draw him out," David said.

"After what he did to Marcus, there's no way he'll surface. Especially with Abasi in the wind." Harvard took a drink. "He's got to know Abasi's out for payback. Far as I can tell, that boy never bothered to hide where his loyalty lay, and it sure wasn't with Tommy."

"As long as Tommy's alive and his organization thriving, Elle's life is at risk." David drained his beer and put the bottle in the sink. "As far as we can tell, the James Syndicate is the only organization that knows about Elle's new identity and where she's hiding. Once Tommy's dead, we can bury any mention of her along with him, and that should remove any immediate threat. She'll always have to be careful, cover her tracks and keep her head down, but we can help her do that by laying a false trail elsewhere—for anyone still searching for her."

Harvard smiled. "I hear Brazil is nice. Lots of criminals hiding out there. Would be easy to make everyone think Elle had joined them."

"Yeah, once we've dealt with Tommy."

Harvard slapped a hand on David's shoulder. "Julia's busy going through all the info everybody collected. Lake's got his Scottish team scouring news reports and social media for intel. Even Harry's come out of semi-retirement to trawl the dark web for any mention of Tommy's whereabouts. With this many heads working on the problem, something's gotta give. In the meantime, get some rest. You're gonna need it." He buttoned his jacket. "I'm going to take my own advice and go to bed. After I hug my woman tight. If you've got any sense, you'll do the same."

With a casual salute, Harvard sauntered from the kitchen. David grabbed two bottles of water from the fridge and a bag of cookies from the cupboard—in case Elle needed sugar when she woke—and took his friend's advice.

He went to bed and curled up beside his woman.

Once Elle opened her eyes, it took her a second to figure out that she was in one of the safe house bedrooms. It was night. The room barely lit by soft, muted glow. Slowly, her environment began to register. The quiet stillness of the house. The muffled sound of traffic. And...breathing.

She turned her head to find David lying beside her, his eyes open, his gaze on her face.

"How you doing, Ellie Blue?" he whispered.

With his gentle question came a rush of memory and awareness. Marcus had been brutally murdered. She would never talk to her brother again. He'd never hug her and tell her he loved her. She wouldn't get the chance to show him how much his protection had meant to her. And he would never get the chance to change his life, to find redemption.

The knowledge was a dull ache in her chest. A steady weight, pressing her into the bed, making it hard to breathe. Her eyes felt puffy and tender, her throat bruised. But there was also a sense of acceptance within her. Marcus was gone. And there was nothing anyone could do to change that.

"I hurt," she whispered to David, answering his question as honestly as she was able.

"I wish I could fix it for you." The faint but warm light from a small lamp in the corner of the room, which someone had thrown a T-shirt over, cast shadows over his beautifully masculine face.

"It feels like someone's reached inside of me and ripped out a piece. From here." She took his hand and pressed his palm to her upper chest, right in the middle, feeling its warmth through the thin fabric of her T-shirt. "I can feel the jagged edges of the space they left behind. It's raw in there."

He didn't say anything for a long time while he lay there watching her. His warm hand against her chest. Her hand covering his. As though his touch could take away her pain.

"I was married." David's whispered words weren't what she'd expected.

Elle didn't move, didn't talk, didn't press. This was his story to tell. His confidence to share. Not hers.

"Long time ago," he said. "I'd grown up in foster care and used fake ID to get into the military when I turned sixteen. I met Celeste at the bar near my base. She was a waitress. I was nineteen when we married, and she was a couple of years older. Celeste was the first person who ever loved me, the only person. Not long after we married, I was recruited for a black ops team. I had...*unusual* skills that I'd acquired during my childhood. They made me attractive to them. From there, I slid right into the CIA. My first mission, I screwed up somehow, and the enemy followed me home. Only, I wasn't there at the time, so they killed my wife to teach me a lesson."

When he said nothing more, Elle put her hand on his chest, placing her palm in the exact same spot as his was on hers, feeling the warm cotton of his T-shirt underneath her fingers. "Do you still feel that jagged place?"

Dark eyes captured hers. "It's still there. I've just become more accustomed to it. It's a part of me now."

"Is she the reason you didn't want to be with me?"

"Yeah."

Elle licked her lips. "Will you tell me about her some-day? What she was like? It'd be nice to get to know the woman who loved you. I bet we would have totally hit it off."

"One day. I'll tell you one day."

"I'd like that." Her smile was sincere, if a little subdued.

"I'll tell you this part now, though," he said. "When Celeste died, it ripped a hole in me. If you're ever taken from me, it will cleave me in two. There wouldn't be a hole, Ellie Blue, because there wouldn't be a me."

She couldn't tear her eyes from his as her hand curled into a fist in his shirt. "I'd very much like you to kiss me now," she whispered.

With a slow, sensual smile that made her melt, he whispered, "As you wish."

~

As soon as David told Elle about his wife, he knew their situation wasn't the same. In fact, it was as different as you could get. He was much more experienced now, more skilled, had more connections he could use to protect Elle. And Harvard was right: she was in the thick of it, whether he removed himself or not. You couldn't bring danger to someone's door when it was already in the house.

The thing that'd struck him the hardest as he spoke was the knowledge that he wouldn't survive losing Elle. He wasn't sure if he'd ever truly loved Celeste. He'd felt affection for her, sure, and enjoyed being with her. But love...

Whereas he very much suspected he was falling deeply in love with the woman in front of him. She'd become as essential to him as water. As air. With every shared breath, every touch, her presence seeped into him. They were intertwined now. She didn't only occupy a place within him that could be ripped out. She was in every cell of his body.

He feared there would be no David without Elle. And if she was taken from him, if she died, the world would turn bloody with his grief before he joined her.

"I'd very much like you to kiss me now," she whispered.

He couldn't help but smile as he gave her a line from one of her favorite movies: "As you wish."

His hand moved from her chest to her face, cradling her cheek as she closed the scant distance between them. Her lips were as soft as satin and tasted of tears. There were no words to comfort her. None he could give anyway. All he could do was show her she wasn't alone. For her, he'd live up to the knight in his name by doing everything he could to spare her pain, to vanquish her enemies, to prove his adoration.

Their kiss was a gentle joining, a languorous exploration. Two people losing themselves in each other, giving up more of themselves with every touch. It was the kind of kiss that left only longing behind when it ended, which was always far too soon.

As they slowly separated, Elle's eyes opened with effort, as though her eyelids were too heavy. She blinked at him, and he watched their color shift from blue to gray to lavender in the light. Extraordinary eyes on a woman who more than lived up to them.

"I don't want to stop," she confessed.

"I don't want to either, but you've had an emotional day, and I'd hate for you to do something you might regret."

"Idiot," she whispered. "This isn't a spontaneous decision. I've been trying to get you into bed for years. I know the timing isn't perfect, but I...I need to feel...alive. I need to feel something good, something real." Her shoulders moved in a tiny shrug. "I need you," she said, as though that explained it all.

"You humble me," he told her.

"I don't mean to." Her brow furrowed slightly as she tried to figure out what he was telling her.

David didn't need her to understand. All he knew was that Elle was laying herself bare before him. Allowing herself to be vulnerable because she saw the reward as too great not to risk everything. It was a gift he would always cherish—that this remarkable woman wanted a broken soldier such as him.

"As long as I'm able," he vowed, "I will always do my best to give you what you need."

The way her eyes softened, darkened, made his chest swell with pride.

His.

More importantly, he was hers. Always hers.

He was so lost in her that he couldn't see an exit. He didn't know when it had happened, and he hadn't recognized the feelings when they'd hit him. But he knew them now. He was madly in love with Elle Roberts.

"You'll need to be quiet, Ellie Blue," he said. "The house is full, and unlike your teammates, I want what's between us to be only for us."

"I can be quiet." She frowned. "I think. I hope. How about we see how this goes?"

With a chuckle, David rolled Elle onto her back and leaned over her. "You're too damn adorable for your own good." He brushed back her blue hair from her tear-stained face.

"And very horny, so less talking and more moving."

His lips twitched again before he grew serious. "I'm

clean, Elle. I promise I'd never lie about something that would harm you."

It took a second for her to catch his meaning. "I know you wouldn't. I'm clean, too, and on the pill. Now, can we stop chatting?"

"As you wish," he said again as his hand slipped between the mattress and the small of her back.

He pulled her to him, their bodies flush against each other as he nuzzled the crook of her neck, breathing deep. Sherbet-scented Elle. Delicious. He ran his tongue up the side of her throat to nibble on her earlobe, hearing her gasp as she pulled him closer. Her soft, full breasts pressed against his chest, making him want nothing but skin between them.

Patience.

He'd waited so long to have his hands on Elle, and he wasn't about to rush it.

Swirling his tongue around the shell of her ear, he pushed up her shirt until it sat just under her breasts. She moaned in frustration. David smiled as he caressed her smooth, soft stomach while whispering against her ear, "I'm going to make you desperate for me, Blue."

"I already am," she gasped as she tried to move his hand to her breast.

"You're nowhere near desperate. I want you so out of your mind with need that you don't know where you are, and you can't string two words together. I want you flying out of control, unable to think, only able to feel what I'm doing with you."

Before she could answer, he covered her mouth with his in a kiss that was long, and slow, and thorough. By the time he moved back to her throat, she was undulating against him, making breathless little mewls of protest.

"You've got to stop making noise, or I'll have to gag you," he threatened.

"Would you really?" She didn't sound too worried about the prospect.

David leaned back to look at her. Flushed cheeks, heavy eyes, and swollen red lips. Damn, she was beautiful. "Only if you wanted me to."

Her brow puckered. "I don't want anyone to hear us either, so if I start screaming, you should probably shove something in my mouth."

Freaking adorable. "I'm sure I can find something," he said.

"Men." She tugged at the back of his neck, wanting his mouth again.

"Nuh-uh." He knelt up beside her. "I haven't unwrapped my gift yet."

Savoring every second of the first time he undressed Elle, he slowly slid her T-shirt over her head, watching it slide across her breasts like a caress. All he'd removed from her when he'd carried her in from the car was her shoes and jeans. Which meant she now lay before him, clad in lavender lace.

"I'm going to bankrupt myself buying lingerie for you," he whispered as his hands traced over her skin, mapping every inch of her body not covered by flimsy lace.

"David," was the sweet feminine complaint that came from her lips. "Too slow."

"Just slow enough," he corrected as he bent to press kisses across her collarbone.

Her hands fisted in his hair, trying to make him move to her breasts. Instead, he smiled at her before laving her belly with his tongue. Followed by a nibble to her hipbone. Kisses down her thighs.

The sweet, heady scent of her need almost made him

hurry. But he was David Knight. His self-control had been refined in fire. What was that saying? 'Good things come to those who wait.' Well, he'd waited a lifetime for the woman beneath him.

Sitting up, he tugged off his T-shirt and tossed it onto the floor beside Elle's clothes. The low moan that escaped her as she stared at his chest went straight to his already straining groin.

"Gimme," she muttered as she reached for him.

"Not yet."

"Why?" She pouted.

"Because I want to go slow, and if you get your hands on me, this will be over far too fast."

"I'm very conflicted hearing that," she said.

With a grin, David moved down the bed. Eyes on her face, he hooked his thumbs into the sides of her panties and lowered them down her legs. She writhed before him. A wanton feast of seduction that was agony to resist. He was a man starved, and Elle was everything he needed to feel sated again.

Once the panties were gone, he caressed her from ankle to thigh before trailing his fingers through the curls covering her heat.

"Brown," he muttered.

"Did you think I'd dye it blue to match my head?"

He cocked his head. "What I think is that you aren't anywhere near as desperate for me as you should be." He climbed off the bed.

"No!" Her eyes went wide as she reached for him. "Trust me, I'm desperate. I'm so, so desperate. If I could think of another word that meant more than desperate, I'd use it right now."

"Trust me, we can get you far more desperate than this." David knelt beside the bed, hooked his hands under her knees and tugged her to him, spreading her legs wide as he did so.

Her fragrance made his mouth water, and the sight of her pink, swollen flesh made him so hard he thought he might come in his jeans like a teenage boy. Unable to wait for a second longer, he leaned forward and kissed her sweet, wet center.

27

Every muscle in Elle's body coiled tight under the barrage of sensation racing through it. Her fingers grasped handfuls of David's hair; whether to keep him in place or pull him away, she didn't know. It was too much pleasure. Her head spun, and her breaths were little more than desperate gasps for air. She was about to scream. She knew it, and she couldn't stop it.

But she had to. She had to be quiet. She didn't want her team rushing in to save her from this. And she didn't want them to turn something precious to her into teasing jokes.

"I can't," she gasped. "I can't keep quiet. I'm going to scream. David?"

His magical ministrations halted. "Use the pillow."

Blank. Her mind was blank. Nothing he said made sense. Suddenly, a pillow appeared on her chest, and her arms wrapped around it.

"Scream into the pillow," he told her before kissing her belly and then moving lower.

Her hands grasped fists of pillow as he licked and nibbled and teased. Too much. It was all too much. Her thighs clenched; only David's hold kept them apart. Her back bowed. Her neck arched. She brought the pillow to her mouth and bit it hard as she screamed into it.

The world was an explosion of color and light. Elle's limbs shook with the strain of release as her insides clenched to the point of pain. Over. And over. And over. Until she thought it might never pass—this wonderful, torturous, long agony of pleasure that held her in its grip.

The room spun and shifted. The pillow fell to her side. Through a daze of ecstasy, she felt hands and lips caressing her body. Her bra loosened and slid down her arms. Warm hands massaged her breasts before lips followed their path.

A deep voice whispered words to her in a language she didn't understand, yet hearing it made her soul ache. Elle floated in the aftermath of her climax, her body boneless as David stroked and kissed it. Each touch felt like a word. Joining together to make long, beautiful sentences that spoke of adoration, caring, and possibly of love.

She reveled in his touch. Soaking it up like a desert flower straining for rain. It seeped into her, renewing the dry, dark areas she kept hidden, acting as a balm to her wounds of grief and loss. Making her feel whole for the first time in her life.

As though he had all the time in the world, David lavished her with sensation after sensation, driving her body out of languid satiation and into rabid need. There were no demands this time, no teasing words. She was lost in a maelstrom of sensual intent, where thought and speech were unimportant. All that mattered was what they could express with their hands, their mouths, and their bodies. It was a sensual dance. Bodies entwined. Moving together until it was difficult to tell where one ended and the other began.

Slick and ready, Elle lifted her hips in wanton invitation and wasn't denied. As the warm, hard length of his shaft slowly entered her, she wrapped her arms tight around him and clutched him to her. She gasped as he filled her. Seeking his mouth in a desperate kiss. Breathing in each other's desire as he rocked his body against hers.

Her small frame tight against him, her mind swimming in pleasure, she let him take her to the precipice of release. And as they fell together, all Elle could think was, *So this is love.*

Spent and breathless, David toppled to her side and held her close. They lay there, tangled limbs and sweat-slick bodies, petting each other with the gentle caresses of a couple still drugged from lovemaking. It wasn't long before Elle fell asleep, lying as close to David as she could get.

THE NEXT TIME ELLE WOKE, SHE FOUND HERSELF DRAPED across David's chest, her ear pressed to the steady beat of his heart. The small clock on the dresser told her it was still before dawn, and the silence of the house told her the team had yet to wake. As was so often the case, as soon as her eyes opened, her brain started working. And this time, it wasn't dulled with the fog of grief.

Thoughts swam through her mind, floating to the top in no particular pattern or order. David's touch whisking her away from everything. Abasi's goodbye. The care and support of her friends, her team. Marcus lying bloody and discarded on the steps of Benson Security. David holding her while she wept. Ryan feeding her junk food. Abasi giving her his necklace...

Elle rode the waves of emotion that accompanied each memory, embracing both agony and joy, knowing they were all evidence that she lived when Marcus couldn't. It was a bittersweet agony, having felt like she'd gotten him back after saying goodbye so very long ago. She wished they'd had more time together, but truth be told, she wasn't sure she'd have liked what she found if they had.

The brother she'd known as a child had morphed into a man capable of horrendous acts. She wasn't naïve. Her brother hadn't grown into a good man. Nor had he been evil. Perhaps he'd just been cornered, trying to make the best of the only options available, clinging on to what honor he had left by protecting his sister. She'd never know why he hadn't escaped from his life when he was able. There had to have been plenty of opportunities over the years. Maybe he'd truly believed he needed to be close to Tommy to save her. Or maybe he'd become so entrenched in the darkness that he couldn't see a way out.

Either way, one thing she knew for certain, her brother had loved her, and he'd died to protect her.

As the faint glow of the orange streetlights cast soft shadows over the characterless bedroom, her eyes fell on the necklace Abasi had given her. Dog tags. Military identification. Strange, when neither Abasi nor Marcus had ever been in the armed forces. She stretched out her hand to hook the chain and brought the tags closer.

There was no engraving. They were nothing more than two blank metallic rectangles with rounded corners. She held a tag between thumb and forefinger; it was thicker than she'd expected. Running her finger along the edge, she felt an indentation.

Her heart jumped.

Very carefully, Elle pressed the tip of her fingernail into the indentation and pushed—and a concealed flash drive connection popped out of the bottom of the tag.

Holy Hidden Data, Batman!

David rumbled beneath her as she examined the hidden flash drive.

"Sleep," he grumbled.

"Bathroom," she replied, pressing a kiss to his jaw before climbing over him and out of bed.

Clad in an oversized tourist T-shirt, this one in pink, she left the room, taking her laptop and the dog tags with her. The only place in the house that didn't have someone sleeping in it was the kitchen, so that's where she headed, creeping through the house on quiet feet.

Hating to have to wait for anything but knowing it was necessary, Elle left her things on the kitchen table while she jumped in the shower. It was the fastest shower in the history of mankind, but at least she was clean when she returned to the kitchen. It was far too easy to forget things such as showering once she got sucked into a project.

She gently closed the door behind her, grabbed an energy drink from the stash Ryan had hidden at the back of the cupboard, and sat at the table. As soon as her laptop was up and running, she plugged in the flash drive.

Code scrolled across the screen instantly, and Elle almost fell off her chair. No. It couldn't be. Energy drink forgotten, she started to type commands into the machine, opening files, reading through coding and notes. Finding everything Marcus had left behind—and there was a lot.

The sun had made an appearance by the time she'd gotten her head around the contents of the drives. After gulping down her abandoned drink, she shut the laptop and headed for the stairs, which she took two at a time.

"Hey, what's going on?" Ryan called from the living room, where he'd been asleep on the couch. "Why are you running around?"

Elle didn't reply, because she was already crashing through the door to the bedroom she'd shared with David. She found him sitting up in bed, the sheet gathered around his hips, his hair standing on end, and a gun in his hand.

"Elle," he grumbled, putting the gun away. "Do you want to get shot?"

"They weren't dog tags." Elle jumped onto the bed and bounced her way to David. "They're flash drives."

"What the hell's going on?" Callum demanded from the doorway. "Why are you shouting?"

"And running?" Ryan asked from beside their boss.

One by one, her team crowded into their room.

Megan pointed a finger at David. "You might want to pull that sheet up a teeny bit more."

He slapped a pillow over his lap.

"What's happening?" Joe asked as he arrived. Like David, he'd grabbed a gun at the first hint of a disturbance. It hung in his hand at his side.

"Right now?" Megan asked. "David has *morning issues*. And, apparently, Elle isn't wearing any underwear."

Elle looked down, noticed her T-shirt had ridden up and tugged it back down to modesty levels. "My bad."

"Somebody get me bleach for my eyes," Callum muttered.

"Amen," Ryan said.

"Elle," David said evenly, "can this wait until we're all dressed and downstairs? With coffee?"

She shook her head, still bouncing on the bed because she couldn't contain herself. "The dog tags Abasi gave me were actually flash drives. Marcus left me the key to their information vault." She beamed at everyone. "With the information on these drives, I can access their secure servers and plunder at will. I have passwords, server locations, and the decryption code for everything they've saved." She held up the tags. "Everything we need to bring the James Syndicate to its knees is on here. All we have to do is use it."

There was a moment of stunned silence, and then the

room erupted. Elle grinned at her teammates as David's hand cupped the back of her head.

"You are a gift, Ellie Blue," he said before kissing the living daylights out of her. When he stopped to take a breath, he ordered, "Everybody out."

And then, as the door closed, leaving them alone, he pressed her back onto the bed, where they celebrated the good news in a way Elle very much appreciated.

28

———

There's a scene that often appears in older Hollywood movies. It shows a guy pacing outside the delivery room, anxiously waiting to see whether he's had a son or daughter. That's exactly how David felt when Elle banished him from the bedroom so she could dig through the information Abasi had given her.

Worse, when she finally emerged—with manic eyes and wild hair—it was only to demand that they change location. Apparently, she needed more screens and faster machines, and the only place with both that wasn't currently under police guard was Rachel's pharmaceutical company.

After calling Rachel and demanding access to her building, Elle wanted to leave straight away. But Callum would have none of it. He stood his ground and told her they weren't going anywhere unless she put on something more than a T-shirt. To which Ryan added that it would be nice if her hair didn't look like she'd stolen it from Troll doll. At that point, Elle had threatened online vengeance on them all before stomping back upstairs—still hugging her laptop.

Two hours later, once David had managed to get some food into her that wasn't stuffed with caffeine or sugar, a fully dressed Elle took over the tech lab at TayFor while her team waited in the conference room upstairs. Every now and then, David went down to check on her progress and feed her, only to be met with glazed eyes and a stream of excited jargon that went right over his head. Then, much to his amusement, she'd forget mid-sentence he was there and start working again.

Just as well his ego wasn't fragile; otherwise, he'd have been in pieces. Instead, when she tuned him out, he kissed her on the head, took one last look at her tiny frame in front of the bank of computers, then headed back upstairs to tell everyone there was nothing to report yet. After the last update, he'd returned to the bowels of the building, to the room where Elle worked. Finding a comfortable chair, he'd stretched out in the corner to watch over her. And maybe doze some, seeing as Harvard was in charge of security for Rachel's company, and it was airtight.

When night fell, Harvard and Ryan appeared with two rollaway beds, which David helped them set up in the corner of the room.

"How's it going?" Harvard asked as they watched Elle's fingers fly over her keyboard while the screens in front of her changed almost as fast.

"I have no idea." David grinned. "I only understand every tenth word she says—at most."

"Must be weird for you," Ryan mused. "Being the useless one for a change. I mean, all you can do is sit around and wait while your genius girlfriend does all the work. It's tough for a man of action."

Harvard and David stared at him.

"What?" Ryan shrugged. "I'm always the useless one, so I know what I'm talking about. My advice? Fill the time with gaming or naps. It'll fly by."

"What's happening upstairs?" David asked Harvard.

"A whole lot of pacing and cursing. Police have amped up the pressure on Lake to get us to come in for questioning. Tessa swears she's going to start Armageddon if we don't turn up soon. She's been covering for us but can't do it for much longer. Her superiors are putting the pressure on. Not only that, but Downing Street's demanding she do her job. Her rank might carry a lot of weight, but nowhere near enough to stand up to a force like that."

He ran a hand over his shaven head as Elle started humming a tune while she worked. "Meanwhile," he continued, "the media's all over Marcus' murder. Turn on any news channel, and it's wall-to-wall footage of his body, along with speculation about the syndicate and impending gang wars. The whole situation is a powder keg that could blow up in our faces at any second." He frowned, watching Elle. "Is that—"

"The *Star Wars* theme tune," David and Ryan said at the same time before grinning at each other.

"It means things are going well," David said. "If it's not, we get Darth Vader's theme music."

"If she starts making sound-effect noises while miming the Death Star blowing up—run," Ryan said.

The humming suddenly stopped, and Elle stood, sending her chair crashing to the floor behind her. "Booya, Vader! The Death Star plans were definitely in the main computer," she muttered before taking a deep breath and shouting, "David! It's done. I'm done. We're done."

And then she started doing this strange little jig where her hands and feet alternately went up in the air. It took him a second to figure out what it was, then it struck him. "She's doing the Ewok dance, isn't she?" he asked Ryan.

"Dunno. Never seen this before. Hoping I never see it again."

"David," she hollered.

"I'm here," he said with amused indulgence. "Turn around."

She spun to face them. "David, I did it. I cracked it all—even the stuff Marcus and Abasi couldn't get into. Tommy James is going to jail. Or hell." She grinned. "Hell or jail. Who cares? We've done it."

She ran across the room and launched herself at him. "Isn't that awesome?" Elle beamed at him, her arms wrapped around his neck and her legs around his waist.

"Very." He beamed back.

She was so freaking cute, dressed in her outfit from the day they ran to the safe house—blue hair in low bunches, green slogan T-shirt, lavender jeans with an unfortunate hole in the knee, and pink Dr. Martens. Had there ever been a sexier woman?

Movement caught her eye, and Elle noticed they weren't alone. "Harvard, Ryan, what are you doing here?" She looked around. "This isn't the bedroom. Where are we? Wait! I recognize that lava lamp, and I call dibs." Her head whipped back to David. "Why are we in TayFor's basement?"

"Uh, because you demanded we come here?" David said through a grin.

"Anybody else got the urge to study her for a psych paper?" Harvard murmured.

"Somebody should," Ryan agreed. "When she zones out like that, all she can see is code. Doesn't notice anything else. I once swapped out her chair for a beach ball. Was really funny watching her try to figure out where it came from when she arrived back on planet Earth."

David glared at him. "That won't happen again."

"No." Ryan inched behind Harvard. "No, it won't. It was juvenile. I've matured since then."

Elle placed a hand on each side of David's face and

turned his head to face her. "We need a team meeting. And an energy drink. Oh! And the toilet. I really need the toilet." She climbed down and ran for the bathroom. "Call a meeting. We're going to win." She screeched to a halt outside the door. "Wait? What time is it?"

"About nine," Ryan said.

"Morning? Night?" Elle hopped from one foot to the other.

"Night," David said.

"We can still have a meeting, right? It's not too late, is it? No, it's not too late. We need to have a meeting. This is important. Gather the team!" She disappeared through the door.

"Guess we're having a team meeting," Harvard said to Ryan, both of them looking a little stunned.

"Guess so." And with that, they headed upstairs to round everyone up.

Leaving David alone to listen to the very loud rendition of the *Star Wars* theme tune coming from the bathroom.

ELLE STOOD AT THE END OF RACHEL'S CONFERENCE TABLE and looked out over the sea of black, gray, and olive drab that made up her team. One day, she'd invest in colorful T-shirts for everyone. Like a Benson Security uniform. Yeah, that sounded good. Although she was pretty sure Callum's head would explode if he wasn't wearing a gray Henley.

"Remember," Rachel said from the other end of the table, where she sat in a larger, more ornate chair. Her throne, Elle assumed. "You aren't at home. This isn't your table, so no scratching your initials into it...Ryan."

"That was an accident," Ryan said.

"For the love of Prada, how can you *accidentally* etch your name into wood?"

Before Ryan could reply with something equally nutty, Elle interrupted: "We need to start. I have too much stuff in my head, and if I don't get it out soon, there will be brains everywhere. All over your fancy conference table, your tasteful walls, that expensive suit you're wearing. Everywhere."

Rachel sighed wearily. "I honestly don't miss working with any of you."

"Liar," Ryan said through a cough.

"That means I'm starting, right?" Elle bounced on the balls of her feet. "Yeah, I'm starting. Okay, here goes. Pay attention because this is going to blow you away." She tapped her laptop, and a detailed mind map appeared beside her on the huge screen suspended from the ceiling.

David, who sat at her side, put a hand on her arm. "Take a deep breath. You've got plenty of time to get it all out."

She nodded and gave him a thumbs-up. "So, this is the structure of the James Syndicate." Elle pointed at the image. "I've color coded it. Red is sex trade, pink drugs, et cetera. There's a key to the color coding in the left-hand corner." She hit the enter key, and another image appeared beside the first. "This map shows all the areas where there are James Family operations. I've tried to color code each one, but often they do lots of different types of business in one location. Where the color's darker, it represents a bigger hub."

"They're worldwide," Ryan said. "Didn't realize they had that much reach. I mean, I grew up hearing whispers about the James Syndicate. Guess I always thought they were only a London gang."

"I didn't know either," Elle said. "The hacking I did into their phones years ago showed me only their immediate concerns. It didn't give me this sort of depth or an overview. I'd only scraped the surface." She changed the slide again, this time to a map overlaid with photos—most of them mugshots. "These are the people in charge of each area. I've got images for most of them, plus names and contact details for everyone." The slide changed again. "This is the command structure. Tommy at the top, and Marcus sitting underneath him as king-in-waiting. Off to the side, you find Cutter, basically in the position of a classic Mafia consigliere. Only, he isn't there to be impartial; he's Tommy's man all the way."

"Tommy always had a backup in place in case your brother didn't work out," Megan said. "Didn't he?"

Elle nodded, rubbing at the ache in her chest that manifested whenever she thought of her brother. "I don't think he ever really trusted Marcus." She swallowed and carried on. "Anyway, as you can see, this shows the managers and captains within the organization. Most of the top-level people are based in London. Each has their own specialist area—Marcus' was money laundering, brokering deals, and gunrunning. He was trying to shut down their sex-trade business and cut their ties with terrorist groups, but he wasn't clean by any stretch of the imagination." She lowered her head. "He wasn't a good man."

David placed his hand on her back. "He was still your brother, and it's okay to love him for how he was with you."

Unable to help herself, she leaned down and placed a grateful kiss on his lips.

"This never bloody happened when I was in the SAS," Callum grumbled.

"Anyway." Elle straightened, feeling much better. "This is the tip of the iceberg. I've downloaded everything I could from their servers, decrypted a huge chunk of it, and we have more than enough to sink Tommy forever. My original thought was to go all Panama Papers on this, but the only person that would benefit is me. I'd be safer, but the bad guys would disappear only to pop up again later in a different location, doing the same thing."

"We need to take this to the authorities. *All* of the authorities," Joe said.

"That's what I'm thinking too. Before this"—Elle pointed at the screen—"everything I'd managed to get on Tommy was local, crimes that a London police force would deal with. This, on the other hand, is global. It's what I wished I'd found before I left. Every police force and intelligence agency on the planet will want this information."

Callum rubbed a hand down his face. He was clearly tired, the lines on his face more prominent than usual. Maybe he should call Isobel. She made a mental note to suggest it after their meeting.

"Do we call all our contacts?" Callum said. "Then figure out a way to give each of them the information? I can see them fighting over us. Or over who'll run the operation. Some idiot's bound to want everything we have, and us too, all to themselves." He was sitting in his wheelchair to give his legs a break from his prosthetics. It was something he never used to do in front of them—let them see him without his legs. But since meeting Isobel, Callum had loosened up a whole lot, to the point of trusting that his team didn't think any less of him because of his disability.

"What about Tessa Sharp?" Dimitri leaned his elbows on the table. "She ran the Met side of the joint-forces op that took down the Abramovich organization. I mean, she plays well with others, has helped us out before, and she has experience in taking down an international crime ring. Could we get her to coordinate the other agencies and act as our point of contact on this?"

"Tessa's pretty pissed at us right now," Ryan said. "Not sure she'll help."

"For a chance at another career-making bust, she'll get over her hard feelings," Dimitri drawled.

Everyone looked at Callum. "It's a good idea," he said. "She'd understand the need to coordinate the response from different agencies before this information leaks. She'll also get why we're leery of trusting anyone, seeing as it was one of her boys who handed over Elle to the James Family. Which she's still pissed about, by the way. I'll sound her out, see if she's willing to play this our way."

"What about Abasi?" Elle asked. "He spent just as long looking out for me as Marcus did. And he watched my brother's back. Shouldn't we try to warn him the police will be closing in?"

David threaded his fingers through hers. "Not sure how we'd do that, Blue. He didn't leave a contact number."

"Oh." She forced a smile for her team's sake. "There must be a way we can get a message to him though, right? I mean, he gave us this information in the first place. Plus, I think, under different circumstances, Abasi and Marcus could have been better men. I want to give him a chance to have a different life."

"We'll do what we can to give Abasi a way out," David promised.

"There you go again," Callum complained. "Making decisions for the team. You have no idea how to work with others, do you?"

David did that one eyebrow thing at Callum, who wasn't as impressed by it as Elle was. "Technically, I'm not part of this team. I'm not part of any team. I'm an independent contractor."

"Aye, well, we'll see about that. Seems to me you'd be a whole lot easier to handle if I was officially your boss."

Callum spun his chair around and headed for the door. "Elle, get the info packaged up for the cops. I'll leave you to decide the best way to do that. And make sure Lake and I have access to everything in case this goes sideways. I'm off to call Tessa and Lake. Somebody order food that isn't pizza. It looks like it's going to be another late night, and we'll get hungry. We'll meet back here when it arrives."

"No, we won't," Rachel called after him. "We have a canteen for dining. The food stays there, not in my boardroom."

"Pity it's the weekend," Ryan said. "Otherwise, we could have eaten at the canteen. They do good noodles. Cheap too. We should have a staff canteen at our office."

"For a dozen people?" Julia said. "That seems like an unnecessary expenditure."

Ryan wasn't listening, he was too busy waxing lyrical about all the foods their fictitious in-house chef could make for them.

Elle felt a tug on her hand and she tumbled into David's lap. She put her arms around his neck and kissed his chin.

"I think Marcus planned to use this information to take Tommy down," she told him. "I think he was going to get out of the business."

His arms squeezed her tight. "I hope you're right, Blue. I really do."

Elle hoped so too.

29

They'd set up a meeting with Tessa and a couple of her trusted officers at the offices of Benson Security's lawyers. It had been decided that only Elle, David, and Ryan would enter the building to hand over the information to the Metropolitan Police. Dimitri, Megan, Callum, and Harvard would act as their protection and backup. They weren't taking any chances when Tommy was still searching for Elle, and they didn't know who they could trust.

Joe, Julia, and Rachel stayed at the safe house to comb through the data Elle had decrypted so far. Julia wanted them to compare the names they'd found in Tommy's records to the police staff rolls they'd acquired, hoping they might weed out his contacts inside the force. It was something Elle could have done much faster; once she'd written a program for the task. But Julia had insisted it was something they could do to help while they waited for Elle to take over. It was clear she wanted something to keep herself occupied, and as usual, Joe indulged her—dragging Rachel in to help too. Something she was super thrilled about.

"I don't like this," David said as they drove up one of the

many narrow, winding streets that made up the City of London. "Most of the roads are one way, and the rest are pedestrian-only. Makes it too easy to predict which route your target would take."

"Although, on the plus side, the buildings being that tall and close together makes it hard for a sniper to get a bead on us." Ryan studied their surroundings.

"Will you two listen to yourselves?" Elle said from the back seat. "We're in the oldest part of London, the part that was almost destroyed by the Great Fire of 1066."

David grinned at her in the rearview mirror. "Think you might find that it was 1666."

"Close enough. The point is, there are buildings here dating back to the Romans. Sitting next to skyscrapers built for international businesses. Down that lane"—she pointed to a dark, narrow passage—"there's a pub that's been around for three hundred years. For goodness' sake, we just passed St. Paul's Cathedral, and the Old Bailey's up there. We've got Fleet Street, famous for its newspapers on one side of us, and the best law courts in Britain on the other. We're surrounded by history and culture, and you two are looking for places we can be ambushed or shot by a sniper."

"How about I do the tourist bit when I'm not playing bodyguard, Ellie Blue?" David flashed her a smile. "Although, I do enjoy guarding that body of yours."

"Yuck." Ryan shuddered. "Don't listen to her complaints. She's probably Googling this stuff to distract herself. You're reading it off your phone, aren't you?"

Elle sighed and put her phone back in her pocket. "One day, you'll wake up to discover I've legally changed your name to Rita Granger, Queen of the Desert, while you slept."

"It has a nice ring to it," he said. "I could make it work."

"Coming up to a bottleneck. It's clear from our end."

Callum's voice came from the phone sitting on the dash. "Dimitri, how does it look from your end?"

"Clear," Dimitri answered from the car behind them.

"I'm not seeing anything either," David added, his eyes still scanning their surroundings.

They took the turn into yet another one-way street without incident, their car in the middle of a three-car procession. It would have seemed impressive and very important *if* the three cars hadn't looked like they'd driven straight out of a junkyard.

"Couple more minutes, and we'll be there," David said. "Ryan, keep your gun handy. Just in case."

"Your Spidey-sense tingling?" Ryan asked.

"Just in case," David repeated.

"Roger that, superspy." Ryan unholstered his weapon.

"THIS IS MIND-NUMBING," RACHEL COMPLAINED AT THE laptop screen in front of her. "It's like searching for a rusty needle in a haystack made of needles."

"So...*not* a haystack then." Joe grinned from the opposite side of the kitchen table, where he had his own laptop open.

"I don't see why we couldn't have done this at TayFor or, even better, my apartment. We'd be much more comfortable there."

"Security," Julia muttered from the seat between Rachel and Joe. "We can't risk using your company building too much. Someone will notice us, and it would put all your hard work as CEO in jeopardy. Also, the James Family might be watching your apartment."

"It has fabulous security," Rachel pointed out. "Much better than my last place." Which the Benson Security team had bypassed on several occasions, purely to annoy her.

"Harvard checked it out himself and says it's practically titanium."

"Practically being the operative word." Joe lifted his mug. "Refill?"

"Dear Coco Chanel, please, no." Tapping at her keyboard with one of her signature red manicured nails, she scrolled through yet more names that meant absolutely nothing to her. "Why can't we wait until Elle's written a program for this?"

"Because we might find something useful in the meantime." Julia checked the list she'd printed out and placed on the table between them. "Just open one of the lists Elle gave you and make a side-by-side comparison with the police list I gave you. Any name that's on both will turn yellow. Once you find a name, add it to the central list on the cloud."

"Why are there so many different police forces in London?" Rachel complained. Because, seriously, her brain was beginning to atrophy.

Julia seemed puzzled. "Is that a rhetorical question, or do you actually want me to answer?"

"She's complaining, Jules. Let her be. It's how she copes with anxiety." Joe sat back down with his filled coffee mug.

"I'm not anxious," Rachel lied. "I'm bored."

They all had their different coping mechanisms. Hers was being a bitch. Julia's was pointlessly combing through data lists rather than waiting for Elle to do it a fraction of the time.

She glanced at her iPhone, which sat within reach on the table beside her. "Shouldn't they be at the lawyers' offices by now?"

"Around now," Joe agreed. "But London traffic can be a bitch."

"Really, Joe?" Julia said. "That word is rude and an insult to women."

"Sorry, baby." His eyes sparkled. "London traffic can be a bastard."

Julia rolled her eyes. Something Rachel hadn't even been aware she knew how to do.

Rachel glanced back down at her laptop screen and startled. "Oh, I think I may have done something wrong. My lists are glitching."

"No," Julia said. "It isn't you. My screen's acting up too. Joe?"

He tapped a key on his laptop to wake it up. Then said some words that Julia definitely didn't approve of. "We're being hacked. Are we connected to the internet?"

"Of course," Julia said. "We're working on cloud documents because we need to share."

Rachel sucked in a breath. "My screen's gone blank."

"Check your local files," Joe said. "Julia, can you check the cloud?"

She picked up her phone and used it to enter their cloud location. "I can't get in."

Joe picked up his phone and dialed. "Lake. Check to see if you still have access to the information Elle stored for us." He paused. "Son of a bitch. No, we've got nothing either. Yeah, that's what I thought." Another pause. "I don't know how many copies she made or where she saved them. We were in a hurry. Callum told her to give you and him access, but beyond that..."

"She wouldn't save it to our servers," Julia said. "Not until the code had been thoroughly checked. It would have been too risky to put something that dangerous in our vault." In visible distress, Julia turned to Rachel. "Could she have left a copy at TayFor?"

"Harvard and I told her not to, for the exact same reason. Nobody could guarantee there wasn't something malicious in the data she'd downloaded that would corrupt our servers."

"Did you catch that?" Joe said to Lake and then nodded. "Portable hard drives?" he asked the women as he put his phone on speaker and set it on the table.

"She must have saved some hard drive copies," Rachel said. "She's Elle; she thinks about that sort of thing. Doesn't she?"

Joe ran a hand through his thick hair. "We've been under a lot of pressure, especially Elle. Time was moving fast. Is it possible she didn't save a local copy?"

"The amount of data is vast," Julia said. "We paid a fortune for a cloud vault large enough to store it in. I'm not sure she could have gotten it onto a portable drive. Also, I'm sure we would have noticed if she'd saved another copy. It would take hours to transfer. It took that long to get it onto the cloud."

"I'm calling in Harry," Lake said. "If the data's out there, he'll find it or restore our access to it. Worst-case scenario, he can tell us what happened to it."

"We know what's happened to it," Rachel said, grimacing at her former teammates. "Someone found out we have it, which means there's a leak amongst the people we've told. Obviously, Tommy James has set his Russian hackers on the trail of his data. What else could it be?"

"Who's in the loop about the data?" Lake asked.

Everyone looked at Julia. "Us, Abasi, Tessa and whoever she trusts at the station, and our lawyers."

"Did anyone think to check out the identities of the lawyers' other clients?" Rachel asked. "I met Ms. Patel a couple of times and didn't take to her."

There were no jibes about her not taking to anyone. Instead, there was an answering silence that made her stomach lurch.

Julia held up her phone, the color gone from her already pale face. "I can't get through to the team."

Rachel scooped up her phone and tapped on Harvard's image. It rang but went straight to voicemail.

"It doesn't mean there's trouble," Joe said evenly. "We don't have comm units, so they're using their phones to communicate with each other. It could be that their phones are just busy."

"I'm calling the Met," Lake said. "Joe, call the law firm. Julia, keep trying to get hold of the team. I'll be in touch." The line went dead.

For once, Rachel couldn't think of even one bitchy thing to say. Instead, she tapped Harvard's image once again and hoped this time the call went through.

"OKAY," DAVID SAID. "THERE'S THE LAW FIRM ON THE corner. We're on the home stretch, people." The sight should have made him relieved, but instead, all he felt was wary. Every instinct he'd honed over the years in the field was telling him that something was off. He just couldn't put his finger on it.

"Callum?" David called out to the speakerphone. "How's it looking up ahead?"

There was no reply. Although it was clear their car was fine, as it was still in front of them.

"Callum?" David repeated. No answer. "Dimitri?" Nothing. A chill ran up his spine. "Check the phone, Ryan."

Ryan reached for the phone as Elle twisted in her seat. "I can see Dimitri and Megan. They're fine." She waved at them, then mimicked for them to call. "Megan's holding up her phone. That girl can't mime to save herself. If I had to guess, I'd say she's lost reception too."

"This cell's dead." Ryan tossed it back on the dash.

"Dead!" Elle beamed. "That's what she's miming. Hold on. I'll check to see if there's a connection from my laptop." She tugged the machine out of her messenger bag and opened it.

"Don't bother, Elle. We're aborting," David said. "Ryan, open the window and signal to the other cars." He pressed the accelerator, speeding up until he was almost bumper to bumper with Callum's car.

Ryan gestured out the window, waving for them to carry on and hurry up about it.

Callum's car sped up, and David put his foot down to follow.

"My laptop can't find a Wi-Fi signal to connect to either," Elle said. "It's as though something's blocking it."

Yeah. That wasn't good. "Put the laptop away and hold on tight," David said. "We're getting out of here."

Out of nowhere, a car shot from a side alley meant only for pedestrians. The fit was so tight that its sides scraped the walls, and sparks flew. David slammed on the brakes as the car slammed into the side of Callum and Harvard's vehicle.

Elle screamed as he shifted gears to reverse into the space that'd opened up between theirs and Dimitri's car when David accelerated. He didn't make it.

Another car smashed through wooden garage doors and into their path. It sped through the gap between cars and crashed into the wall of the building opposite. David couldn't stop in time, and they slammed into the crashed car, sending both vehicles into a spin that had them bouncing off walls on either side of the road before they stopped. Like pinballs in a machine.

"Out, out, out," David ordered, shoving at his warped door, feeling it stick.

Ryan was already out, gun up, opening the door for Elle, who scrambled toward it.

David undid his seatbelt, twisted in his seat, and slammed his feet into the door until it opened. Smoke from the car behind them billowed into the alley. People shouted. Someone screamed. There was the sound of glass shattering.

David held up his gun, aiming at everything, scanning the area for threats as he made his way around the front of the car to get to Elle. Two armed men climbed over the wrecked vehicle behind them, heading straight for her.

"Run," David shouted. "Ryan, get her out of here." He fired at the men, giving Elle cover.

Three gunshots rang out from behind him, echoing through the narrow alleyways and streets, bouncing off the buildings. David spun and threw himself beside the car, searching for the shooter.

There was a grunt. A thud.

Elle screamed.

David poked his head out to see what was happening, and a volley of shots barely missed him.

"Ryan?" he shouted. "Elle?"

When there was no answer, he risked sticking his head up. And stopped breathing. Elle was being carried toward a passageway. Her eyes panicked as she struggled against a man much larger than her, his hand covering her mouth. David could make out the dark outlines of two more men at the end. A car in the sunlight behind them.

They had her.

They were taking her to Tommy.

A bullet whizzed past his head. He was pinned. Stuck. While Elle was being taken.

There was nothing he could do but call out to her. "Elle," he bellowed. "I'm coming for you!"

Two more shots rang out, forcing David to focus on what was happening around him. Forcing him to wait instead of going after the woman he loved—despite every fiber of his being demanding that he chase her down.

He roared into the sky. Then assumed the cold mask of clarity he wore for every mission. He had a job to do.

Then, he would get Elle.

And eliminate every man who'd touched her.

"Clear this end," Dimitri called from the other side of the wrecked car. "I'm coming over."

"No. Somebody's firing at me." David pressed himself flat to the ground, lying on his stomach to peer under the car. A man stalked toward them from the direction of Callum's vehicle. He wasn't wearing the shoes Harvard or Callum wore. David stretched out his arms, gun in hand, and fired at his legs.

There was a wail. The man struck the ground, panic making him shoot wildly, aiming at nothing. David had no choice but to stop him. He took aim and fired again. The gunfire stopped.

"Callum?" David yelled as he got to his feet. "Harvard?"

"We're clear," Harvard snapped. "Coming through."

"Dimitri," David called. "Come over but watch your back. Have you got eyes on Ryan?" He shouted orders as he made his way around to the other side of the car.

The wooden door to the private passageway they'd carried Elle down had swung shut. David wanted to empty his gun into the wood. He breathed deeply. Slowly. Evenly. Until his heart rate slowed again.

Patience. Planning. Pressure.

The three rules he lived by. First, you waited while you sorted out your course of action, then you exerted pressure where needed. He'd get Elle. Soon. But first, his team.

David tore his eyes from the door—and spotted a boot-clad foot sticking out from under a downed office sign. He clambered over the hood of the car and shoved the wooden panel aside to reveal the person lying underneath.

Ryan.

He lay on his back. Unconscious. Blood pouring from his head and two bullet wounds to his chest.

"Man down," David shouted, stripping off his sweater, then his shirt. He pressed the cotton T-shirt to the holes in Ryan's chest. "We need an ambulance."

Dimitri rounded the car. "Hell, no." He knelt beside David. "Pulse?"

"Haven't checked." Pressing Ryan's chest hard, he worked to stop the bleeding. "We need an ambulance now," he called.

"Already rung; the phones are working again. Somebody must have been jamming the signal," Harvard said as he appeared behind Dimitri. "Shit. Head wound." He got down on his knees and gently checked Ryan's head. "We got a pulse?"

"It's there, but it's faint." Dimitri sat back on his heels. "I can't believe this is happening. Ryan, hell. How am I going to tell Megan? She's going to think this is her fault because she wasn't here to help." He leaned over Ryan. "You'd better live, you food-stealing bastard," he said, devastation written large on his face.

"I'm worried about this head wound," Harvard said. "I'm not sure if the bullet went in or skimmed. There's a lot of blood, and I don't want to risk making things worse by moving him too much. Gimme your shirt, Dimitri."

He unzipped his hoodie, took off his T-shirt, and handed it over. Harvard pressed it to the head wound while Dimitri shrugged back into his hoodie.

"Where's Elle?" Dimitri said.

"They got her." David felt the fury—cold and relentless —curl in his gut. "Took off before I could get to them."

Dimitri clenched his hands into fists. "And the news just keeps getting better. If something happens to Elle too…" He took a deep breath. "What do you need?"

"Right now? To get Ryan to a hospital. After that, I'm going after Elle. What about Megan?"

"Knocked out by the airbag. Two office workers offered to keep an eye on her while I came to back you guys. Far as I can tell, she's fine, but there might be a concussion."

David heard the relief in Dimitri's voice and didn't blame him for it. "There's nothing you can do here. Go check on your woman."

"Ryan—"

"We've got this covered," Harvard said.

With one last pained glance at Ryan, Dimitri jogged off.

"What's the status on Callum?" David asked Harvard.

"He's bruised and bloody but otherwise fine. I left him standing guard over one of the guys we pulled out of the car that slammed into us. Other one died in the crash."

"Does he need backup?" They could send Dimitri if needed. Once he'd checked on Megan.

"He's got it covered." Harvard's jaw tightened. "This is bad." He jerked his head toward Ryan, who was deathly gray.

"Yeah. We need that ambulance."

Not only for Ryan's sake but also for Elle's. Every minute he was delayed in getting to her put her a minute closer to death. There was absolutely no doubt in his mind that Tommy would kill her and do it bloody. David looked down at the man whose blood covered his hands. Elle couldn't cope with losing someone else she loved, and Ryan was as much of a brother to her as Marcus ever was, maybe even more so.

"I've seen wounds like these before," Harvard said, his voice low. "It didn't end well."

"This time will be different." He had to believe that. For Ryan. For Elle. For all of them. Ryan might think he was the useless one, but there would be no London team without him. The team might not realize it, but Ryan was the glue that held them together. He was the one who fit in where needed, who allowed his teammates to let off steam at his expense because he cared about them. The one who quietly used his talents without jostling for power or position. He was a friend, son, brother, and protector to every other member of the team.

Yeah, Ryan had to live.

"You know we were set up." Harvard scanned the surrounding destruction. "Takes a lot of local knowledge to pull off something like this in a short amount of time. We would have had to scout the route, figure out where to put the interception vehicles, and plan a clean exit. No way we could have done it in a few short hours."

"Somebody we talked to is working for the James Syndicate."

"We didn't talk to that many people."

"No." David's voice was pure death. "Which should make it easier to find out exactly who's behind this."

Footsteps ran toward them, and a voice called out, "It's Tessa, don't shoot."

"Roger that," Harvard answered.

The police commander rounded the car, dressed in plain clothes for their meeting. She had two more officers with her. All of them were clearly enraged.

"Ambulance is two minutes out," Tessa said. "We were up in your lawyers' offices when we heard the crash." She glanced at her two men. "Secure the scene; let me know when our team arrives."

The men jogged off.

Tessa crouched beside Ryan to get a closer look. "Damn it to hell," she whispered. "Anybody else hurt?"

"Megan got knocked out," David said, still applying pressure to Ryan's wounds. "Elle's been kidnapped."

"I promise you"—she stared him in the eye—"we will find the people who did this."

"Not if I find them first," David told her. "I'm getting Elle back. I don't care what you do, but know that I won't let you get in my way."

"Bloody macho warrior men." With a shake of her head, Tessa stood. As sirens drew closer, she spotted a discarded firearm amongst the rubble.

"Fucking guns," she spat out as she passed it.

30

Elle wrapped her arms around her middle, rocking in place on the back seat of the car they'd stuffed her into. A strange roaring filled her ears like a jet engine was close by. Vaguely, in the back of her mind, where reason still existed, she realized she was hearing her blood rush through her veins. That same part of her brain calmly noted the facts of what was happening to her. She'd been kidnapped. Punched in the jaw. Carried down a passage between the buildings. Stuffed into a car with three James Syndicate thugs.

And now, they were heading north.

To Tommy.

It didn't matter. None of it mattered. Because all she cared about were the images in her head.

Her pulling out her laptop to see if it could connect them to their team. The vehicles screeching out of nowhere. Their car hitting the wall. Ryan jumping out. Someone firing at David. Ryan opening her door for her, yelling at her to get out. Her scrambling to stuff the laptop back in her messenger bag before climbing out of the car. David shouting something she couldn't catch. Ryan glancing over her shoulder toward Megan's end of the street. His gun coming up.

"Get down," he snapped, shoving her behind him.

Crouched low, he moved to the rear of the car, arms outstretched in front of him, gun aimed and ready. Elle slid down the wall, stupidly protecting her laptop with her body by swinging her messenger bag to her back. She couldn't see David. Ryan pressed his side against the car, using it as cover. He glanced back at her. Checking on her.

Three popping sounds.

Quiet gunshots.

Was there such a thing? Frantically, she looked around. Trying to figure out what was happening and what to do next.

Ryan grunted. It was a deep, guttural sound. The kind of noise that sounded wrong.

His eyes met hers. There was panic in them.

"Run." He barely mouthed the word.

Elle couldn't move. Her gaze was stuck on Ryan. Something was wrong with him.

"Ryan?"

Red, red blood appeared on his chest like an inkblot, spreading across his pale blue shirt.

The whole thing happened in seconds, but it took Elle a lifetime to watch. Blood poured down his face, dripping onto his shirt. His gun slipped from his grasp and clattered to the ground as his eyes rolled back. And then he crumpled, folding in on himself as though his bones had evaporated. He struck the hard pavement with a dull thud only she would have heard in the chaos surrounding them.

And then Elle did run.

But not away. She ran toward Ryan but made it only a few steps before a man appeared in front of her. She kicked out, exactly as Joe had taught her. The man grunted and fell back against the wall, causing a business sign already hanging by a thread to fall to the ground. On top of Ryan.

"No!" she screamed, lunging for her friend.

A blow to the jaw snapped her head sideways and made her vision blur. An arm grabbed her around the waist, pinning her arms to her sides. A hand covered her mouth as her feet left the ground. All she could see of Ryan was his boots peeking out from beneath the rectangle of boldly painted plywood.

She screamed against the palm clamped to her face, the muffled sound only loud in her head. She kicked. Struggled to get free. Fighting to get back to Ryan. To her team. To David.

It was pointless. The hold on her was too strong to break.

As he swung her around toward a dark, narrow passageway, her frantic gaze searched for David. He was nowhere to be seen. And then a voice roared, the words carrying straight to her like arrows.

"Elle, I'm coming for you!"

David.

The wooden doorway to the passage slammed shut with everyone she loved on the other side of it.

"David!" she screamed against the hand.

He had to fix things. He had to find Ryan. He had to find her.

He had to.

Before it was too late for all of them.

As she was shoved into the back of a waiting car, Elle felt her mind begin to close down. Like programs shutting, one by one, on a computer screen. Until the only two left open were a video of Ryan, bloody and falling, playing on an endless loop—and a file marked "David Knight, Spy."

DAVID, CALLUM, AND HARVARD WATCHED THE AMBULANCE doors close on Ryan. There was nothing more any of the team could do for him now.

"I should have seen this coming," Callum said, his normally Scottish-blue complexion grayer than usual. "Should have planned for an attack here. Now Ryan..."

Harvard clasped a hand on Callum's shoulder while the Scot stood like a rock in the middle of the carnage. "We did everything we could in the time we had," Harvard told him. "We've all agreed that there was no way something like this could have been set up in the time we had. Ryan's injuries aren't on you. Put the blame where it belongs—at the James' doorstep."

Callum rubbed at his chin. "The boy... I know he's a man. A trained one at that and bloody good at his job. It's just, he's like a..." He swallowed, looking away from them.

Like a son to me. His unspoken words hung in the air between them.

"He'll make it," Harvard said. "He's strong."

"Aye." Callum sounded no more convinced than the rest of them.

"Has anyone told the rest of the team?" David asked.

"I called Rachel." Harvard stared at the bloodstains on his suit. "She said she'd grab Joe and Julia and get to the hospital. Never heard her that upset." He gave them a wry smile. "She told me that Ryan's the only member of the team who can take her attitude and not get hurt, upset, or vindictive. Not to mention, he can give as good as he gets. There aren't many people in her life who interact with her the way Ryan does."

David watched the organized chaos of the techs working

the crime scene. He was as worried about Ryan as everyone else, but time was ticking for Elle too.

"I need to go after Elle," he said quietly.

They stood huddled in a corner, out of the way of the huge number of cops swarming the area.

"Aye, *we* do." Callum was firm, his eyes flint.

"That won't work." Although he found himself wishing he could take the team with him, despite being used to working alone. "Cops are going to want to question us. One missing team member is explainable, but the whole team walking out? Not so much. I can't risk them chasing us straight to Tommy. He'll kill her if he thinks the cops are charging in."

"She's important to us too," Callum argued.

"And this is how you show that." David wouldn't be swayed. "Stay here, keep the cops occupied, and let me go in alone. I'll call if I need you." He reached for the gun tucked into the small of his back, being careful to keep it out of sight of the cops. "I need you to get rid of this." He handed it to Harvard. "Used it to end one of Tommy's guys."

Harvard slipped it into his pocket. "I'll wipe it and make sure the cops think it belongs to the gang."

There was no need to ask if it was registered to David; they all knew it wasn't.

Callum's expression was thunder. "Hate sitting this out." He took a breath. "You got a backup weapon?"

"I'll find one."

Callum lifted his shirt to reveal a belt holster. He took out the gun and slipped it to David. It was small but effective and better than nothing.

"It'll do until you get something else." Callum scanned the area as he spoke. Aware that they had a couple more minutes at most before someone became curious about their huddle.

"How you gonna find her?" Harvard said.

"I bought half a dozen of those digital tracking disks you put on your keys so you can find them. I hid them all over everything she wears. They're under the insoles of her boots, inside the casing of her laptop, sewn into the waistband of her jeans. They aren't as good as our usual tech, but they work." He held up his phone. "I know exactly where she is."

"Sneaky bastard," Callum muttered with approval. "Guess I'm on distracting Tessa then. Well, she deserves it." He was particularly angry with the cop because she'd taken away his prisoner before he could get any useful intel. "Be careful out there, and keep in contact. If we have to make a break for it to back you up, we will. Remember, you still have Joe. He's waiting for your call. And, Knight? Keep in mind that there are people who won't be happy if you end up in a bad way because you didn't call for help. We're a bloody team."

David nodded, his throat strangely tight.

He watched as Callum strode toward the police commander. "Tessa, what the hell's going on? We cannae stand around all day waiting for you to get to us. We've a seriously injured man, a woman with a concussion, and another who's in danger and needs finding."

Harvard gave David a chin lift before sauntering toward the car with the dead gang member. Obviously, he'd already decided on a place to dump David's gun.

"No bloody way," Callum roared, attracting everyone's attention.

It was enough to allow David to slip behind the barrier and into the crowd. Although his hands had been rinsed clean, Ryan's blood was on his clothes, blending with the black until only he knew it was there. Years of experience had taught him that black hid most of his sins, which is why he wore it all the time. Elle had been right: it was his uniform.

And didn't that say everything about his life?

Two streets over, he helped himself to an old Ford Escort and joined the steady stream of London traffic. All the while keeping an eye on the screen of his phone and the dots that represented the woman he loved.

"Hold on, Ellie Blue," he whispered. "I'm coming for you."

It was as close to a prayer as he'd ever gotten.

HER KIDNAPPERS WERE TAKING ELLE HOME. THAT KNOWLEDGE was like a bucket of cold water, jarring her out of the shocked daze that ensnared her.

"Bet you never thought you'd see this place again." The guy sitting in the back with her chuckled. "You're in for it now. Tommy don't tolerate people betraying him. You're gonna end up like your brother—in pieces." He threw back his head, laughing louder and exposing his Adam's apple.

Elle swung her arm, hitting him hard with the side of her fist. He clutched his throat, choking as he turned a fetching shade of purple. Just because she was small didn't mean she hadn't learned how to hit.

"What the hell?" The guy in the passenger seat snapped right before he slapped her. "Keep your hands to yourself, bitch." He carried on talking, mainly to the guy she'd hit.

Elle tuned them out, her attention focused on the house she'd grown up in. It was a faux Georgian manor house, built at the height of the eighties McMansion era by Tommy himself. Not by his own hands, of course, because Tommy rarely dirtied them for any reason. No, all he'd done was point at a house in Mayfair he'd liked and said "Gimme one of those" to his builder.

She supposed there was nothing wrong with the house itself. With its box shape and symmetrical layout, it was pretty enough. The stone was beige, the trim white, and the roof a deep slate gray. It was amazing how tasteful and classy a house of horror could be.

As they rolled up the wide driveway to the front door, past the immaculately tended gardens, Elle couldn't help but wonder how many bodies lay buried under the roses. Tommy would be arrogant enough to do it. To bury his enemies on his property so he could look out his window and gloat. He'd never think that anyone would find them. In his mind, he was one of the original Untouchables.

Guess that made her Eliot Ness.

Because one way or another, she was bringing this Al Capone wannabe down.

Who was she fooling? Not even herself. Big talk and bravado weren't going to give her confidence. She was outnumbered, outgunned, and about to walk into the lion's den while defenseless. It couldn't get any worse.

The car slowed to a halt in front of the oversized front door with the three white marble steps leading up to it. Steps just like the ones they'd dumped Marcus on. Elle's stomach lurched, and she pressed a hand to it. If she weren't a smart, aware woman, she'd believe that she'd led Tommy straight to her team. That she was responsible for the bullets that hit Ryan. For the knife that killed Marcus.

But she *was* smart and aware. And she knew she wasn't any more responsible for those acts than Leia was responsible for Kylo Ren. Or Diana Prince was to blame for Steve's death. No, none of this was on her. It was all on Tommy James—psychopath, murderer, and evil despot.

As one of the thugs dragged Elle from the car and shoved her toward the steps, the front door swung open.

And there he was.

The man she'd believed was her father.

The nightmare overshadowing her life.

The reason she'd run from everything she'd ever known.

She wanted to vomit, but instead, she cocked her head and watched as he sauntered down the steps toward her. Through eyes of suicidal bravado, she noted that he was shorter than she remembered.

"You have *not* aged well, Tommy," she said, ignoring the tremble in her voice as she lifted her chin. There was no way in hell she was going to her death submissively. She would fight every step of the way, in any way that she could. And the best way to fight Tommy was by using her brain.

"No?" He shared an amused smile with his boys. "Now, that's funny, see, because you ain't gonna age *at all*." He jerked his head toward the house. "You know where to take her."

Grabbing an arm each, Tommy's soldiers frog-marched her into the house and past a smirking Cutter, who was leaning in the doorway to the sitting room. He held a large knife in his hand.

Elle wanted to claw out his eyes for what he'd done to Marcus.

Instead, she smiled at him. "I see you're still overcompensating for your teeny-tiny penis, Cutter. Wouldn't one of those knives they include in a Swiss Army key chain be more appropriate?"

One of the guys holding her started coughing, and Cutter's face turned red. "Gonna enjoy cutting you, bitch."

"I'm sure you will," she said sympathetically. "It's the only way you can get it up, isn't it? You know there are pills for that."

His eyes gleamed with maliciousness. "Your brother screamed like a baby in the end."

The words were a wound to her soul, one she refused to let him see. Instead, she rolled her eyes, knowing the act was awkward but doing it anyway. "Everybody screams in the end, Cutter. You're going to find that out when my guy comes for me." Because even if David didn't get there in time to rescue her, he sure as hell would avenge her. "I'm betting you pee yourself too."

He took a furious step toward her, but Tommy intervened. "You seriously gonna let her get to you?"

Cutter glared at her with such menace it made her feel faint. With a nod to Tommy, he turned and disappeared into the sitting room.

"Always with the smart mouth," Tommy said with a shake of his head.

"Am I supposed to act polite while you drag me off to maim and kill me?"

"It might help. Might make me go easier on you."

For a brief second, Elle's grief and fear almost made her crumple. And then something occurred to her, and she laughed. Sure, it sounded hysterical. But it felt damn good. The men shared bewildered looks. Which made her laugh even harder. It was official—she had lost her mind entirely.

"What's so funny?" Tommy demanded, standing in front of her.

"What's funny?" Elle gasped for breath. "David Knight is going to come in here like death himself. He won't leave a single one of you standing. Especially if you harm me, because that man loves me." She leaned forward, straining against the hold the men had on her. "He's going to cut a path of complete destruction, miles wide, through your organization. And what he misses, my team will get in the clean-up. You think you're scary, but you don't have a clue what you're dealing with here." She laughed again. "Hell, I didn't even know until I found out his full name. David Knight makes the guy in *Taken* look like an amateur, and he's coming for *you*. Don't take my word for it; ask some of your CIA contacts about him. See what they say. A smart man would let me go before he rains hell down on them."

Of course, she was exaggerating. She hadn't a clue what David did in the CIA. But she had seen what he'd done since this whole situation exploded. Her man was scarily skilled.

Tommy didn't reply, so she carried on. "You thought you'd captured him in Amsterdam and what happened there? Huh? The guys are dead. The building up in smoke. Or how about those men you sent to pick me up at the police station? Also dead. *He* took them out. One man against three, and he didn't even break a sweat. The whole thing was over in seconds, and he walked away without leaving a trace. In. A. Police. Station. You sure you don't want to just let me go, and we can forget all about this?"

Tommy hesitated, a wariness in his eyes that made her want to gloat. Then those same eyes hardened. "Get her downstairs. Don't listen to a word she says; it's all bullshit." With that, he turned and followed Cutter into the sitting room.

Elle gazed up at one of the guys holding her. "If you get me out of here, I'll tell David to spare you."

For a second, he actually seemed to consider it, but then he shoved her forward. "Shut up, bitch."

31

___

David wasn't surprised that Tommy James had spent barely a day in hiding before returning to his home. It was pure arrogance. At first, David thought his motivation might be protecting his status and power. But truth was, Tommy had been getting away with doing whatever he wanted for so long that he thought he was bulletproof. From the Georgian mansion house to the luxury cars and parklike setting, the whole setup screamed that Tommy was too important to touch. Too distanced from the muck he created to get any of it on his expensive suit. Elle was right. He thought he was untouchable.

And David planned on proving him wrong.

The whole property was wired with cameras, motion detectors, and sensors. Tommy had soldiers positioned both in clear sight—outside the doors of his house and at each corner—and patrolling the property more covertly.

With eyes everywhere, the wise move would have been to wait until after nightfall to enter the building. It would definitely be a whole lot easier then, but unfortunately, Elle didn't have hours to wait for his arrival. And he didn't want her in there one second more than she'd already been inside.

"Could smell your aftershave," he said softly to the man who soundlessly came up to stand beside him. "If I didn't recognize it, you'd be dead."

"How about we argue over who'd kill who first later?" Abasi said.

Marcus' best friend had dumped his James Syndicate uniform of suit and tie in favor of jeans and a long-sleeved T-shirt, both in black.

"They've got Elle," David told him as they watched the guards patrol Tommy's garden from behind a tree in a bushy part of a neighbor's property.

"I heard." Abasi reached under his shirt at the small of his back and produced a gun. "You won't get in from here."

"How did you find me, anyway?"

"Unlike the dickheads in there"—he pointed at Tommy's house—"I know how to work a computer. I learned from the best. And she must have hacked all the cameras in the surrounding properties. That's how I saw you sneaking, ninja-like, across the Freemans' lawn."

In his haste to get to Elle, David clearly wasn't thinking straight; otherwise, he would have realized someone could hack the neighborhood. "How do we get in then?"

Abasi didn't argue the "when" of their break-in. He knew as well as David that time was running out for Elle. "Follow me." He cocked his head back toward the road, where David had abandoned his stolen car.

Taking one glance at the pitiful vehicle, Abasi shook his head. "We'll take mine."

His was a sleek black SUV with illegally tinted windows.

"How are you for firepower?" David asked once they were ensconced inside.

Abasi's eyes were sharp. "You need something?"

"All I've got is Callum's backup gun. It won't get me far." He held it up.

Without another word, Abasi opened the glove compartment and produced a 9mm 15-round SIG Sauer P226—with an extra clip. "That do?" He handed it to David.

"Nicely." The semi-automatic was his weapon of choice in most situations, and he was happy to have one in his hand now.

As he checked the gun, Abasi talked. "Marcus and me, we knew something like this was coming." His eyes closed briefly. "Maybe not exactly like this, but you get the drift. We knew we'd need a way in and out of the house, and seeing as Marcus set up the security system..."

"He made a back door."

"Yeah."

They wound their way through the streets, coming in behind the property, where the houses were smaller and closer together. A large, rustic-looking pub took up a corner of one of the streets. Abasi drove into the parking lot behind it and parked in a spot reserved for management.

He pointed to the corner, where the trees and bushes were thickest. "There's a gate through there. It opens up to a narrow alleyway that's too small for cars and blocked at both ends. The alley runs between the bottom of the back gardens for the rows of houses on two streets. At the end of the alley, there's a private garden, which the residents share."

"The garden backs onto Tommy's property," David guessed.

Abasi nodded. "The northeast corner, to be precise. Tommy made sure the wall was fortified, and there are several cameras—none of which have worked for years. The security room receives a loop that changes depending on the season, time of day, and the weather." He cocked his head. "It utilizes a program Elle wrote for Tommy years ago. One of the many he didn't understand. I like to think there's a certain kind of harmony in his weakest point being created by the work he made Elle do for him."

"What about his army patrolling the place?"

"Tommy likes them big and dumb—picks them because they look the part rather than knowing how to do the job. We designed their patrol patterns and shifts years ago, leaving gaps in this corner. Nobody's ever said anything about it. Don't think they noticed."

David nodded; that sounded like Tommy. All flair and no substance. The man had been getting by on reputation and arrogance for years.

"Once we're in and over the wall, then what?"

Abasi pulled out his phone and brought up an aerial image of the house and grounds on Google. "I've often wondered how many people know how much you can find out about where they live from this thing." He pointed at the screen. "We're going in here. We skirt the pool building, using the hedges for cover. Our access is the mudroom door." He tapped a longer part of the building attached to the cube shape of the main house. "That's where the problems start. The cameras in this part of the building definitely work, so we need to take them out. This part of the house doesn't get much in the way of security cover. It's for staff, and Tommy doesn't give a shit about them. But there are still cameras."

"Any idea where Elle would be?"

"Depends how Tommy wants to play it. If he starts out slow, questioning her in the hope she'll give up everything she knows, then she'll be in his study." He pointed to the front corner of the main house. "If he just wants to hurt her, she'll be in a hidden room off the wine cellar that he uses for *interrogations*." This time, he pointed to the back of the house. The rooms were in opposite directions.

The way Abasi said the word made the meaning clear. "He's got a wet room."

"Several. But this is the one he likes to play in."

"Okay, it's clear it'll get nasty once they know we're there. What are the chances of Tommy killing Elle if he thinks he's being raided?"

"One hundred percent." His jaw tightened, and his eyes went flat. "He hates your girl."

"Then we need to split up, take a location each. You take the office, and I'll take the wet room."

Abasi shook his head. "Won't work. The problem isn't getting into the house; it's getting out. As soon as Tommy knows he's under attack, he'll call in every syndicate member he can find. The house is gonna be overrun by guys who want to prove themselves to the boss by taking us out. We need to watch each other's backs. It's our only chance of getting out of there alive."

"And you were going to do this alone?" David cocked an eyebrow at him.

"At night. Stealthily. In and out without anybody noticing, leaving Tommy with a bullet in his brain."

"Elle doesn't have until nighttime." David ran a hand down his face. "Okay, best guess, where's Tommy more likely to take her?"

"If I'm wrong..." For the first time since he'd met Abasi, the man seemed unsure of himself.

"Everybody dies. That's what happens if we pick the wrong location and Elle pays the price. Everybody. Dies."

Abasi let out a stream of curses. "Best guess, she's in the

basement. Cellar entrance is off the kitchen, at the back of the house."

David nodded. "Then let's get going."

They climbed out of the car, and as Abasi rounded the hood to join him, David paused.

"Gimme one sec," he said as he fished his phone from his pocket. And then, he did something he'd never thought he'd do after years of working alone—he called his team. "Joe? Yeah, Knight here."

"What do you need?" was Joe's instant response.

"I'm going after Elle. Abasi is with me, and it's possible we'll need backup."

"I'm at the hospital with Julia and Rachel. Ryan's been taken into surgery, and Megan's being kept in overnight for monitoring. Which means you get me and Dimitri. Where are you?"

As he proceeded to fill Joe in, Abasi signaled him.

"One more piece of information you might want to pass on," the mobster said.

"What's that?"

"The name of the person who sold you out."

OH, THIS ISN'T GOOD. THIS REALLY ISN'T GOOD.

This situation was right up there with the time Leia fell into the trash compactor on the Death Star and nearly got crushed to death. It was that level of not good.

Instead of taking Elle to Tommy's study, where she'd expected to go, his goons had taken her downstairs. They'd walked through the fully stocked wine cellar—which was laughable in itself because Tommy couldn't taste the differ-ence between white vinegar and a good Chardonnay—until they reached the back wall. One of the guys took a bottle of wine from the shelf.

"None for me, thanks," Elle said, earning a glare.

He reached into the gap left by the bottle and tapped a code into a keypad. The rack swung outward to reveal a white door, which opened onto a room beyond. Not just any room. This was a sterile, windowless space, decorated in plain white tiling and with a drain in the middle of the concrete floor. Next to that large, ominous drain was a metal chair screwed into the floor. And on the wall behind the chair hung a massive mirror. Two-way? She didn't think so.

The men led Elle to the chair and shoved her into it. As one divested her of her messenger bag and the laptop inside, the other cuffed her hands behind her, fastening them to the back of the chair. After he was done, he secured her ankles to the chair's legs. She was completely immobilized. Then, with brutish smiles, they left the room, taking her bag with them and closing the door firmly behind them.

Holy Torture Chamber, Batman!

She was going to die. There was no doubt about it. Everywhere she looked, something new fueled her fear. A heavy-duty hook in the ceiling above her, chains hanging from it in a coil. A stainless-steel bench and sink fitted with a spray nozzle on a hose that could be used for washing down the room. A tall metal cabinet, its glass panels filled with tools and equipment you'd find only in an operating theater. Or an abattoir.

Yeah. She was totally going to die.

Even if David made it in time to rescue her, how would he find her in the super-secret torture room? She'd lived in the house for sixteen years and hadn't known it was there. Which meant that not only was it designed for easy cleaning, but it was also built with soundproofing. Yet another thing to add to her list of things that were terrifying about her current situation. She was in a room designed to capture her screams.

Had they brought Marcus to this room? Was this where he breathed his last? Had his blood poured into that drain? Only for them to wash it away before they threw him out like trash?

No. She couldn't think about that.

And she couldn't think about Ryan either. If he died…

No.

Elle had to concentrate on her current situation. What would Leia do? She'd goad and torment her captors until an opportunity to escape presented itself. Right? She could do that. She knew Tommy's weak spots. She knew things about his team that even he didn't know. Surely that would buy her some time.

The door swung open, and the man she'd believed to be her father swaggered in—followed by a smirking Cutter. Her plan was about to be put to the test.

"What did you do with the hard drive, Elle?" Tommy said.

"I'm afraid I don't know what you're talking about."

The strike came out of nowhere. A backhand across her cheekbone that happened so fast she didn't see it coming. Her head snapped to the side as pain burst across her face. Slowly, she turned back to face him.

Cutter was grinning now, malice in his eyes. But Tommy, he looked like he'd just ordered a coffee instead of smacking the woman who was supposed to be his daughter.

"Your laptop's missing a hard drive," he said evenly. "A hard drive that's got all of my fucking information on it. Information you stole with the help of that useless shit I called a son." He spread his hands. "Now, my hacker people managed to delete the online copies you'd made and move my information to a more secure location. All that's left is the copy you planned to hand over to the cops. I want it. You're going to give it to me. It can happen the easy way or the hard way, your choice."

"I'm guessing both choices come with pain, right? Think I'll pass. How about a third option? I tell you who's snitching on you to MI6, and you let me go. How about that?"

Tommy drew back his fist and punched her in the gut. The chair didn't move an inch as the air was stolen from her lungs. Panic swelled within Elle. She couldn't breathe. Her diaphragm had stopped working. She gasped for air, but nothing happened. She was going to suffocate to death. In a room full of air. While Cutter laughed.

Suddenly, the muscle spasm passed, and air rushed back into her lungs.

You can take this. You can do it. Even Leia was tortured by Darth. If she can suffer through it, so can you.

All she had to do was get them to turn on each other. "Have you ever wondered where Cutter disappears to a couple of times a week?" She watched Cutter stiffen.

"I don't give a shit where he goes or what he does," Tommy said. "I care about what you did with my information. Where have you put it?"

"I honestly don't know where it is. The hard drive was in the laptop last time I opened it. But I do know where Cutter goes and what he does when he's there."

"Let me at her," Cutter exploded. "She's dicking us around. I'll make her talk."

Tommy considered Cutter thoughtfully before backhanding Elle again. This time, he burst her lip, and she tasted blood.

"He's talking to his contact at MI6." Elle forced out the words. "He heard they were closing in on you, making a case, and he's cutting a deal. His testimony for immunity."

"Bullshit!" Cutter lunged at her, a knife in his hand.

Tommy stepped in to restrain him while Elle smirked at Cutter. She didn't even care that it hurt her bleeding lip.

"I'm gonna slice the bitch," Cutter shouted.

"You're gonna do what I tell you to do," Tommy snapped. "She's playing you. Get a fucking grip."

When he was convinced Cutter wouldn't stab her to death before he was done with her, Tommy turned back to Elle. "I know where he goes when he disappears. He heads to an underground club in Soho, where he fucks teenage boys."

Cutter, was frantic as he took a step toward his boss. "Tommy, I—"

Tommy held up a hand to stop him. "Don't give a crap what he does with his dick. All I care about is that he's loyal and gets the job done."

Cutter paled, as though he was about to faint. "I didn't know you knew…"

"If it mattered, I'da said something." Tommy ended the discussion. "Now you." He pointed at Elle. "I shoulda killed you with your mother. You've been nothing but trouble for me since the day you were born. Bastard child of a whore and her cop lover. Should never have let my boy talk me into keeping you."

"Your boy? You mean the one you killed? The one you threw away like yesterday's garbage?" She struggled against the cuffs, wanting to get at him and claw off his evil, smug face.

"You ruined him," he roared, spittle flying. "You're to blame for his death. You!"

She shook her head. "No. Marcus' death is all on you and your pet psychopath. You took a good, smart, funny boy and turned him into a monster of a man who had trouble telling right from wrong. You did that. The same way you take everything good and warp it until it's nasty and unrecognizable. And do you know why you do it? Because you know what you are, and you can't stand the sight of yourself. You're a freak, a monster, a belly-crawling slug who has to hurt people to feel like a man. You're pathetic."

This time, his fist came at her face.

And the world went black.

32

Callum was sick and tired of answering the same questions over and over. Tessa had confiscated his phone and separated him from Harvard when she found out David had made a run for it. Since that moment, he'd spent his time dealing with a pissed-off cop instead of being out in the field, supporting his people.

It was becoming increasingly difficult to keep a lid on his temper while he sat in his lawyer's office, going over the same old ground. He hadn't even been able to contact the hospital to find out how Ryan was doing. And who the hell knew what trouble Elle was in. His team needed him, and he'd had a gutful of playing nice.

Callum shoved back his chair and stood to face the irate cop. "I'm done."

"Get your backside back in your seat," Tessa snapped. "I've got dead bodies with bullet holes and your team running around my city with guns. This isn't the Wild West; this is London. You don't get to take the law into your own hands."

Ms. Patel cleared her throat. "I think you'll find that my client was merely defending himself from a brutal attack and that Benson Security has permits for every weapon they carry."

"That is not the issue here, and you know it." Tessa pointed at Callum. "You let a member of your team walk away from *my* crime scene when you knew I needed to talk to him. Now he's off playing vigilante instead of letting the police do their job. I demand that you tell me where David Knight went."

Callum glared at Tessa before turning to his lawyer. "I can go, right?"

"Unless Commander Sharp wishes to charge you with something."

"You planning on charging me over this cock-up?" Callum asked the cop.

Before she could answer, the door to Ms. Patel's spacious and tastefully decorated office slammed open, and Rachel strode in with Harvard at her back. Behind him, a cop was running to catch up.

"Mr. Carter," the cop shouted. "Our interview isn't over. I insist you return immediately, or I'll have to charge you with perverting the course of justice."

Harvard shut the door in his face.

"What's going on?" Tessa demanded, glaring at both of them. "This is a police interview; you can't come in here."

Harvard spoke to Callum. "Rachel just sprung me. I know what you know."

In other words, nothing.

"Rachel?" Callum said. "Has something happened to Ryan?" *Is he dead?* That's what he meant but couldn't say. Not out loud. Not where it might become something solid and real.

Her blazing eyes snapped to his. "They took him straight to the National Hospital for Neurology and Neurosurgery. He's in surgery. A small-caliber bullet shattered part of his skull when it glanced off his head, but it didn't penetrate his brain. They need to repair his skull and monitor the swelling. The concussive impact of the bullet might have caused severe brain damage. They won't know for certain until he wakes up." She paused, and the rest of her words hung in the air—*if he wakes up.* "He has a collapsed lung that needed more surgery. They removed two bullets from it. They just missed his heart."

Harvard took a step toward Rachel, obviously intending to comfort her. She moved away. "No," she told him.

That's when Callum took a closer look at his former partner. Her face was flushed, her hands were shaking, and her shoulders were rock solid. She was fighting to remain in control. He'd assumed it was grief, but now he saw it was fury.

Callum shared a worried glance with Harvard as Rachel kept talking. "When I was at the hospital, David called Joe, and he in turn called me."

Callum crumpled back into his seat. "Elle?"

Rachel glanced at him. "I don't know how she is. He was on his way to rescue her."

"Bloody hell, Rachel, give a man a break. Today isn't the day to let someone think the worst." Relief, frustration, anger surged through him.

Rachel stared at him as though not really seeing him. That's when he realized her designer handbag and ever-present iPhone were nowhere in sight. It was almost as though she were naked.

"As I was saying, David spoke to Joe," she said. "Who passed on the information to me, and I came right here." Visibly seething, she stared down their lawyer and then Tessa. "He told Joe the name of the person who passed on information to the James Syndicate. The person who set up our friends."

With speed Callum didn't know Rachel possessed, she pulled back her arm and punched Tessa hard in the face. And she didn't stop there. She followed the dazed cop, punching and slapping until she had Tessa backed up against the wall.

The whole thing lasted no more than a second or two before Harvard grabbed Rachel and carried her to the other side of the room.

"Tessa?" Callum frowned as he got back to his feet. "Is this true?"

Tessa wiped her mouth with the back of her hand, then tugged at her clothes to straighten them. "That's assaulting a police officer," she said. "Your lawyer can explain the penalty for this crime. My constables will be in directly to take you to the station, where you will be charged and processed." She strode toward the door.

But Callum beat her to it and blocked her exit. "Is. This. True?"

"Are you insane?" Tessa snapped. "Do you honestly think I could be bought off by Tommy James?"

Rachel, who'd managed to pull herself together enough for Harvard to put her back on her feet, glared at Tessa. "I will ruin you. No matter how long it takes. No matter how much of my personal fortune I have to use to do it. Your unhappiness and the sullying of your stellar reputation has, from this moment on, become my mission in life. Until the day I die, I will make you suffer for betraying our trust and for what you've done to Ryan and Elle. You have my word on that."

"That's going to be hard to do from prison," Tessa said. "Counselor, please deal with your client."

"She isn't my client," Ms. Patel said. "I represent Benson Security, and Ms. Ford-Talbot no longer works with them." She turned her attention to Rachel. "I hadn't realized we'd met, but now I remember you, and I'd be happy to help you to achieve your new goal." Her cold gaze returned to Tessa. "This isn't the first time I've heard rumors about Commander Sharp."

Tessa's cheeks reddened as she retreated from Callum, giving off trapped-animal vibes that turned his stomach. He liked Tessa, trusted her. Counted her as an ally. Surely, they were wrong about her? This had to be a mistake they'd easily clear up.

With manic eyes, she swept her gaze over all of them and uttered the words that damned her, "You can't prove anything."

She'd just confirmed everything Rachel had accused her of. "You really did it," Callum said. "You sold us out? What did you get for it? Where are your thirty pieces of silver? You didn't only betray us; you betrayed everything you stood for and made a mockery of the police. I'm sorely tempted to walk out of here and let Rachel have you."

There was banging at the door, and a voice called out, "Commander Sharp, I have an update."

"You'd better open that door, Callum," she said.

Emotion roiling inside him, Callum stepped aside and threw open the door.

A uniformed officer hurried into the room, his face flushed with excitement. "Forensics discovered a hard drive in one of the Benson Security cars. We believe it came from Elle Roberts' laptop. Detective Sumner thinks she removed it from her computer when their car was struck and stuffed down the back of the seat. This is great news, isn't it, Commander? The James Syndicate data isn't lost."

"Mr. McKay," Ms. Patel said smoothly, "would that be the same data that includes every officer on the James Syndicate payroll?"

"Aye, that it would." Callum folded his arms as he

watched Tessa pale. "Ms. Patel, who do you know in the Met that can be trusted? I've a sudden need to give a statement to someone other than Tessa here."

"Funny you should ask." The lawyer reached for her phone. "As it would happen, my uncle's on the force. I'm sure he would be happy to help. I believe you know him, Commander. Assistant Commissioner Sturgis? Wasn't he your commanding officer at some point? Isn't it a small world?"

Rachel took a deep breath, straightened her shoulders, and pointed at the lawyer. "I like you," she said before striding from the room. Obviously, she was finished giving Tessa a piece of her mind.

"Harvard"—Callum stopped the man as he went to follow his fiancée—"find out where David is and what he needs. See if you can help. I'll deal with this."

"Got it, boss," he said, even though he barely worked part time for Benson Security anymore.

As Harvard left, Callum studied Tessa, who appeared to be rallying herself in front of her subordinate—a man who appeared more confused than excited. No doubt Tessa was working out another set of lies for the commissioner.

Callum couldn't stomach any more from her. "Why did you do it? We've had drinks together. You celebrated the birth of my daughter. I took you to Gordon Ramsay's restaurant after you blackmailed me into it. I thought we were...friendly."

Tessa's gaze flicked to the lawyer and then to her officer, who wisely picked up on the atmosphere in the room and made a hasty retreat. Once he'd left, Tessa said, "If you think I'll say anything that might incriminate me further, you're going to be sorely disappointed. I will say this though, it isn't easy for a woman to reach my rank. It requires a certain degree of finessing to make it happen."

"Aye, well, I hope it was worth it." Callum glanced at their lawyer. "I don't think she needs to be here for this."

"Neither do I," Ms. Patel said. "If you would excuse us, Commander Sharp, we have a meeting with Assistant Commissioner Sturgis."

Shoulders back and head held high, Tessa strode to meet the officer waiting in the outer office.

Unable to look either of them in the eye while she did so.

33

David's phone vibrated in his pocket while he crouched behind Tommy James' pool house. He pulled it out, read a text from Harvard saying he was on his way, and showed it to Abasi, who nodded.

As soon as he'd returned the phone to his jeans, Abasi signaled that the patrol had passed, and it was time to run for the cover of the hedges. Crouched low, gun in hand, both men made it without incident. From there, it didn't take long to get to the door leading into the mudroom.

Peeking out from the cover of the hedge, Abasi pointed to the camera above the door. "Think you can shoot that out?" he whispered.

"Yeah, but they'll hear it."

The other man reached under the back of his shirt and came out with a silencer. He handed it to David.

"You couldn't have given this to me back in the car?" He screwed it onto his gun while Abasi shrugged.

David didn't hesitate—he took aim, shot once, and knocked out the camera. They were running as soon as he'd finished.

With their backs pressed to the walls on either side of the door, they waited to see if anyone would investigate. Nothing. Abasi glanced through the window in the door and jerked his head at David. They were clear.

The door was unlocked, but their entry triggered the sensor. Abasi keyed in the code on the pad beside the entrance to disarm it. David fished out his phone again and handed it to Abasi, who typed in the code for the rest of the team. That done, they hurried through the room and down the short hallway to the kitchen door.

The house was eerily silent, even though they could hear at least one person moving around in the kitchen.

Abasi leaned into him. "If they had her in the office, we'd hear voices. Definitely downstairs."

A measure of relief surged through David. They were heading in the right direction. They'd get her. Every instinct told him to hurry, that Elle was running out of time, but he forced himself to use caution. He couldn't help her if he was injured or managed to get himself killed.

With another jerk of his head, Abasi signaled for David to open the door while he covered him. Slowly, carefully, he opened it a crack and saw two young women at the kitchen island. One appeared to be poring over a cookbook, the other polishing dishwasher marks from crystal glasses.

David held up two fingers before indicating it was safe to enter.

Abasi went first; his gun trained on the women, who startled when they saw him but, strangely, didn't make a sound. "Cara, Susan, I need you to get into the pantry."

The taller woman turned gray. "Did he send you to kill us?"

"No." Abasi's eyes hardened. "If this goes as planned, you two will be able to walk out of here forever."

The shorter woman's lips trembled. "I overheard them say we're to go to a brothel in Germany."

It was clear they didn't believe Abasi would just let them go.

"I'm with the CIA," David lied. "We're raiding this house as part of an investigation, and Abasi here is undercover. If you do as we say, we promise you'll be protected."

The women shared a look and began to shed silent tears. With encouragement from Abasi, they hurried across the room and entered the large walk-in pantry. Abasi handed them the key.

"Lock it from the inside," he said. "Don't come out unless we come for you or you hear the cops."

They nodded hurriedly, then the taller one's eyes widened with terror. Abasi spun just in time to avoid the fist of one of Tommy's soldiers.

"Lock it now," David told the women as he turned to see Abasi aim at their attacker.

"No gun," David snapped before jumping on the soldier's back and trapping him in a headlock until he passed out.

"You need to teach me how to do that," Abasi said with clear admiration.

"No problem. But let's wait until after we're done here. Where can we put him?"

Abasi pointed to one of the many doors leading off the vast kitchen. "Walk-in fridge."

He bent to grab the guy's feet while David took his arms. Together, they dragged him into the fridge and hid him at the back.

Abasi handed David some nylon twine. "Best I can find for tying him up."

"I've got it. See if you can dig up something to gag him with." He set about hog-tying the unconscious man.

Meanwhile, Abasi grabbed an onion off the shelf, opened the guy's jaw, and wedged it in his mouth. "That should do it."

When they were done, they stood side by side and surveyed their work.

"Looks like we're going to spit-roast him," Abasi said.

With a shake of his head, David divested the soldier of his weapon before they shut the door firmly behind them.

"Cellar?" he said.

Abasi pointed to the last door in a row of three. "There's a camera directly above the door as you open it," he warned. "Tommy's bodyguards will probably be waiting in there too."

David considered him. "Do they know you've abandoned ship?"

"Not unless Tommy's told them. Far as the world is concerned, the Albanians killed Marcus. They might think I disappeared to get some payback."

"You want to risk it?"

"You got my back?" Abasi raised a brow.

"Don't ask stupid questions." David motioned toward the door. "Leave it open a crack, and I'll take out the camera."

"Just remember, any place I get shot, you get shot too."

"Stop complaining and get on with it."

"American dickhead," Abasi muttered as he tucked his gun into the back of his jeans and opened the door.

ELLE CAME ROUND TO THE SOUND OF HER TEETH CHATTERING. *Cold. So cold.* Her whole body ached with it. Something hit her in the face, and it took a second to realize she was being drenched in icy cold water.

She blinked rapidly, bringing the world back into focus. But she wished it hadn't because all she could see was Tommy standing over her, the spray hose from the sink aimed at her head.

Noticing she was awake, he shut it off and tossed it back into the sink. "Where's the hard drive?" He flexed his fists.

"I-I can u-understand why sh-she had an affair," Elle forced through chattering teeth. "There is n-nothing a-attractive about you."

This time, he didn't bother to hit her. Instead, he kicked her hard in the shin. The pain blinded her, stealing her ability to think. She couldn't even scream. All she could do was scrunch her eyes tight and wait for it to pass.

"Remember the first time we did this?" Tommy said once she'd opened her eyes again. "You couldn't have been more than twelve. No, thirteen. That's right. Marcus begged for you then too." He kicked her other leg.

This time, Elle screamed. The sound echoed off the hard, cold tiles and bounced back at her. She could hear laughter and knew it was Cutter, but she couldn't make herself look at him. So much for being brave like Princess, no, *General* Leia. She'd bet Leia had no problem thinking through the pain.

Tommy crouched in front of her. "I planned to get rid of you. You were screwing up important jobs, and I figured I could get somebody else to do them. Somebody who didn't make me sick to look at them. But Marcus, he wanted his sister. Even though you were no more related to him than any other bitch. So, we made a deal. Do you know what I made him do in return for leaving you alone that time? He ever tell you? No?"

Elle's stomach churned. Whatever was coming, it would be bad, and she didn't want to hear it.

"I took him with me when I went to teach somebody a

lesson. The moron had stolen from me and bragged about it. You can understand why I couldn't let that slide. I had Cutter here hold the guy down while Marcus cut off his fingers, one by one, and we stuffed them down the guy's throat. He did a good job, Marcus did." Tommy leaned toward her. "I think he enjoyed it."

With no warning for her or Tommy, Elle vomited all over him.

"Bitch," he exploded as he sprang away from her.

The disgust on his face would have been amusing if she wasn't still trying to empty her already empty stomach. He cursed and spat at her but wouldn't come close because they were both covered in vomit. It was almost the worst thing that could happen to vain Tommy James. And Elle loved it.

"Better get that hose of yours, Tommy. Looks like you could do with a wash," she taunted.

Fury, dark and malevolent, contorted his features. "Clean her up while I get changed," he ordered Cutter.

As he strode toward the door, Cutter's phone rang. He glanced at the screen and called after Tommy, "Wait up, it's the cop."

Tommy turned back slowly. "See what she's got for us," he said, his eyes on Elle.

"Tessa? What you got?" Cutter said into his phone.

Elle stilled. Tessa? It couldn't be.

A vicious smile appeared on Tommy's face. "Paid Tessa Sharp a fortune for the details of when and where you were meeting with the Met. Worth every penny."

If Elle hadn't already emptied her stomach, she would have vomited all over again. Tessa had betrayed them. They'd known the woman for years. Relied on her. Trusted her. How could she have done this to them?

Cutter's eyes caught Tommy's. "You're gonna want to

hear this, boss. Tessa's been made, so she's making a run for it. But she knows where the hard drive is."

"Does she now?" Tommy reached for the phone.

34

Abasi strode down the stairs to the cellar as though he owned the place. "Boss in there?" he asked the guys standing guard beside a door that had been hidden behind a rack of wine.

"Yeah," the one on the left said. "Where you been? Cutter's been looking for you."

"I bet he has." Abasi moved to the left, taking their attention with him.

Which meant David was free to reach up through the gap at the top of the door and yank the wires out of the camera.

"Cutter in there too?" Abasi asked. "Who're they dealing with? The Albanians?"

"Naw, they found the girl. Boss is working her over. Got no clue why," the guy on the left said.

"Don't know. Don't care," the other added.

"Cutter says we get some time with her before he finishes her off." The left guy smirked.

"Ain't it great to have a job with perks?" Abasi reached behind him for his gun as the men laughed.

David was faster. He'd pushed the door open and shot both in the chest before Abasi even had his gun in his hand.

"You ruin all my fun," Abasi said dryly as David stalked across the room to join him.

"Do you know the code?" David nodded toward the keypad on the door.

"Not to this room. Only Cutter, Tommy and the two dead stooges have that code. We need to make them come out to us."

"Any ideas?"

They stared at the door.

"If we do anything to spook them, they'll kill Elle," Abasi said, stating the obvious.

"Can you call Cutter and tell him you know he's looking for you? That you're upstairs waiting for him?"

Abasi stared at him like he was an idiot. "Yeah, because he'll rush straight up the stairs to get to the guy he knows wants to kill him."

"What if we just bang on the door and mumble something?"

"Mumble something?"

"Come out, boss, it's urgent," David said. "That kind of thing."

"You haven't been around many gangsters, have you? Tommy won't come out because his bodyguard tells him to. He'll wait until he's ready, then shoot the idiot who pissed him off."

"Then how the hell do we get him to open the door?"

"I'm thinking," Abasi said as a muffled scream came from the hidden room.

"Think faster," David snapped. "He's hurting her."

"Shit, shit, shit, shit, shit." Abasi paced.

The wet room had gone deathly silent, and David's skin was electric with the tension.

"I've got it." Abasi pulled out his phone. "I'll call one of the captains and get him to call Tommy with something urgent. Keep your gun trained on the door. This is going to happen fast. And remember, Cutter's mine."

David raised his weapon.

Just stay alive a little bit longer, Blue. I'm coming for you.

~

"You've got my hard drive?" Tommy said into the phone as he stared at Elle.

His eyes were cold and flat, letting her know he was contemplating the best way to end her.

"What do you mean the fucking techs have it?" he bellowed.

Elle couldn't help but smile. The drive, and everything on it, was in police custody. Even the cops Tommy had in his pocket couldn't get to it now. Chain of evidence was sacrosanct. There were systems in place to ensure no one could tamper with any of it. The drive was out of Tommy's reach.

And it was all down to pure dumb luck.

If Megan hadn't chosen a laptop with an easy access drive that didn't require a screwdriver to remove it, or if Elle had still been using her original machine, she wouldn't have been able to get to the hard drive. So, frying her baby had been worth it, as it meant she'd been carrying a laptop with a removable hard drive. One she'd decided to leave behind after their car was struck. If Megan hadn't gone shopping and Elle hadn't hidden the drive, everything that'd happened would have been for nothing. Megan would get a kick out of this for sure.

Tommy ended the call with a furious stab at the screen and tossed the phone back to Cutter.

"What do we do?" Cutter asked.

For once, Elle kept her clever comments to herself.

"We've got some time before they access the drive," Tommy said, still staring at Elle as his own phone began to ring. He took it out and glanced at the screen before silencing it. "You think you've won, don't you?" he said to her.

"I never thought this was a game," she told him. "It was never about winning or losing. It was about stopping you."

"See?" Tommy spread his hands. "That's where you went wrong. You can't stop me. Nobody can stop me. You think the cops are gonna come in here and arrest me? I own the fucking cops."

"Not all of them," she pointed out.

"Enough. And even if they do come for me, I'll just shift countries for a while and conduct business elsewhere while I work on my tan. You've achieved nothing here—except for getting Marcus killed."

It was pointless arguing with him. "Ticktock, Tommy. Better run away before the cops get here. Hurry along now."

"I wish I could spend weeks taking you apart." It was clear he meant every word. "Instead, I'll let Cutter here have some fun for a while before he finishes you off."

Elle let her disgust with him show. "You should have left me alone, Tommy. I left you alone."

"That was your mistake." He turned his back, dismissing her. "I need a minute to think, and I can't do it in here with this smell." He glanced down at his suit and winced. "I'm going to change. When you've finished with her, meet me upstairs. She's no use to us now. And, Cutter," he said as he reached for the door handle, "don't take too long. We got to pack."

"I don't need a whole lotta time to make her pay," Cutter said as he slid one of his many knives from its sheath.

The cold light from the bulbs above Elle's head glinted

off the blade as a calm acceptance stole over her. She was going to die. It would be painful, and it would cause someone else joy. But there was nothing she could do about it.

Was this how Marcus felt at the end?

Was this the same acceptance she'd seen in Ryan's eyes before he collapsed?

As Tommy swung the door open and stepped out of the room, Cutter bore down on her. Elle wasn't proud; she shut her eyes, not wanting to see the glee on his face as he tortured her. Steeling herself, she waited for that first cut.

But it didn't come.

Instead, there was a soft thumping sound, and then something heavy thudded to the floor.

Elle's eyes flew open to see Abasi bearing down on Cutter, his gun aimed at the man as he backed him up against the wall. Meanwhile, David stepped over Tommy's body and into the room, coming straight for her.

"Is this real?" she asked, fearing it was a hallucination brought on by pain she could no longer feel. Had she tuned out Cutter while he used his knife on her? Had she gone to a happier place, one where David saved her and all was right with the world?

"Yeah, Blue, this is real." He clasped the back of her head and pressed a gentle kiss to her forehead.

"If this was a dream, you'd totally say that, so it doesn't help convince me," she said as he crouched in front of her and worked on releasing the ties from her ankles. "Say something I couldn't imagine you saying."

"When this is all over"—David finished with her legs and moved around her to unlock the cuffs. Was he picking the lock? She needed to learn to do that. It would so come in handy—"we're getting married."

Elle's heart skipped a beat, and then she started laughing. "You *are* real."

"And I'm serious. We're getting married."

"You can't ask me to marry you while I'm being tortured." Her brain wasn't working as well as it should have because it took her another second to realize he hadn't asked at all. He'd just told her.

"You aren't being tortured. That part of your day is over. Now you're being rescued. By the man you're going to marry." He came back around to the front of the chair and scooped her up into his arms. Cradling her to him as a groom would when carrying his bride over their threshold.

Stupid custom. She'd never understood it.

"Could you two hurry up and get your arses out of here?" Abasi said. "I need a private word with Cutter."

"He's all yours," David said as they headed to the door.

"Abasi," Elle called out. "I'd better see you again—big brother."

She saw his shoulders tense at the term of endearment before they walked out of the torture room. Elle didn't avert her gaze from the sight of Tommy lying on the floor. She wanted to see him, wanted to know he truly was gone.

"Is he absolutely, for certain, dead?" she asked David.

"Shot him in the heart."

"That's impossible." Elle snuggled into him, letting him carry the weight of her thoughts as well as her body. "Tommy didn't have a heart."

"Clear up here," Harvard called from the top of the stairs. "I see you didn't wait for us before you started having fun." He motioned to Tommy's body. "Never were any good at sharing."

"And you always managed to turn up just as the work was over," David said. "Is there anybody still standing?"

"A few, but Joe has them trussed up like Thanksgiving turkeys." Harvard smiled at Elle. "Good to see you made it."

She tried to smile back but it was proving difficult. "Someone will have sent for more soldiers, we're not safe yet."

"Don't worry," David said. "The team will protect us until we get out of here."

"What team?" Her head was filled with fog.

"Our team," he said.

"I heard that," Harvard called. "Should I tell Callum you're on board?"

"Smug bastard," David answered.

As he held her even tighter, emotional exhaustion got the better of her, and she fell asleep, knowing she was safe in David's arms.

35

It had been almost a month since the day Tommy kidnapped her, and in that time, David had barely touched her. Sure, he slept beside her at night and was caring and attentive during the day, but there was a distance between them that Elle didn't understand. She wasn't sure if he found the bruises Tommy left on her repulsive—although, they'd mostly gone now. Or if the whole experience had brought back old memories that he couldn't shake. Or, maybe, he really just wasn't *that* into her.

That's why she'd decided it was time to seduce her man. And to do it, she'd called in help. She'd asked Megan to shop for her. Unfortunately, she hadn't made it clear when Megan needed to turn up with her purchases. For all Elle knew, she'd gotten sidetracked and followed something shiny to her doom.

While the rest of the team had gone to their various homes after Tommy was killed, Elle and David remained holed up in the safe house, mainly to avoid the many government agencies who wanted to ask her questions. As far as she was concerned, she'd given them all the answers they needed. Her testimony, together with the data from the hard drive, was more than they needed to bring down the James Syndicate. Tommy James had stolen enough of her life; he wasn't getting any more. He wasn't getting it all the way he had with Marcus.

Elle had spent much of the past month mourning her brother. Not the man he'd become, but the boy who'd sacrificed everything for her. The boy who'd loved animals and dreamed of becoming a vet. The boy who'd sneaked her ice cream and told her bedtime stories. Her heart would always ache for that boy, the brother she'd loved so very much. The Marcus she'd known before Tommy twisted him.

She'd also spent a lot of time wondering about Abasi. After that day at the house, he'd disappeared, and there was no trace of him anywhere. All he'd left behind was the body of the man who'd killed his best friend. The police had found Cutter pinned to the wall of Tommy's study with his own knives. After one had been used to cut his throat. Out of all the stupid things occupying Elle's mind, one of the dumbest was why Abasi had moved upstairs to kill Cutter. Why not just do it in the torture room? If he ever surfaced again, she planned on asking him about it.

As for the rest of the team, Megan recovered from her mild concussion and was pleased to hear the laptop she'd chosen had saved the day. Of course, it didn't make up for missing a gunfight. Rachel, meanwhile, had made it her life mission to ruin Tessa Sharp—who'd tried to escape to Europe but had been picked up by Interpol. To achieve her goal, Rachel had joined forces with her darker-skinned doppelgänger. It was scary watching Ms. Patel and Rachel together. Elle kept waiting for one of them to explode purely because nature couldn't allow them both to occupy the same general space at the same time. So far, it hadn't happened, but fingers crossed...

Despite Tessa being charged with several offenses and

facing a lengthy prison sentence, Rachel didn't deem it punishment enough. She was currently suing the ex-police officer for everything she could think of while giving copious interviews to the media about the officer's betrayal. By the time she was done, Tessa Sharp's name, reputation, and everything she held dear would be gone.

Of course, Rachel's mission to destroy the cop wasn't just because she'd betrayed the team. She was doing it for Ryan. It was her way of coping.

Elle placed a palm against her roiling stomach as it spasmed with the ache she associated with Ryan. They all had their different ways of coping with what'd happened to him. Elle's was currently denial. One day, she'd deal with it. But...not yet.

Spotting Megan on the path up to the house, Elle swung the door open.

"You should use real handcuffs." Megan stepped inside. "These won't hold him."

It was clear Elle never should have involved Megan in her plans. But her choice of someone to help was sorely limited. Julia would faint if she even thought about buying naughty cuffs, and Rachel was too busy destroying a dirty cop. So that left Megan. And, apparently, Megan's help came with lots of unwanted sex advice. None of it good.

"The whole point of these handcuffs," Elle said as she followed Megan through the house to the kitchen, "is that he has to *want* to be restrained. Not that I'm forcing him to stay where he doesn't want to be." Elle didn't know why she bothered. It wasn't as if anything she said would make an impact. Megan did Megan. Full stop.

"Whatever." Megan had already tuned Elle out. "I still don't see why we couldn't have just swung by your apartment at the office to pick up the pink cuffs you already have."

"Uh, cops? Crime scene? TV cameras? Any of this ringing a bell?"

Megan waved a dismissive hand. "I would have gotten us past them. I spent years sneaking past my brother, I'm an expert. Anyway, I picked up some other stuff for you while I was in the shop. And something for me." She grinned. "I bought a corset that will knock Dimitri on his backside when he sees me in it."

"Just as long as the rest of us don't see it, I'm sure it will be great." She eyed the brown paper bag Megan had given her with suspicion. "I'm almost too scared to see what else you got."

"Don't be a wimp," Megan said as she raided Elle's chocolate stash.

With a sigh, Elle peered into the bag. "Cinnamon lube? What the heck am I supposed to do with that?"

"I'm sure you'll figure it out."

Elle already had—it was going in the bin. She lifted two furry pink disks adorned with long pink tassels from the bag. "You got me nipple pasties?"

"To match the cuffs!" She was so pleased with herself that Elle felt embarrassed on her behalf.

"I'm going to use the cuffs on David."

Megan scrunched up her nose. "Well, I suppose you could stick those on him too, but I don't think it would be very sexy."

"Okay, we're done here." Elle turned her friend around and propelled her toward the front door. "Thanks for shopping for me. Let's never do it again. Now go away."

"You know you're making this way too complicated," Megan said. "When I want to seduce Dimitri, I just strip and stand in front of him. That always works. You should try it."

"Not all of us feel comfortable getting naked in front of people. We're still new. I'm still nervous. You, on the other hand, would strip for a busload of tourists without batting an eyelid."

"Whoa," Megan said as Elle shoved her out of the house. "Being horny makes you mean."

"Love you too." Elle shut the door in Megan's face.

DAVID WAS EXHAUSTED. EVER SINCE PULLING ELLE OUT OF Tommy's wet room, he'd had nightmares about it. And when he wasn't waking in a cold sweat, terrified he'd been too late to save her, he was waking up several times a night just to check she was still breathing.

It was inevitable he'd finally crash.

Which is exactly what he'd done when he'd gone to bed that evening.

And it was also why someone had managed to get the drop on him while he'd been asleep. A very smug, blue-haired someone, who currently sat astride his naked body—when he was certain he'd worn pajama bottoms to bed. Not only that, but Elle had also managed to lose her clothes while he'd been out cold. Well, most of them. She appeared to have curtain cords dangling from her breasts.

When he reached out, intent on pulling one of the cords to see what happened, his wrists caught on something. Glancing up, he found himself secured to the headboard by a set of fluffy pink cuffs.

"Elle, why am I cuffed to the bed?"

"For sexy times." She grinned.

The sight made him relax for the first time in weeks. Between mourning for Marcus, denial over Ryan, and anxiety over the violence she'd experienced, Elle hadn't been her bubbly self since he'd rescued her. Until now. And he couldn't have been happier to see her back to normal.

Except for one teeny, tiny detail. "Why are you wearing curtain cords on your breasts?"

She glanced down. "I suppose they do look like something you'd use to tie back your curtains. But these are nipple pasties. Megan bought them for me."

"There's a lot to unpack in that sentence," he said.

For a second, David thought he might still be asleep and having the weirdest dream he'd ever had. Then Elle bounced on top of him, making the tassels fly in different directions.

She puffed out a breath toward her forehead, moving her hair out of her eyes. "I spent half an hour trying to make them go in circles but couldn't get it to work. I suspect you have to use the same movement you use with a hula hoop, and I could never get the hang of that."

Her expression was expectant, as though waiting for him to say something.

When nothing came to mind, he said, "I can't hula hoop either."

"This isn't working," she said, her shoulders slumping.

"If you tell me what you're trying to do, maybe I can help you figure out where it went wrong." Although, he already suspected that the moment it'd all started to go south was when she'd involved Megan. Wisely, he kept that observation to himself.

"I was trying to initiate sex." She looked woeful. "You've hardly touched me in weeks, and I'm worried you've gone off me."

David didn't know whether to laugh about her thinking pasties and handcuffs were the way to go or cry with relief that the problem was something he could easily fix. "Ellie Blue," he said as gently as he was able. "You've spent the past month in mourning and recovering from being beaten. Getting physical seemed like a dick move when you were obviously coping with a helluva lot of trauma and loss. I wanted to give you time to heal and to take care of you while you did it."

"I'm not sure I'll ever get over what happened to Marcus...and Ryan," she said with her usual guileless honesty. "But I feel...stronger, more like myself, every day."

"I can see that." He wished he could hold her, comfort her, but the damn cuffs were getting in his way. Sure, he could snap them, but she'd gone to so much trouble to seduce him with them that he wanted to see what she had in mind.

"So, you still want to be with me?" she asked, looking so damn vulnerable.

David rocked his hips up into her, letting her feel just how much he wanted to be with her. "Does that answer your question?"

"No, that tells me you get hard when a naked woman bounces around on top of you."

She was so damned adorable. "Elle, I'm crazy about you. I love you so much I can barely think straight. I want you every minute of every day. Does *that* answer your question?"

She melted against him, pressing those crazy pasties to his chest. "I love you," she whispered, her heart in her eyes.

"I know."

A wide smile lit up her face. "My man, quoting *Star Wars* at me. Could you get any more perfect?"

"Uncuff me and we'll see," he teased. "For future reference, you don't need props to seduce me. Being near me is enough. But if you want to *initiate sex*, just say, 'David, I want to have sex.'"

She leaned in to press a kiss to his jaw. "David, I want to have sex."

"Your wish is my command. Although, how about we save the cuffs for another time?" When she had a better idea of what to do with him while he was in them. "Maybe lose the pasties too, unless you're really attached to them."

"That's the problem," she said mournfully. "I really *am* attached to them. You had to glue them on, and I'm scared it will hurt to take them off."

"Blue," he said, trying not to laugh. "Don't worry about the pasties. I'll get them off you, and you won't feel any pain at all."

"Promise?"

"Promise."

With a happy sigh, Elle reached above him to unlatch the cuffs, brushing his face with the curtain cords. Although he didn't make a sound, he couldn't keep his body from shaking.

"You're laughing at my boobs, aren't you?"

There was no containing it after that. The laughter just burst out of him.

With his hands freed, he tumbled his woman onto her back beside him. "Never change, Ellie Blue," he said before kissing her thoroughly.

By the time he was finished, she was rubbing up against him and mewling with need.

Just how he liked her.

"Now," he said. "Let's see what we can do about these things." He tugged on a tassel, and Elle groaned in pleasure. "Well, this is going to be fun," David said as he lowered his mouth to her breast.

FIRST EPILOGUE

Every member of Benson Security's London team, plus a couple from the Scottish head office, where Ryan had worked before moving to London, had assembled for their teammate.

"He's still in a coma," the doctor told the waiting room full of brooding men and women.

When he took a step back, Elle completely understood. En masse, they were pretty intimidating. And that was when they weren't all frowning at you.

"What about his injuries?" Rachel asked. "Are they healing?"

Like all the core members of the London team, Rachel had spent as much time as possible by Ryan's bedside. They each had a different way of trying to reach him. Julia read recipes to him. Megan described all the ways she was going to beat him in training. Dimitri talked about an online game they both played. Joe kept him up to date with everything happening with the James Syndicate case. Rachel ordered him to wake up and get better. Harvard apologized for Rachel. Callum just sat glaring at him before stalking out, leaving Isobel to explain to an unconscious Ryan that her husband was too upset to talk. Elle joked with him and explained all the geek-culture references she thought he should know while David hovered over her, ready to wipe away any stray tears that might fall.

They just wanted him back.

It was as simple as that.

"We're very pleased with his progress," the doctor said. "As you know, we reconstructed his skull with titanium mesh, and it's functioning nicely. The swelling in his brain has gone down, and the gunshot wounds to his chest are healing rapidly. Physically, he's doing far better than we expected."

"Then why won't he wake up?" Elle asked, her tone making David put his arm around her shoulder to comfort her.

"The truth is, we don't know. The trauma to his brain was massive. It isn't only the bullet wound itself, you understand. It's the pressure waves caused by the force of the bullet. The waves can cause catastrophic damage to the brain. We won't know what effect they've had on Ryan until he regains consciousness."

"Will he?" Julia asked, sounding close to tears.

"We very much hope so." The doctor smiled at them all. It was full of sympathy. "All I can tell you is that he's healing well, and there's nothing more we can do other than wait until he's ready to wake."

"How long will that take?" Rachel demanded.

"I'm afraid I can't say," he said.

With a nod of his head, the doctor escaped the room. Leaving the team to turn to each other.

"We carry on doing what we're doing," Lake Benson said. "We talk to him and make him deal with us. In the meantime, we're moving him to a private room, where he'll be more comfortable. There are facilities in the private wing that'll make it easier for his family when they visit."

Elle pressed into David at the mention of Ryan's family. His grandparents and great-uncle and great-aunt, as well as his parents, wandered in and out of his room, their expressions devastated. Watching them broke the already bruised hearts of his friends. Each and every one of them was desperate to ease the Granger family's burden. Unfortunately, nothing short of Ryan waking would do that.

"Lake's right," Callum said. "It sucks, but all we can do is wait. Julia will set up a roster for visiting, so we can ensure someone's with him around the clock. Other than that, it's back to work for all of us."

Elle watched her friend as he lay sleeping on the bed. His head was bandaged, as was his chest. Drains and tubes and monitors surrounded him.

"It's okay." David held her tight. "All that stuff will disappear soon enough, and he won't look so scary."

She wrapped her arms around his waist. "What if he doesn't wake up?"

"Then we'll spend the rest of his life keeping him company while he sleeps."

"I miss him." She wiped her tears on his black sweater as she tried to make them stop.

"We all do," Rachel said from behind them.

Elle lifted her head to find the whole team filling the room. None of them were ready to leave just yet. With all of her heart, Elle hoped Ryan wasn't ready to leave them either.

There was nothing they could do but leave their friend alone in his bed as they went on with their lives. Each of them carrying an ache where he should have been.

Some of the team headed for the hospital's carpark,

where Lake wandered over to Elle and David. "I hear you're joining the team," he said to David.

"Stuff it, Benson," David grumbled. "I don't want to hear it."

"Hear what?" Lake rocked back on his heels. "Hear my recollection of the many times you told me you'd rather die than become part of a team again? Is that what you don't want to hear?" His lips twitched in what passed for a smile with the man.

"What will your wife say if you go back to Scotland with a broken nose?" David asked. "Should we find out?"

This time, Lake did grin. And the transformation was blinding.

Holy Hotness, Batman!

"Go to hell," David grumbled, turning her away from Lake, who was now laughing out loud.

It sounded like rumbling bubbles of joy.

"Why are we leaving?" Elle protested, looking over her shoulder at the man who'd started Benson Security.

"Because he's messing with me, and I don't want to break his nose now that he pays my wages."

That seemed like a decent enough reason to Elle. "Can we go say goodbye to Ryan first?"

"Of course we can, Ellie Blue."

Her hand in his, he led her through the garage to their car.

SECOND EPILOGUE

Seven months later
National Hospital for Neurology and Neurosurgery
London

R yan Granger opened his eyes.

Find out what happens to Ryan
in Benson Security 7, Reset.

Preorder here!

ABOUT THE AUTHOR

Janet is a Scot, living in New Zealand and is married to a Dutch man. She writes contemporary romance and romantic suspense with a humorous bent – this is mainly due to the fact that she has an odd sense of humour and can't keep it out of anything she does! If she wasn't a writer, she'd like to be Buffy the Vampire Slayer, or Indiana Jones. Unfortunately, both of these roles have already been filled. Which may be a good thing as Janet has no fighting skills, wouldn't know a precious relic if it hit her in the face, and has an aversion to blood. When she's not living in her head, she's a mother to two kids and several pets.

Janet loves to hang out with her readers. You can chat with her in her Facebook group, which is full of awesome readers. And don't forget to sign up for her newsletter too!

www.ingramcontent.com/pod-product-compliance
Lightning Source LLC
Chambersburg PA
CBHW020924110726
47900CB00001B/288